WAR BOUND

WAR BOUND

ELVEN ALLIANCE BOOK TWO

TARA GRAYCE

Sword Cross
Publishing

LIST OF CHARACTERS

Book 1 - Fierce Heart:

- Ashenifela – Essie's horse
- Averett – king of Escarland (humans)
- Brina – daughter of Weylind and Rheva. Princess of the elves. Younger sister to Ryfon
- Daesyn – human man from elf legends who formed a heart bond with the elven princess Inara
- Edmund – prince of Escarland. Brother to Averett, Julien, and Essie
- Ellarin – late king of Tarenhiel. Late husband of Leyleira. Father of Lorsan.
- Elspeth – princess of Escarland. Nickname: Essie. Younger sister of Averett, Julien, and Edmund
- Farrendel – prince of Tarenhiel. Younger brother to Weylind, Melantha, and Jalissa
- Illyna – a friend of Farrendel that he made during the war.
- Inara – elf princess from legends who formed a heart bond with the human Daesyn
- Jalissa – princess of Tarenhiel. Sister to Weylind, Melantha, and Farrendel

- Julien – prince of Escarland. Brother to Averett, Edmund, and Essie
- Leyleira – former queen of Tarenhiel. Grandmother to Weylind, Melantha, Jalissa, and Farrendel. Great-grandmother of Ryfon and Brina
- Lorsan – late king of Tarenhiel. Father to Weylind, Melantha, Jalissa, and Farrendel. Son of Leyleira.
- Master Wendee – chief diplomat for Escarland (humans)
- Melantha – princess of Tarenhiel. Sister to Weylind, Melantha, and Farrendel
- Paige – queen of Escarland. Wife of Averett. Good friends with Essie.
- Rheva – queen of Tarenhiel and Weylind's wife
- Ryfon – son of Weylind and Rheva. Crown prince of Tarenhiel. Brother to Brina
- Vianola – late queen of Tarenhiel. Mother to Weylind, Melantha, and Jalissa.
- Weylind – king of Tarenhiel (elves)

Book 1.5 – Elf Prince

- Fingol – friend of Farrendel's from the war. Skilled with carving wood
- Iyrinder – bodyguard for Weylind.
- Sindrel – chief diplomat for the elves

Book 2 – War Bound

- Albert – Nickname: Bertie. Essie's oldest nephew. Son of Averett and Paige.

- Charles Hadley – owns the largest weapons manufacturing factory in Escarland. Father to Mark Hadley
- General Freilan – Escarland's top general/head of the armies
- Lance Marion – human inventor friend of Essie's and Farrendel's
- Lord Bletchly – one of the lords in Parliament
- Lord Crelford – one of the lords in Parliament
- Lord Fiskre – an elderly lord in Parliament
- Lord Kranshaw – one of the lords in Parliament who actively hates elves
- Mark Hadley – Son of Charles Hadley.
- Phineas – Nickname: Finn. Essie's youngest nephew. Son of Averett and Paige
- Thanfardil – elf in charge of the train system

LIST OF ELVISH

- Amir – prince
- Amirah – princess
- Dacha – father (informal)
- Daresheni – Most honored king (or more literally, great king)
- Elishina – heart bond
- Ellonahshinel – heart of the forest
- Elontiri – welcome, greetings, hello
- Eshinelt - green paint used in elven wedding ceremonies
- Isciena – sister
- Laesornysh – death on the wind
- Linshi – thank you
- Macha – mother (informal)
- Machasheni – grandmother
- Sason – son
- Sasonsheni - grandson
- Sena – daughter
- Senasheni – granddaughter
- Shashon – brother
- Shynafir – fierce heart

CHAPTER
ONE

Dead trolls haunted Essie's nightmares.

She struggled to drag herself from the images of dead bodies and blood and battle. A nightmare. Just another nightmare.

A hand shook her shoulder, gently, pulling her all the way awake. "Essie."

She rolled onto her back, blinking up at him. "Did I wake you?"

"No." Farrendel, her elf husband of three months, withdrew his hand, his silver-blond hair cascading over his shirt and still perfectly unfrizzy and detangled thanks to the magical elf conditioner. Or possibly magic elf hair. Essie hadn't decided which it was yet.

He rolled into a cross-legged position on his side of the bed. And it was definitely his side of the bed, pressed underneath the window while she curled against the far side of the rounded, elven bed grown into the wall, leaving several feet of space between them. "Are you all right?"

"Just tired." Essie swiped her hair from her face, staring up at the ceiling, visible in the pre-dawn gray. If she hadn't woken him, then he'd already been awake dealing with the aftermath of his own nightmares. "And you?"

It had been only two days since Farrendel had killed a hundred trolls with his destructive magic after the trolls ambushed her, Farrendel, and the rest of the royal elf family. Between her nightmares and Farrendel's, neither of them had managed to sleep much in the nights since.

It was sad, really. Only reason she was even staying in her husband's rooms was to more conveniently wake him from his nightmares. At least this was a whole lot better than tromping up and down two flights of stairs between his room on one branch and her room on another branch of their section of the elven treetop palace to wake each other from nightmares.

It had given them the chance to learn more of each other's quirks. Elves had a magic barrier around their treehouses keeping them warm and bug free even though their windows were just openings without glass. Farrendel, however, liked to sleep with that magic barrier left open on his window, letting in the cool breezes all night long. Essie had hauled an entire mound of blankets into his room just to stay warm through the night.

For his part, Farrendel claimed she snored. Or, as Essie insisted, breathed loudly.

Farrendel glanced at the window. The sky was the deep gray of pre-morning. If there was a hint of light on the horizon, the thick foliage of the elven forest hid it from view. "I do not believe I will sleep more tonight."

Essie scooted closer and took his hand. At the touch, she felt the connection of the heart bond warm in her chest. After two days of being this aware of the heart bond, she was becoming used to the feeling. Mostly. "Do you want me to stay up with you?"

"No. I will not disturb your sleep any longer." He leaned over to press a light kiss to her forehead before he tugged his hand free from hers. With a graceful motion, he swung over the windowsill and dropped onto the small porch that surrounded the small treehouse bedroom built high in the branches of Ellonahshinel, the elves' palace at the outskirts of their capital city of Estyra.

Shedding his shirt, Farrendel flipped over the porch railing, landing on a foot-wide branch. He dashed along that branch, then spun on his heels, kicked out, and pushed off, alighting on a branch only four inches wide with the ease of a great, hunting cat.

After crawling to his side of the bed, Essie rested her arms on the windowsill and leaned her chin on her arms. What did she want more? More sleep or to gaze at Farrendel while he performed death-defying feats of agility?

When she'd first come across Farrendel exercising like this, she'd thought it his way to stay in shape since he was Laesornysh, an elven title meaning Death on the Wind, given because he was the foremost elf warrior.

But was there more to it? Perhaps these early morning workout sessions were a way he stayed sane, working out his mental stress through exhausted muscles. How early did he wake each day, driven from his bed by nightmares?

She ought to know. She was his wife.

But they had only known each other for three months. Theirs was a marriage of alliance made out of desperation to draw her people, the humans of the kingdom of Escarland, and his people, the elves of the kingdom of Tarenhiel, together after decades of tension. They hadn't had a proper courtship or time to fall in love like a normal couple.

Instead, they'd been married within two days of meeting, and she'd found herself living in the elves' treetop home. Still, she and Farrendel had managed to build the beginnings of a relationship. Somehow they had even formed an elven *elishina*, a heart bond.

Would she and Farrendel have a chance to make more progress in their relationship? Instead of time to themselves, they had an impending war to deal with.

The real reason the elves had been so desperate for peace with her people was the threat of war from the trolls to the north. A war that someone was trying to start by planting some of her kingdom's new rifles and repeater guns among the trolls, making it appear that Essie's older brother Averett was aiding the trolls.

They had a spy in Escarland. A spy in Tarenhiel. A mess no matter where she turned.

After letting herself doze for another half an hour, Essie sighed and forced herself to get up. They were leaving for Escarland today, and she would have plenty of time to sleep on the train if she wanted to.

A peek out the window showed Farrendel still flipping, spinning, and running along the branches. Burning the rest of his restless, nightmare-fueled energy.

Stepping out of the treehouse bedroom that appeared grown into the branch, she crossed the small porch and navigated the set of stairs formed out of the branch. At the bottom, she entered the main room, which consisted of a small countertop and cabinet area while cushions filled the other side to form a sitting area.

She went through the next door over, up a similar staircase to a matching treehouse bedroom on the next branch. Inside her room, she changed into her elf-style tunic and trousers. After brushing her hair, she left it loose and flowing.

She would miss this in returning to her homeland. The elves in many ways were traditional and staid, but practically so. They didn't go in for lots of frills and an excess of fabric in their dresses, nor did women have to wear dresses all the time.

In Escarland, Essie would be expected to wear a corset and yards of fabric once again. It would be scandalous to wear her hair unbound like this.

But...she was a princess of the elves now. Maybe it would be her role to introduce elf fashion to Escarlish culture.

In the past three months, she had proven her place among the elves by showing them she could become one of them. But in Escarland, her people needed to learn to respect the elves, not just hate them as enemies. She would wear the elves' clothing and hold her head high while she was doing it.

With that in mind, Essie packed the rest of her elven clothes, as few as there were. She hadn't lived in Tarenhiel long enough to have more clothes made for her, nor did elves tend to have large wardrobes.

Once she was finished, she returned to the main room and placed her bag by the door, waiting to be loaded onto the train.

Essie blew out a long breath, trying to calm her tight chest and churning stomach. Would her family like Farrendel? How would he react to being in Winstead

Palace in the bustling capital city of Aldon, so different from the elves' earthy and calm capital of Estyra?

It wouldn't be an easy thing, bringing her elf husband home for the first time. But they had weathered the disapproval of his family. Surely it would be no different with her family.

As Essie set out a cold breakfast on the small table, Farrendel entered from his room, his hair wet. She gave him a wry smile. "I guess I don't have to ask how you slept. You slept as badly as I did."

His mouth tipped at the corners. An attempt at a smile, at least.

A knock came from the outer door of the main room. Essie started and glared at the door. "We aren't due to leave for several hours yet."

Farrendel shook his head. "No. I will get it."

Essie set out the last of the cold meat, cheese, and fruit for breakfast, trying to pretend she wasn't curious about their early morning caller.

When Farrendel shut the door and returned to the table, he carried a canvas-wrapped package. He held it out to her. "It is for you."

For her? She set it on a section of the table, untied the twine holding it shut, and opened it, revealing a pile of deep green silk, with glimpses of other fabrics beneath. "What's this?" She lifted the first dress from the package. She recognized the dark green silk as one she'd picked out one of the times she and Farrendel visited Estyra. "The seamstress finished the rest of my clothes?"

"Yes." Farrendel glanced at her, then looked away. But she'd caught the uncertain look in his ice-blue eyes. "I did not want your family to think me stingy with your care."

It was sweet of him to worry. She stood on her tiptoes and kissed his cheek. "Thank you for caring."

Farrendel shifted, still not looking at her. "It will probably not matter. Once we are in Escarland, you will have all the things you left behind there. You will not need these."

Essie let out a breath that was something between a sigh and a laugh. He was still worried that, once she returned home, she wouldn't want to return to Estyra with him. It was, perhaps, a valid worry. She'd left home for that diplomatic meeting three months ago fully expecting to return in a few days. Instead, she'd found herself married and on the way to a new home, though she hadn't realized then how special this treetop palace in Estyra would become.

Returning to Winstead Palace would be interesting for both of them. She missed her family. Terribly. It would be wonderful to see them again, even if for only a short time with the cloud of war hanging heavy over them.

It would also be uncomfortable, trying to bring Farrendel into her family. But she was determined. This would work. This had to work. She would hold her two families together if she had to do it with a white-knuckled grip.

Essie set down her new dress, eased her arms around Farrendel's waist, and held him. "I have decided that I'm going to dress like an elf even in Escarland. Your people needed to see a human fitting in with their society in order to respect me. But my people need to see me embracing your culture to respect your people as allies rather than enemies. I might be returning home, but I'll still be a princess of the elves. Your Elspetha Shynafir."

Farrendel lifted a hand and gently cradled her chin,

tracing his thumb over her cheek. "Are you sure? I do not wish for you to feel out of place in your own home."

Was it possible to melt from the inside out? Essie leaned into Farrendel. "Of course I'm sure. This will be tough but don't worry. My family will love you. My brothers might take a while to come around, but my sister-in-law and mother will love you right away. You'll see."

Farrendel wrapped his free arm around her in an awkward, unpracticed way. Not only were they still figuring out how to be a married couple, but elves weren't the hugging type.

The more touchy-feely, hugging family culture in Escarland was going to be a shock, that was for sure.

Farrendel stepped back first. "I will do my best. As you did with my family."

"And I will stand by your side like you did with your family." Essie rested her hand on his chest, feeling the steady beat of his heart.

They shared a heart bond. Surely they could withstand this and keep their peoples from going to war with each other yet again.

CHAPTER

TWO

F arrendel shifted on the moss of the train platform in Estyra, faced his family, and tried to keep his breathing steady, his expression neutral. Behind him, the train waited, sleek and silver on rails formed of tree roots stretching into the vast forest. Their bags had already been loaded, as had their horses and the gifts he had picked out for Essie's family. All that awaited now was to say farewell to his family.

This was a diplomatic meeting. He was not going to war. He would not end up captured and tortured. His sister Jalissa was coming along as the official ambassador. She stood next to him, serene with her hands clasped in front of her.

More importantly, he would be with Essie. Even now, she held his hand, their first two fingers clasped with the backs of their hands pressed together tighter than was proper in public. But he did not care if his family saw and was embarrassed on his behalf. He needed the steadiness that her presence gave him at that moment. Both the grip of her hand against his, and the connection of the heart bond tugging deep in his chest.

Even with Essie's protection, he and Jalissa would be stepping into a kingdom that had been their enemy a mere fifteen years ago. A kingdom that had reason to imprison and torture him simply for being an elf. Her brother Averett had promised peace, but would he keep that peace when presented with two elves in his own castle?

Well, three. Jalissa had a single female guard coming with her, more as a formality than anything. If Escarland wanted to cause trouble, one guard or ten, it would not matter.

None of them knew what to expect. While the human kingdoms seemingly practiced sending diplomats to each other's kingdoms all the time, it was not a Tarenhieli custom. Not even his brother, King Weylind, had left Tarenhiel except to go to war.

A war Farrendel would be called to join the moment he returned from this trip to Escarland. Visiting Escarland might be terrifying, but it was preferable to becoming the weapon of death to protect Tarenhiel, as was expected of him.

After a long, tense moment where his family stared back, as if waiting for a cue to tell them it was time to say farewell, Farrendel's niece Brina stepped forward. A smile tipped her mouth. "I am jealous. I have heard the human cities are a sight to behold."

Farrendel shifted and glanced at Essie. She had told him much about her home, but he could not picture it.

Essie touched Brina's arm. "Maybe we can take you for a visit in the future. When things are less tense. I'd love to show you Aldon."

As Brina moved to talk to Essie, Farrendel's nephew Ryfon faced him. Ryfon straightened his shoulders. "I will help hold Tarenhiel until you return."

Farrendel barely kept himself from stumbling back at those words. He had been barely older than Ryfon when he had been captured and tortured. When his father had been killed rescuing him. He would not allow history to repeat with Weylind and Ryfon.

He reached out and gripped Ryfon's shoulders. "Do not join the fighting. You can help your father best by taking on duties here at Estyra."

Not that Farrendel thought Weylind would allow Ryfon anywhere close to the fighting. They had all learned their lesson after what had happened in the last war. No, Weylind would hold the trolls off, if they attacked in the next two weeks, and wait for Farrendel to arrive before he made any large-scale counterattack.

This was what the battles and torture had turned Farrendel into. He was Tarenhiel's weapon. Until he had met Essie, that was all he had thought he would ever be.

Ryfon nodded and stepped back as Weylind's wife, Rheva, strode forward to give a quick farewell while Weylind spoke with Jalissa.

When Rheva moved to exchange a stiff farewell with Essie, Weylind gripped Farrendel's shoulders. "Stay safe, shashon."

Farrendel swallowed back the frantic clawing in the pit of his stomach. He and Jalissa would be essentially alone in Escarland. The most vulnerable Farrendel had ever been, except for his capture by the trolls.

Guards would not do any good should Escarland turn on them. If that happened, they would be better served by Farrendel's magic than with guards Weylind could not afford to spare. Not that Farrendel truly believed he would be called on to fight against a betrayal by Escarland's royalty. Essie would not allow it. But that did not satisfy the part of him that panicked over any risk like this.

Since he could not allow Weylind to see his fear, he forced his face neutral and gripped Weylind's shoulders in return. "I will."

But Weylind did not release Farrendel. If anything, his grip tightened, as if he was loath to let him go. "I am trusting the Escarlish king with the protection of my family. Your magic is strong, but even you cannot stand alone against their army should they turn on you."

Surely King Averett of Escarland would not risk war— a war he had sacrificed his own sister in a marriage alliance to prevent—by allowing injury to either Farrendel or Jalissa.

Farrendel glanced at Essie beside him, her focus on his and Weylind's conversation now after Rheva's short farewell.

Essie stepped closer, wrapping her arm around Farrendel's waist as she faced Weylind. "My brothers will keep him safe. I know you don't trust them, and you probably don't trust me a whole lot either, but war between our peoples is the last thing Averett wants. Nor does he want to have me grumpy with him over not liking Farrendel. So your family is safe."

Essie? Grumpy? Farrendel tried to picture it. The few times he had seen her grumpy, she usually turned weepy, then back to talkative and sunny fairly quickly.

Essie sighed and shook her head. "I'm talking too much again, aren't I? You're giving me your bewildered look. Which, honestly, doesn't look a whole lot different from your panicked look or your indulgent look, but I can tell."

Here he had thought he was doing an admirable job of keeping his expressions to himself. The public train station was hardly the place to be expressive.

Weylind gave him an almost pitying look before he released him, as if he still felt guilty about pairing Farrendel with such an exuberant human. Now was not the time to give yet another correction that, no, Farrendel did not mind being married to Essie in the least. She would never be tame enough to truly fit among the elite of elven society, but Farrendel would not want that for her.

King Weylind moved to Essie, hesitated a moment, then gripped her shoulders. "Look after him for me, isciena. This is going to be harder for him than you know."

Farrendel stiffened but could not allow either of them to see the way those words twisted. Weylind understood. He knew how Farrendel struggled with change and new places.

Would Essie be as understanding? She had only seen him at his best in places where he felt as safe and controlled as he ever could feel. She might consider his nightmares his worst, but the ones she had seen so far were the manageable ones.

What would she think if he lost the tenuous balance he currently maintained? His life had tilted out of control once before, and it had taken all of his family's tenacity to drag him back to this level of sanity.

Essie glanced at Farrendel before she returned Weylind's gesture with her own, smirking as she did so.

Farrendel tried to imagine what she was thinking but failed.

As Weylind stepped back, Essie muttered under her breath. "Elves love their cryptic warnings."

As it did not seem something that required his response, Farrendel remained silent.

His sister Melantha was next, and the last person left for farewells. She gave him a quick embrace of his shoulders, her black hair dark against the deep red of her dress.

Farrendel gripped her shoulders, not sure what to say. He had always been closer to Jalissa than Melantha, since Jalissa was a mere hundred years older than him rather than two hundred years as Melantha was. But Melantha was the strong sister. The one who had carried the burdens the tragedies in their family had left to her.

Melantha's gaze flicked to Essie, and for a brief moment, her mouth curled before she tamed the expression. "Do not let yourself be tainted by the humans."

Farrendel gritted his teeth, forcing the churn in his chest to still. He had argued enough with Melantha over this already. He did not want to part now with yet another argument.

She did not linger for a reply, even if he had found one. Instead, she glided away, skipping over Essie entirely.

If Essie noticed the slight, her smile did not waver. Farrendel suspected her smile performed the same function as his impassive expression. They were both a mask to conceal emotions best kept hidden from those around them.

Jalissa pivoted and embarked on the train, her guard trailing behind her. Essie made a waving motion with her hand but halted. It must have been a human gesture Farrendel had yet to learn.

After a final nod to his family, he steered her onto the train. The dark green of the cushioned seats contrasted against the silver of the train's walls while large windows looked out onto the forest and kept him from feeling too enclosed.

As he sank onto one of the benches, Essie perched on the bench next to him, peering out the window. "I'm excited to be awake this time. I missed seeing much of the Tarenhieli forest last time. It will probably be a shock to you when we reach Escarland and see our rolling, treeless fields stretching out to the horizon. Though, I guess you will have the same problem I had back then. We will arrive in the evening and cross the kingdom in the dark, so you won't see much except for the last stretch before Aldon, and that's rather urban."

The train eased forward, gliding smoothly down the rails as it picked up speed. Essie leaned even closer to the window, coming within inches of plastering her nose to the glass.

Across from him, Jalissa quirked one eyebrow. He let his own smile flicker onto his face for a moment while Essie's back was turned. Yes, he fully expected Essie to chatter the entire train ride. And, no, he did not mind. As long as Essie was talking, she did not demand a response from him.

The last time Farrendel had left for a diplomatic meeting like this, he had come home married to a stranger to form a marriage alliance between Tarenhiel and Escarland. Now he could not imagine his life without her in it.

Essie turned out to be a very adaptable, understanding human, but what if her family was not of the same disposition?

What if he could not convince her family of how much Essie meant to him? He could not even fully convince his own family of how right Essie was for him.

After two hours of alternating between staring out the window and regaling them with past trips she had taken and sights she would like to show them in Aldon, Essie flopped back onto the bench and glanced between them. "Aren't you bored? The two of you have barely moved in two hours. What do you normally do on a long trip like this? Our trip to Lethorel took most of a day, but I napped during that one as well. I'll probably nap later, but not right away. Do you have any games you like to play?"

Jalissa started, as if the suggestion was an immense relief. She gestured to the row of drawers set below the benches. "I believe there may be games in one of these from when we were children."

Essie immediately plopped onto the floor and started searching through the drawers. When she located the games, she pulled all of them out until she held one up. "Elven checkers. I know how to play this one. Though, you guys might use different rules than my family does."

Elven checkers? Was that what they called the game in Escarland? Farrendel reached to pull the folding table from the wall to set it up in the aisle. "It is *eshalma* here. Jalissa?"

Jalissa lifted her shoulders. "I suppose I will play."

After they had set up the game, a board with eight points and played with colored glass marbles, Farrendel played the worst eshalma game of his life. Essie was too fascinating the way she chattered through the game, exclaiming over good plays whether they were hers or someone else's, and bouncing in her seat in that way that said she could not sit still even if she tried. With Essie, he did not mind being distracted.

As Essie made another play, her focus on the board, Jalissa met Farrendel's gaze, her mouth twitching before she gave a small huff, glancing toward the ceiling.

Farrendel raised an eyebrow back. Right now, he did not care if his sister was laughing at how much he was staring at his wife. As Essie would probably curl up and fall asleep on his shoulder once she wound down for a nap, Farrendel being unable to take his eyes off Essie would not be the worst offense against propriety.

As evening descended, they neared the border station at the Hydalla River, which formed the border between Tarenhiel and Escarland.

Essie had indeed fallen asleep against his shoulder. Her head rested heavy, cutting off circulation to his arm. But she was warm against his side. Her breath wafted against his neck, fluttering the collar of his shirt.

As much as he wanted to let her sleep, she would want to be awake for crossing the border. With his free arm, he gently shook her. "Essie, it is time to wake up."

Her breath caught, then she made a groaning noise in the back of her throat before she pushed off him. She swiped her hair from her face and rubbed at her eyes. "Are we there already?"

"Yes." The windows behind Jalissa showed the broad expanse of the Hydalla River, its ripples flecked with the orange of the sunset.

Once the train eased to a halt at the station, they waited on board as their luggage was moved from the train to the boat. It took only moments to board the boat, and then they were moving into the current, headed toward Linder Island, a barren, rock island in nearly the center of the river.

Essie rushed to the bow railing, focused on the Escarlish shore with her face turned to the breeze. Farrendel joined her, but he glanced over his shoulder at the Tarenhieli shore growing farther away by the moment. He forced away the churn deep in the pit of his stomach.

Unlike the last time he had been there, Linder Island now had a jetty for their boat. A string of roots grew out of the water up to a tiny, one-room structure built on their side of the island. The roots connected to the rest of their root-system communication system. Farrendel had heard the humans used wires to achieve the same message transfer.

The boat docked, and the gangplank lowered. Farrendel hesitated, but Essie gripped his first two fingers in a handhold and all but dragged him off the boat.

Across the minuscule island, a stone building had been built on the Escarlish side with a wire running to the top of it. A steamboat waited next to their new jetty, smoke belching from the stacks.

This was the result of the treaty between their peoples. Their two communication systems met here, on this island, where the soldiers stationed here could pass messages back and forth with a quick walk.

A far too quick walk. Farrendel barely had time to brace himself before Essie was tugging him across the way.

An Escarlish captain met them beside the stone building. "Princess Elspeth. It is good to have you back on Escarlish soil."

Farrendel was not sure how Essie would want him to

present himself. He settled for standing straight and still beside her, hoping he appeared non-threatening. Beside him, Jalissa held her head high, her expression neutral.

"It's good to be back." Smiling, Essie glanced past him to the steamboat tied to the dock behind him. "Is the boat ready to leave now?"

"Yes, Your Highness. We've kept the steam pressure up so we can leave immediately." With a sideways glance at Farrendel and Jalissa that was too quick to discern his thoughts, the captain led the way to the steamboat.

The steamboat was painted a crisp white with black lettering in Escarlish naming the ship the *Swift*. Red wheels studded with paddles stuck out of the boat on either side toward the rear while the smokestack rose black against the sky, a bright red strip decorating the top.

Jalissa grimaced up at the plume of smoke puffing from the ship's smokestack.

When Essie glanced at Farrendel, he forced himself to attempt a smile. But he could not hold the expression in place for long before the tightness of his shoulders ran tension into the rest of his muscles.

Essie led Farrendel, Jalissa, and Jalissa's guard up the gangplank onto the steamboat. The crew retrieved their luggage, then the steamboat shoved off Linder Island.

In the bow, Essie leaned against the rail and bounced on her toes. She pointed. "The outpost is flying a royal pendant. It could be for me, but I think one of my brothers is here to meet us. I wonder if it's Julien or Edmund? That isn't Averett's standard, so it can't be him."

Farrendel forced his breathing to remain steady, even as he glanced over his shoulder at the blurry smudge of the far, Tarenhieli shore. In moments, he would be on

19

Escarlish soil for only the second time in his life. His kingdom's survival might rest on the impression he and Jalissa gave the Escarlish dignitaries. He trusted that Jalissa would make the correct impression, but would he?

He had not made a thorough study of human customs. What if he offended them?

All too soon, the steamboat eased to the dock. Smoke puffed into the sky as the paddle wheels reversed to slow the boat before it lightly bumped a piling. Soldiers rushed to tie the boat in place.

Jalissa joined Essie and Farrendel, her face set in a serene mask. Her flowing, deep burgundy dress highlighted the rich, brown-black of her hair and eyes. She would show the humans exactly how stunning and composed a princess of the elves could be.

If only Farrendel could keep his own bearing as poised.

Essie tugged her hand free of Farrendel's. When he glanced at her, she clasped his hand with all their fingers, palms together, in the human way of holding hands. "We're in Escarland now. This is perfectly acceptable, and even expected, here."

"I see." Farrendel resisted the urge to glance around, his back prickling with discomfort. This was far too intimate a gesture for public, surely. But none of the soldiers were staring at them as if horrified by the impropriety. A few were staring, but their gazes had the calculating look of threat assessment Farrendel recognized.

"Ready?" Essie's grin was wide, bright as the sun beaming down through the broad leaves of his home.

No, he was not ready. But he had no reason to delay. "Yes."

Swinging their clasped hands, Essie strode beside him down the gangway to the jetty.

At the end of the dock, a delegation of soldiers awaited them. In their center stood a slim human man with brown hair cropped short in the style of the humans. Farrendel was not an expert at gauging age in humans, but this human man was young. Around Essie's age or perhaps a few years older. He was dressed in gray, human-style trousers and a black shirt.

"Edmund!" Essie squealed, dropped Farrendel's hand, and raced forward. She leapt into the young man's arms, hugging him tightly around the neck. He responded by lifting her from her feet, swinging her around.

She had said Edmund was one of her brothers, correct? Farrendel strode after her, not sure where he should stand.

The young human man, Edmund, set Essie back on her feet, holding her at arm's length as he gave her a look over. "Are you all right? I couldn't believe what Avie did. And without giving me a chance to properly investigate him."

The look Edmund gave Farrendel over Essie's shoulder pinned Farrendel in place. It was not a glare but rather something penetrating and calculating.

Essie stepped back and reached for Farrendel's hand again, tugging him forward. "Edmund, this is Farrendel Laesornysh. Farrendel, this is my brother Edmund."

Edmund held out his hand to Farrendel, a smile on his face. "It's a pleasure to finally meet you. I can see by my sister's smile that she already cares for you very much."

He could tell that from just a few moments? Farrendel studied Edmund right back. This brother of Essie's was perceptive.

21

And, there was a test in Edmund's words. This was the kind of test with which Farrendel was familiar. It was the type of probing statement an elf would make.

Edmund's hand remained in the space between him and Farrendel. As if he was expecting some reaction from Farrendel.

Farrendel glanced at Essie. What did Edmund want him to do?

Essie leaned closer and said in elvish, "This is a human greeting custom. You clasp his hand and shake it."

Clasp his hand? That was highly unsanitary. Farrendel had no idea where Edmund had been or when he had last washed his hands. It was a wonder humans as a race had endured this long, if they had no compunction against spreading diseases with every stranger they greeted.

Farrendel swallowed, forcing himself not to stumble back. This visit to Escarland was going to be far more difficult than he had anticipated.

THREE

T hree months ago, Essie had left Escarland mostly married to a mysterious elf prince she didn't know. A marriage of alliance, nothing more.

Returning now, it was so much more, even if it was odd to have Farrendel on Escarlish soil, facing her brother Edmund.

Farrendel eyed Edmund's hand. Elves barely held hands with their significant others, much less clasped hands to shake with a stranger.

Essie leaned in close and whispered, "You don't have to if you don't want to."

It would be a fine line between encouraging Farrendel to learn her culture and yet not force him to do things he was uncomfortable with, like shake a stranger's hand.

Edmund started to withdraw his hand, but Essie glanced at him and shook her head. Edmund needed to give Farrendel just a little more time to decide if he wanted to do this or not.

After another moment's hesitation, Farrendel warily reached for Edmund's hand.

Edmund gripped Farrendel's hand before he had a chance to pull away and gave it a firm shake before letting go.

Farrendel quickly withdrew his hand. Behind his impassive mask, he had to be grimacing and struggling not to scrub his hand on his tunic.

Jalissa swept down the gangway to the jetty, resplendent in her burgundy dress, the silk rippling around her feet as she glided forward.

Edmund bowed. "Princess. Thank you for gracing us with your presence. With your help, I am sure our two kingdoms will be able to put aside our differences and build a lasting peace."

Essie barely restrained herself from rolling her eyes. Edmund could be such a charmer when he wanted to be.

Jalissa stared at Edmund coldly, even as she made the elf mouth to forehead greeting gesture with one hand. "It is my hope we can halt another costly and fruitless war caused by Escarlish aggression."

Essie tightened her grip on Farrendel's hand. The last war had started twenty years ago when her father's advisors convinced him to attack Tarenhiel. Now, the trolls were trying to make it look like Escarland was again the aggressor.

Instead of showing any offense, Edmund smiled brightly, as if the insult went right over his head. "As we have no aggression toward your people, this should be a simple matter to clear up. Now, the train is waiting to take us to Aldon."

Essie stifled her yawn, more than ready to board. It had been a long day, even with her nap. After a night on the train, she would wake just before they reached Aldon.

She led the way past the Escarlish soldiers standing next to the train as the guard escort. Their hands straying to their muskets, the soldiers eyed Farrendel, Jalissa, and the guard.

Essie tightened her grip on Farrendel's hand and worked to keep her smile in place. Hopefully seeing their princess holding hands with an elf and looking happy would reassure the soldiers.

Strolling past the caboose, the baggage car, the passenger car where the soldiers would ride, and the car with the staff and kitchen, they reached the two, luxury sitting and sleeping cars. After boarding the train, Edmund pointed to the largest of the three sleeping compartments in the car. "This one has been prepared for you, Your Highness."

Jalissa nodded, glanced at Farrendel, then stepped inside, followed by her guard. The stoic female elf guard closed the door firmly behind her. Staying up and talking late into the night wasn't the elves' cup of tea.

That left Edmund, Essie, and Farrendel standing in front of the remaining two sleeping compartments.

The train jerked forward, the wheels grinding against the iron tracks. Farrendel winced at the screeching, tipping his head as if to minimize the noise.

After the quiet of the elves' forest and magically powered train and boat, the coal-powered steam engine would be achingly loud to Farrendel. And, for all Essie knew, elves probably had better hearing than humans. It wouldn't surprise her, at this point.

"I was sleeping in this compartment, but if you both need a compartment, there is room in the crew's bunks where I can sleep." Edmund glanced between Essie and Farrendel, his gaze evaluating.

Essie breathed out a sigh. This was going to get embarrassing. There wasn't a delicate way to go about telling her brother that, no, she didn't mind sharing a room with her husband. It was something that would normally be assumed, but their situation wasn't exactly normal. And, really, if it was set up like a normal train car compartment, it had bunks built into the sides. "We'll take the other compartment."

Edmund gave a short nod. "Very well. I was probably going to stay up for a while longer in the sitting and dining car, but feel free to retire. I know it has been a long day."

Longer than he knew. Elves were early risers, and thanks to Farrendel's nightmares, they had risen even earlier than most elves.

But Essie caught the note in her brother's voice. He wanted to talk, if she had a moment.

She gave him a slight nod, then gave Farrendel a nudge toward the compartment. As soon as the door shut behind them, Farrendel's shoulders sagged, even as he swayed with the movement of the train.

The compartment was tight, barely big enough for their travel bags to sit on a bench and two bunks to fill the far wall. After the night and day they'd had, Essie ached to curl up in a bunk and fall asleep.

"You're tired, aren't you?" Essie rested a hand on his arm. Farrendel was probably even more tired than she was. He usually went to bed earlier than this.

He nodded and flinched as the train's whistle pierced the evening.

"Would you mind if I stayed up a little longer to talk

to Edmund?" Essie didn't want to just abandon Farrendel here, especially after the nights of nightmares he'd been suffering. "Do you need me here for the nightmares? Sorry it is so loud. You're probably going to have trouble sleeping, aren't you?"

She forced herself to stop asking questions long enough for him to actually answer. It was a bad habit of hers, talking too much.

"Yes." Farrendel pulled something out of a pocket. It looked like two pieces of moss. "Spend time with your brother. I will be fine."

He stuffed the pieces of moss into his ears, surveyed the two bunks, then swung into the top one with a swift, easy movement.

Yes, he would be all right. He was a grown elf. She didn't have to babysit him. Besides, she wouldn't stay up that much longer. She was nearly as tired as he was.

Easing out the door, she closed it behind her and made her way down the narrow hallway past the sleeping compartments, across the swaying connection between the sleeping and sitting cars, and entered, timing her steps to the rhythm of the wheels on the tracks.

Gaslights flashed by outside the square windows behind the plush benches lining the sitting area. A marble-topped, low table sat in the center of a cluster of upholstered chairs. If not for the clacking wheels, chugging boiler, and swaying rhythm, it could have been a sitting room in Winstead Palace.

Edmund lounged in one of the chairs, cradling a mug of coffee. How he managed to sleep after consuming coffee, she would never understand.

Another mug waited on the table in front of the chair across from Edmund. Essie sank into the chair and picked up the mug. Its warmth seeped into her hands. She breathed in the rich, savory smell of chocolate. "I missed our late-night talks. And hot chocolate. How I've missed hot chocolate."

"They don't have hot chocolate in Tarenhiel?" Edmund leaned back in his chair.

"Not that I've seen. Elves live in the trees, and they tend to only eat hot meals once a day. I think they don't like making cook fires any more than they have to." Essie sipped at her hot chocolate, closed her eyes, and gave in to a small moan. "Oh, this is good. I wonder if they have a way to enchant something to heat up a pot of water. I would love to have my cup of hot chocolate in the mornings."

"If the elves can't figure it out, I'm sure Lance Marion might be able to do something."

Lance, a local inventor, worked with Averett frequently when trying to pair magic and machines. If anyone could think of something, he could.

"I'll have to stop by his shop while I'm in Aldon." Essie sipped at her hot chocolate, closing her eyes for a moment at the sheer bliss of the warm drink.

"I'll make sure you are supplied with all the chocolate you need." Edmund eyed her over the rim of his coffee mug. The light tone dropped from his voice. "Seriously, Essie. Anything you need. I will get it for you."

"I know." Essie stared down at the mug in her hands. Edmund would be able to do it, too.

This small talk was nice, but she could feel its sharp edges. Was Edmund waiting for her to open up to him? Or was he figuring out a way to tell her something important? She couldn't quite read the message in his silence.

She took a fortifying swig of the hot chocolate, set it

on the table, and met Edmund's gaze. "If you have something to ask, then go ahead and ask it. We've never been the type of family to tiptoe around."

Edmund set aside his coffee. "I'm not sure how to ask this. You and that elf seem to be getting along well, and I don't want to ruin anything between you. Yet..."

"What are you getting at?" Essie tried not to tense.

"After I learned you'd married him, I did some digging. In my way. You know."

"You did some spying and all that." Essie rolled her eyes. Edmund could be so secretive when the entire family knew exactly what he did. As a member of the Intelligence Office, he had the means to dig up all the facts he wished.

What had he found about Farrendel? There were secrets Essie preferred they didn't know, for Farrendel's sake.

"I reached out to my contacts and hung around some of the border towns." Edmund didn't smile.

Essie's stomach tightened. What had Edmund learned? Had he found out Farrendel's secrets? She didn't dare ask, in case Edmund hadn't found out everything yet.

"There were a few things I learned." Edmund rubbed at his palm, huffed, and shook his head. "I don't even know how to go about asking this. If you don't know, I don't want to wreck anything. But it's something I think you ought to know."

Edmund could dance around the topic all night if he wanted to. If he had been in the border towns, he'd probably heard Farrendel's worst secret. After all, it wasn't like the circumstances of Farrendel's birth were a secret in Tarenhiel. The fact that he was the illegitimate son of the late elf king was the biggest scandal the elven court had seen in hundreds of years. The only reason it wasn't known in Escarland was because elves kept their scandals to themselves. "If you're asking if I know about the... timing of Farrendel's birth, then, yes. I know."

Edmund's shoulders sagged a moment before he met her gaze. "I wasn't sure the elves would tell you."

"Actually, Farrendel's grandmother told me the whole story the first week I was there. She seemed to think I ought to know." Essie leaned forward and didn't continue until Edmund met her gaze. Something fierce beat inside her chest. "Maybe I needed to know to understand him, but, please, Edmund. This isn't something Avie needs to know. It does nothing to help the alliance between Escarland and Tarenhiel if Avie were to find out he'd married me to the illegitimate elf prince. Farrendel was fully recognized as a part of the elven royal family. As Laesornysh, he has earned himself a respected place in their court. And if the scandal of his illegitimacy still plagues him there, I don't want it to follow him here. He should have at least one place where he isn't defined by it. Please, Edmund."

Edmund leaned his elbows on his knees. "He will have a hard enough time in our court without this hanging over him as well. I will quietly bury my file on this, if that's what you wish. I see no reason why anyone else needs to know. But, Essie? If this ever does get out, I'll be sure to get ahead of it."

"Thank you." Essie picked up her mug of hot chocolate again. She would never take her brothers' loyalty and love for granted. They had protected her for her whole life, and they were still looking out for her now, even if she was in a different country.

Edmund also reclaimed his mug. "You are falling in love with him, aren't you?"

"Yes." Essie grinned and gulped down her hot chocolate now that it had cooled. "You know me. I was bound to fall in love quickly. I am too determined to be happy to spend time moping around. Estyra is beautiful, and Farrendel is so sweet. I know he doesn't look it. He puts on that hard, warrior mask and doesn't let people in easily. I'm hoping he will relax enough that all of you will see the real him instead of only his mask."

"Maybe. But I'm not surprised. You always were the sunshine in our family." Edmund reached over to tweak her nose like he used to when she was little. He glanced down at her tunic and trousers. "You're wearing trousers."

Essie grinned. "I wondered how long it would take you mention that."

"It's rather noticeable."

"It's wonderful." Essie swung her feet. "In Tarenhiel, both males and females wear tunics and trousers for everyday clothing. In their treetop walkways, dresses would just get in the way, not to mention awkward if anyone happened to look up. It's just more sensible for them. Besides, tunic and trousers are so much more comfortable."

Edmund chuckled as he lounged in the chair once again, all tension gone at the change in topic. "You always begged Mother to let you wear trousers. And tried to steal some from us, if I recall."

"Yes." Essie laughed at the memory, even as she had to suppress a yawn. How stifled she'd felt back then. She'd wanted to run and play like her brothers, but it was so hard to climb trees and get into trouble in a dress. Not that she wanted to wear trousers all the time. She loved dressing up in a gorgeous dress as much as the next girl. But it was nice to have the freedom of movement in between the fancy dress wearing times. "It is funny, really. I thought I would be even more stifled among the elves, since they are rumored to be so stuffy. And, in some ways they are. But in other ways, I've found the freedom I've always craved. Perhaps it wouldn't have been that way with another elf, but Farrendel is a rather unusual, scandal-causing elf already."

"I'm glad you're happy." Edmund's smile was soft. "We all worried."

"I know. And I'm probably going to have to reassure everyone several times that I'm fine before anyone believes me." Essie blinked her dry eyes and swallowed back another yawn. She needed her bed soon, that was for sure.

"Probably. Especially Avie. He's been beating himself up for the past three months." Edmund stood and tugged on a strand of her hair. "Now off to bed with you. Don't think I haven't noticed your yawns."

"It was an early morning." Essie swigged the last of her hot chocolate and covered another yawn. "Elves subscribe to the whole early to bed, early to rise thing."

"I bet that was an adjustment." Edmund chuckled as he walked with her to the doors of the sleeping compartments.

"Just a little bit." Essie paused by her door. "Goodnight."

It felt so much like home, being with her brother again. She hadn't realized how much she'd missed this.

This was the price she'd paid, marrying Farrendel and

moving to Tarenhiel. She'd given up her home. Her family.

She stepped into the compartment and clicked the door closed behind her. The tiny room remained dark, except for the gaslights of towns and stations flashing by along with hints of the moon filtering down from the crescent high in the sky.

Farrendel was nothing but a lump beneath blankets on the upper bunk. Was he already asleep? Perhaps. He had been awfully tired, especially after the last few, rough nights.

She eased her boots off and slipped into the blankets of the bottom bunk. After the last two nights sleeping next to Farrendel, the bunk felt cold. Empty. Even if she could hear his steady breathing above her.

Farrendel's steady breathing. The clickety-clack of the wheels. The steady sway of the car. An easy rhythm to lull her to sleep.

FOUR

Essie woke to chilly, early morning air pouring through the upper window by Farrendel's upper bunk. His blankets flapped in the breeze, but he was missing.

Had he slipped out the window? How had he even managed it? The window wasn't that big, and the wind from the train's passing had to be strong.

Where was he? Surely he hadn't fallen out the window or something ignoble like that. This was Farrendel. He could put a cat to shame with his balance.

Essie glanced from the open window to the door. Should she go look for him?

There was a scraping sound outside the window, then Farrendel swung through feet first, landing gracefully on his bunk, hunched in the tight space.

"How...where..." Essie shook her head. She couldn't even manage to get the questions out.

He shut the window and dropped to the floor. "I was on the top of the train. It is getting light, and I did not want to be seen. Your soldiers might think elves were attacking the royal train."

"They might be trigger happy, that's for sure." Essie eyed him. He didn't look any worse for the wear, even though he'd been doing his flipping, spinning exercises on the top of the fast-moving train. She didn't know how it was even possible.

Even after whipping about in the wind, his hair floated in perfect, unfrizzy strands down his back. Elven conditioner was truly magical stuff. Though her red hair was making it work hard. Her hair was still decently sleek this morning, and after traveling all day and sleeping on an unfamiliar bunk, that was amazing.

She stepped closer and gave him a short kiss. More a peck, really. "Good morning, by the way. You must have slept decently well. You didn't have a nightmare last night. First time in three days."

"Yes." Farrendel rested his hands lightly on her waist and gave her a longer kiss.

She smiled as she kissed him back. As long as she and Farrendel kept choosing each other, they would be fine.

After a few moments, she stepped back and patted his chest. "Edmund tends to be an early riser as well and will probably have breakfast laid out in the sitting room already."

Farrendel straightened at the mention of food and grabbed his silver, formal clothing from his bag before he wedged himself into the tiny water closet attached to the sleeping compartment to change and clean up after exercising.

Essie quickly changed into her new, dark green dress, leaving her hair loose. In the mirror, the green of the dress set off the flaming red of her hair. It almost made her want to switch into a different dress or pin up her hair to hide most of it. She shouldn't feel this self-conscious about her hair. Especially when she was only meeting her family today, not the full Escarlish court.

In the mirror, Farrendel appeared behind her, his gaze focused on her rather than their reflections. He ran a lock of her hair through his fingers. "You were correct. Green brings out the vibrant color of your hair."

"It isn't too red, is it?" Essie grimaced at her reflection. The freckles across her nose were more prominent in the morning light.

Farrendel's gaze snapped up to meet hers in their reflections, a furrow on his brow. "No. It is pretty."

If he'd said it in a swoony tone, she might have doubted him. But his tone was so matter of fact, as if there wasn't any other opinion to be had besides pretty, that she couldn't doubt his assessment.

She leaned back against him, his hands on her shoulders. This was nice. It almost made her want to skip breakfast.

Except that her stomach made a loud grumbling noise, making Farrendel smile.

She turned to the door. "How come your stomach isn't growling? You're probably hungrier than I am, considering you usually eat breakfast long before now."

He reached the door first and opened it. "It stopped an hour ago."

In other words, he'd been up so long, his stomach had given up rumbling a long time ago.

In the sitting room, they found toast, jam, eggs, and sausages laid out on the table while Edmund lounged on one of the benches, reading what looked like that morning's newspaper. One of the guards must have retrieved it when the train stopped for water and coal earlier that morning. He glanced at them over the top of the paper. "Morning."

"Anything interesting in the news?" Essie picked up two plates, handed one to Farrendel, and started dishing food onto hers.

Edmund turned a page and flapped it to straighten the paper. "Just a headline about the visit of elven royalty and competing editorials either in favor of the closer ties with the elves or protesting it. Nothing they haven't already printed a dozen times over since your marriage."

There was something to Edmund's tone. He wasn't telling her everything.

But she didn't want to press him for details now. She'd rather focus on being reunited with her family and properly introducing them to Farrendel. The grim realities of trying to stop another war from sparking, the impending war between the elves and trolls, the traitors in Escarland and Tarenhiel, the reaction of Escarland's people, could all wait until later.

She took a seat on the bench with a table in front of her. After thoroughly inspecting the food, Farrendel picked out a slice of toast, a piece of sausage, and eggs. When he sat beside her, he still eyed his food suspiciously.

Had he ever eaten hot food for breakfast? Elves tended to only eat a hot meal once a day for dinner in the evening.

The door at the far end of the car opened, briefly letting in the louder sound of the rushing wind and clacking wheels, before Jalissa stepped inside.

Edmund's paper crinkled as he folded it and set it aside. "Good morning, Princess Jalissa."

She dipped her head in a nod before picking out food with the same wariness Farrendel had. She claimed a seat next to Farrendel, and the two of them discussed something in elvish too quietly for Essie to hear.

As they ate, the rising sun illuminated the rolling hills flashing past outside the rows of square windows now that they had left behind the more heavily wooded part of Escarland near the border with Tarenhiel.

Farrendel turned in his seat, and his gaze remained focused on the landscape even as he absently finished his breakfast and set the plate aside.

"It looks different than Tarenhiel, doesn't it?" Essie swiveled as well to better watch both Farrendel and the scenery outside.

"Yes." Farrendel leaned closer to the window. "There is so much sky."

Essie grinned. At least she wasn't the only one who was mesmerized by seeing a new kingdom outside the train windows, even if Farrendel and Jalissa were more dignified and restrained than Essie had been.

As they approached one of the larger towns that surrounded Aldon, Farrendel's eyes widened, and he came dangerously close to pressing his nose to the glass. "Is that Aldon?"

"No, that's Highborough, a town about ten miles north of Aldon." Essie couldn't help but grin wider. "Aldon is even bigger."

Farrendel's gaze swung to her with something that might have been horror in his eyes before he stared out the window once again.

As they were a royal train, they rumbled straight on through the Highborough station. They had to stop briefly at the coal and water station outside of town for the last amount of water and coal they would need to reach Aldon.

Then they were chugging past the final stretch of rolling hills and smaller villages before they finally crested the rise and the sprawl of Aldon came into view.

Aldon rose along two sides of the Fyne River and spilled into the surrounding hills. A mass of chimneys puffed smoke into the sky while warehouses, homes, and shops clustered along rows upon rows of streets and alleyways.

Near the river, the distinctive bell tower of Hanford University, a world-renowned college for magicians, punctured the skyline. It was a landmark in Aldon, though Essie wasn't sure Jalissa and Farrendel would find that fact interesting.

Jalissa muttered something under her breath. Farrendel's hands clenched at his sides, his expression hard and grim. Gone was the wonder they'd had looking at the cornfields stretching into the distance. This looked more like they'd seen their doom written into the landscape.

"What's wrong?" Essie leaned close to Farrendel, speaking in a low tone.

He glanced from the window, to her, and back. "I knew you humans were numerous but..." He shook his head, still staring out the window as the tracks neared the outskirts of the city. "I did not understand how numerous."

When he didn't elaborate further, Essie took his hand. "That's why we need to build an alliance beyond a simple peace treaty. I believe our kingdoms can be assets to each other rather than enemies. Now, we'll be entering Aldon and arriving at the palace soon. Let's grab our crowns and make sure we're ready."

Farrendel nodded, and they left for their compartment. Jalissa retreated to hers as well to finish getting ready for her arrival as the official Tarenhieli ambassador to Escarland.

In their compartment, Essie dug out her silver, elven circlet made of twining strands with maple, oak, and beech leaves forming a pattern, and settled it on her hair.

The shriek of the steam whistle warning those on the streets that a train would be passing by had Farrendel grimacing and reaching for his moss earplugs. As the train whistle kept blaring, he rested his own, matching circlet on his head. In his formal silver tunic, gray trousers, black boots, and silver-blond hair flowing down his back, he was every inch an elf prince.

Essie swallowed and smoothed the front of her dark green elven dress. Why was she even nervous about this? This was her home. Her family. Everything would be fine.

Metal screeched on metal as the brakes slowed the train as they pulled into the private, royal train station that was walled into the palace complex.

Essie braced a hand against the wall as the train jerked and shuddered. Farrendel rested a hand on her waist to steady her, his feet braced.

With a final squeal, the train juddered to a halt. The shrill steam whistle blared into the morning before a whoosh filled the air as the rest of the steam pressure dissipated.

Farrendel grimaced and removed the moss from his ears. "Are all of your human inventions so loud?"

"We humans do tend to be a loud bunch." Essie took his hand and reached for the door to their compartment. "Are you ready for this?"

Farrendel tensed, almost as if he was trying to think of

a nice way to say the truth since elves didn't lie. His shoulders sagged a fraction. "No."

"Sorry. My family isn't as scary as they seem. I think you've already started winning Edmund over." Essie faced Farrendel and touched his cheek. "They'll love you once they get to know you."

Farrendel straightened his shoulders, and his aloof, hard mask fell into place. Perhaps not quite the reaction she was hoping for, but his hard, warrior edge would make for an impressive entrance, even if he wasn't wearing his swords.

Essie slid the door open, then picked up her skirt so she didn't trip.

Edmund was already gone from his compartment. Probably to prepare the last few things for their arrival.

Essie and Farrendel joined Jalissa, who wore a flowing silver dress. A silver circlet of aspen leaves rested on her dark hair. She stood tall, head high, shoulders back. No princess ever looked more regal.

As the official ambassador, Jalissa led the way through the train and down the steps to the wooden platform. Her guard marched behind her, just as stoic as ever. This particular guard must have been chosen due to her skill at being impassive. She made Farrendel seem expressive.

As Essie and Farrendel stepped from the train, Farrendel stiffened.

The private, royal train station sat off to the side of Winstead Palace, with the tracks running along the outer wall that surrounded the whole palace complex including extensive gardens and a small lake. The roofs of the town crowded against the other side of the wall and spread into the distance. A few people leaned out of the upper windows closest to the palace wall, trying to catch a glimpse of the arriving elves.

Ahead, soldiers and servants lined the walk that joined the main circle drive before the grand entrance to the palace. Edmund waited for them on the walk.

Essie couldn't see anything that would make Farrendel go so hard and cold. She leaned closer and whispered in elvish, "What's wrong?"

Farrendel's gaze was locked on Winstead Palace sprawling before them, a grand edifice of gray stone accented with marble steps and glittering arched windows.

"Are you all right?" She still spoke in elvish and squeezed his hand. "Are we in danger?"

Farrendel's stiff posture cracked enough for him to flick a glance in her direction. "No."

Was that no, they weren't in danger or no, he wasn't all right? Essie couldn't be sure, and now didn't seem like the time to ask.

Jalissa glanced over her shoulder, and Essie thought she caught a hint of worry in the narrowing of her eyes before Jalissa faced forward again.

Stepping forward, Edmund bowed and extended his arm to Jalissa. "Welcome, to Escarland and to Winstead Palace."

Jalissa eyed him, as if deciding if taking his arm would be beneath her dignity. After a moment, she lightly rested her hand on Edmund's forearm in the style of the elves instead of tucking her hand in the crook of his elbow as was the custom in Escarland.

Edmund didn't miss a beat, and instead matched her pace along the walk. The Escarlish soldiers saluted while the servants bowed.

It was all so very official and pompous. When Essie had arrived in Estyra, the walk from the train had been relaxed, with the elves in the town casually greeting their king as he passed.

Then again, she had gone to Tarenhiel as Farrendel's bride. Part of the royal family instead of an official ambassador like Jalissa was. This visit of two members of the elven royal family to Escarland, a human kingdom, was historic. Nothing like it had happened in living memory.

Two footmen in crisp black uniforms and white shirts opened the huge double doors to the palace. Edmund swept inside with Jalissa on his arm. Essie followed, and beside her, Farrendel crept forward like the floor would burn him.

Inside the grand entrance hall, a huge marble staircase wound to the upper floor while paintings of historic battles and kings flanked the walls along with a few busts of those same kings.

Her brother Averett was, thankfully, standing at the base of the stairs rather than waiting on the landing for a cliched grand entrance. He wore his large, gold formal crown, complete with jewels set into the heavy thing, though the rest of his clothing was a nice suit and shirt. He was the only one of Essie's siblings to also inherit red hair, though his was a darker shade of auburn.

Beside him, Essie's sister-in-law, Paige, beamed in a bright pink dress that set off the sparkle in her blue eyes and the shine of her golden-blond hair. Although Paige was four years older than Essie, she had been Essie's best friend even before she'd fallen in love with Essie's brother Averett.

Essie's mother stood beside Paige, dressed in a somber gray dress and wearing a circlet on her faded red hair that had once matched Essie's in color. She still carried herself tall, wearing the circlet of the Queen Mother with dignity.

Julien, the middle of Essie's three older brothers, wore his tan, army uniform. His brown hair was cropped short while a short beard covered his chin.

Averett stepped forward. "Welcome to Escarland. I hope this visit will be the first of many as the alliance between our kingdoms strengthens."

Jalissa gave the mouth to forehead greeting gesture and a small dip to her head. "It is a pleasure to be here. I hope we will be able to put aside our differences to build a more lasting peace."

Essie hung back with Farrendel while Averett completed the official welcome for Jalissa. Essie didn't want to greet her family in this stiff, formal manner.

After a few more preliminaries, a maid stepped forward.

Averett motioned from Jalissa to the maid. "She will show you to your rooms if you would like to freshen up and settle in. We will be dining in an hour."

"Very well." Jalissa followed the Escarlish maid from the entrance hall, her elvish guard trailing behind them.

As soon as she left, Essie turned to her family. They had relaxed, somewhat, but their stances remained tense as they glanced toward Farrendel.

This was ridiculous. They were family, even if Farrendel was a stranger to them.

Essie launched herself forward. "Mama!"

In a moment, Essie found herself enveloped in her mother's warm, soft hug. How she'd missed this.

Her mother stepped back, her gaze searching Essie's face. "How are you?"

"I'm fine, really." Essie stepped into Julien's bear hug. "I missed all of you so much."

Essie squealed as her sister-in-law Paige gave her a squeezing tight hug. "I have so much to tell you."

Paige flicked a glance toward Farrendel as she drew back, but her smile remained in place. "I'm sure. I can't wait to hear all about the last three months."

Averett pushed past Paige to hug Essie next. "Are you sure you're all right? I've been so worried..." He trailed off, and Essie caught the tortured look in his eyes before he looked away.

"You need to stop beating yourself up about arranging a marriage of alliance for me. It worked out better than even I could have imagined." Essie returned Avie's hug before she extricated herself and glanced over her shoulder.

Farrendel stood, hands behind his back, his face impassive. To her family, he probably looked forbidding and hard. But they wouldn't be able to see the way he leaned back, as if he wanted to bolt.

Essie reached a hand to him and waited until he hesitatingly twined his fingers with hers. "I know most of you met him briefly at the wedding, but none of us were relaxed enough to really get to know each other. Everyone, this is Farrendel."

Farrendel remained still and hard as the statues in the palace's garden. But Essie could feel the tremble through his fingers, the wariness in his stance.

Essie tugged on Farrendel's arm to get his attention and spoke in elvish. Hopefully Edmund's elvish wasn't as good as Essie suspected it was. "Farrendel, my love, I know you're nervous, but you're going to scare my family away if you keep putting on your intimidating Laesornysh face."

As he glanced down at her, the hard line of his jaw softened. When he replied, it was in elvish. "Sorry. It is just…"

"It's scary meeting my family. You want them to like you, but you don't want to be vulnerable." Essie quirked a smile. "I know. I had the same thing with your family."

Farrendel's mouth curved upward enough to count as a smile. "You made it look easy."

"I like people, so it *is* easier for me." Essie patted his arm. "Just smile and relax and try not to look so scary. Now we probably should stop talking in elvish before my family wanders off."

They were all staring at them. Averett and Mother just looked bewildered. Paige smiled, her eyes twinkling as if she read something into the situation. Edmund had a smirk as if he had, indeed, understood that entire conversation. Julien had his arms crossed and looked bored.

Essie tugged Farrendel to stand in front of Averett. "Farrendel, this is my brother Averett, though we all call him Avie."

Averett held out a hand. Farrendel's smile dropped for a moment before he pasted it back into place and shook Averett's hand. When Averett let go of Farrendel's hand, Farrendel gripped Averett's shoulders in the elves' restrained version of a hug. "Shashon."

Brother.

The elves didn't have words for brother-in-law or sister-in-law. They believed a couple was so united in marriage, that they used brother or sister for an in-law. Though, they tended to skirt around that by simply not claiming any sort of relation if they didn't want to, making it a huge deal for Farrendel to claim her family as his. Once said, he wouldn't take it back. He would consider her brothers as his brothers for the rest of his life, even if her brothers didn't know it yet.

Essie could've hugged Farrendel right then and there, but she restrained herself and instead gestured to Paige. "This is Paige, my sister-in-law and best friend. I have two nephews as well, and you'll meet them tonight."

"Essie has told me so much about you in her letters. I'm so excited to finally meet you." Paige gave Farrendel a quick hug, and Farrendel went stiff again, glancing over his shoulder at Essie.

Essie grinned back at him and told him in elvish, "I did warn you hugs were common in my family."

His mouth twitched with a grimace before he smoothed his expression and gripped Paige's shoulders briefly. "Isciena."

Edmund squirmed his way into line next, even though he'd had his chance to greet Farrendel at the border. He gripped Farrendel's shoulders in the elven style of hugging and said in perfect elvish, "Elontiri, shashon."

Welcome, brother. Essie sighed and swatted Edmund's shoulder. "So you do know elvish."

"Sorry to break it to you, but your secret language isn't so secret, little sister." Edmund tweaked her nose and strolled away, still chuckling, before Farrendel even had a chance to return the gripped shoulders gesture.

"Your brother is sneaky." Farrendel's tone was flat, almost like he couldn't decide if he should be offended or impressed or simply bewildered.

"Yes, but, for the most part, he uses his great powers of observation and sneakiness for good, though he does enjoy annoying his younger siblings. As my husband, I think you now fall into that category." Essie glared at Edmund's retreating back. In the past three days since realizing they had formed a heart bond, Essie's elvish had improved even faster than it had before. That meant up until a few days ago, Edmund had probably been better at elvish than she was, and she had been working at it for months.

Essie switched back to Escarlish as Julien took Edmund's place with silent footsteps that almost seemed out of place for such a tall, large man. "My brother Julien. He's in the army."

Of all her brothers, Julien looked the most like the portraits of her father that still hung in many places around the palace. Broad shoulders, a round face, soulful deep brown eyes set in deep sockets. He was the quietest of her three brothers, but when he spoke, others listened. His wisdom and strategic insight had promoted him through the army ranks despite his title.

Farrendel had to reach up to grip his shoulders. "Shashon."

Julien patted Farrendel's back, making Farrendel stumble. "Come to the training yard for a sparring match while you're here."

Her brother's way of saying, *Let's see how good you really are and if the Laesornysh legends are true.*

Essie wasn't sure she wanted to see a match between Julien and Farrendel. Even if Farrendel didn't use his magic, he was deadly. Did he even know how to fight in a match that wasn't to the death?

Julien stepped back, leaving Mother the one family member still to be properly introduced.

Essie smiled. "And this is my mother."

Mother wore a soft smile as she also hugged Farrendel. He didn't stiffen as much with her as he had with Paige, though he didn't return the hug. When he clasped Mother's shoulders in the elf version of a hug, his voice had a raspy, almost choked sound to it. "Mamasha."

Mother. Now Essie had a lump in her throat. Farrendel had never had a mother before. Not one he had met in person to address like this.

Essie's mother wouldn't even recognize the word or know the depth of what it meant to Farrendel to say it.

Perhaps Mother did sense something of it or heard it in his voice. Her smile and expression softened still more. "Welcome to the family."

CHAPTER
FIVE

Essie dragged Farrendel away from her family greeting party before they could think to ask awkward questions about where to stash Farrendel at night. She was just going to haul him to her room as if it was the most natural thing in the world.

Except, when she stood in front of her door in the family wing of the castle, she had to pause to take a breath. Her life had changed so drastically the moment Farrendel had come into it. She loved her new life. Her new room in the elven palace. The routines she'd built with Farrendel over their three months of marriage.

But taking him into her old room here in Winstead Palace was such a clash of her old life and new. As if Farrendel didn't quite belong in that room.

Nonsense. That was the wrong way to look at it. Once she invited him inside, there wouldn't be a clash of her previous life and her life as a princess of the elves.

Gripping Farrendel's hand, Essie pushed the door open and stepped inside.

After the sparse quarters that even the royal elves had, her sumptuous suite of rooms was almost a shock. Plush rugs covered the floor. Wood paneling and plaster hid the stone walls with landscape paintings over the soft rose-colored paint. A settee and several padded chairs filled the sitting room while a door next to the fireplace led to the bedroom.

A small bookshelf along one wall held her favorite books and mementos. A set of bookends Averett had given her. A scrap book with items she'd collected on trips throughout Escarland. A porcelain doll that was one of the few gifts her father had given her before he'd been killed.

This room remained just how she'd left it that day when she'd joined Averett on his diplomatic mission to the elves of Tarenhiel. A book sat on one of the marble-topped tables, a velvet ribbon sticking out of the pages. A blanket crumpled on her favorite chair where she'd pushed it off without bothering to fold it or put it away. The servants must have cleaned in here since the surfaces lacked dust, but they hadn't touched anything else.

Farrendel's face remained impassive while he glanced around. Essie would've given anything to know what he was thinking. Probably thinking Winstead Palace was so huge and overdone. Elves, for all their love of fine things, weren't ostentatious. Even their royalty lived simply.

With another fortifying breath, Essie opened the door to her bedroom. Pink velvet drapes bracketed the windows while a floral-patterned blanket covered the bed beneath a gauzy, pink canopy while soft green rugs carpeted the floor. A few trunks and shelves to the left side of the room held her knickknacks and personal items. To the right, a door led into the water closet.

Did the room look as childish to Farrendel as it now did to her? This was the room of a girl who, though she had grown up, still clung to her childhood. Everything was flowers and pink and sentimental items she wasn't ready to part with, even though she hadn't missed most of it in the three months she'd been gone.

Essie let go of Farrendel's hand to let him wander. When she'd arrived in Estyra, she had curiously searched through every cupboard in their main sitting room.

Well, honestly, she had been nosy. She would've been snooping through the room by now, but Farrendel waited by the door, as if asking for her permission.

Essie sat cross-legged on the bed and waved at the room. "Go ahead and look around if you want. Sorry it is so pink. Though, do you elves have the same cultural connotations for the color pink as we humans do? Maybe a pink and floral bedroom isn't as stereotypically girly to you as it would be to my brothers. Then again, you didn't think anything of my red hair, for which I am absolutely grateful, so maybe you don't care about pink either."

Farrendel glanced at her long enough to raise an eyebrow at her chattering before he started wandering around the room.

Essie leaned her elbows on her knees and tried to look relaxed as Farrendel prowled around her room. He didn't touch anything, and he stayed on the rugs as if the stone floor at the edges would bite him. What did he think as he took in the room where she'd grown up? What could he tell about her from it?

She bit the inside of her cheek to stop herself from asking questions. It would be better to let him process in silence and come up with his own questions, if he had any.

But it was so difficult holding back the flood of words. They burned inside her chest, ached inside her throat. It didn't help with Farrendel investigating her room like a puppy sniffing around a new place.

After stalking the edges of the room, Farrendel circled the bed, staring at it for a long time as if trying to puzzle something out. The stare was enough to send a blush to Essie's face.

Halting, he gestured at the bed. "How do human young ones not fall out?"

What? That's what had him staring at the bed so long? Essie blinked, then snorted with her effort not to laugh. "You walk across tiny branches hundreds of feet in the air without so much as a handrail to stop someone from falling, and yet you're worried about falling out of bed?"

Farrendel climbed onto the end of the bed and sat cross-legged facing her, eyeing the edges of the bed as if they were going to reach out to drag him off. Something in his posture remained on edge, as if prepared to whip out his swords at any moment. "It is flat. And large. And in the middle of the room."

The elves slept in beds that were almost nest-like, curved and grown into the living walls of their treehouses. This bed would look odd to him. Then again, this whole room and palace probably looked strange.

"We get used to it, I guess, though rails are put on beds for young children to keep them from falling off." Essie traced the floral pattern of the bedspread with a finger. "Sorry this is all so strange for you."

Farrendel's white-blond hair trailed over his shoulders, all too temptingly silky. "You apologize a lot. You do not have to. Do not apologize for your family or home."

She nearly said *I'm sorry* yet again but clamped her

teeth over the words before they snuck out. "I guess I just want…" For someone who usually had too many words bubbling inside her, they failed her now. What did she want? "I know Winstead Palace probably won't feel like home to you the way Estyra does for me. But I'd like you to feel a part of my family and, at least, not hate it here. But I don't know if that's possible. I can tell you're still on edge, and I don't know if it is my family or because this place is so different than what you're used to or something else. I just…"

Farrendel rested his hand on hers for a moment, but he withdrew his hand and looked away. "I will try."

He looked like he was going to say more, but as Essie waited, Farrendel didn't continue. At least he'd said he'd try. Farrendel would put in a genuine effort. Hopefully Essie's family would put in the same effort. She reached out and squeezed his hands. "Thank you."

His mouth tipped into something almost like a smile. "I like your family. Their protective love for you is admirable."

Trust Farrendel to see their grilling him as something praiseworthy and honorable.

She laughed, and for a moment, sitting there cross legged on the bed facing him, it almost felt right to have him there with her in her old bedroom, fitting in to her old life.

Maybe, just maybe, this visit wouldn't turn into a disaster after all.

ESSIE GLANCED around the table in the formal dining room. Averett held court at the head of the table, with

Jalissa, as the honored guest, sitting to his right. Paige was on his left with Essie and then Farrendel next to her. Edmund and Julien had the places next to Jalissa with Mother at the end of the table. Essie wasn't sure how he'd managed it, but somehow Edmund had claimed the seat next to Jalissa that probably should have been Julien's by right of age.

But her brothers didn't stand on ceremony, especially between Julien and Edmund. Averett was somewhat different. He didn't have the luxury to shed the crown and just be one of the siblings as often as the rest of them.

Still, Edmund probably wasn't going to get far with Jalissa. Her elf sister-in-law could surprise her, but Essie wasn't sure Jalissa would even notice Edmund. Then again, it was hard to tell if Edmund was truly serious or not.

As this was an official welcome banquet, her nephews were eating elsewhere. And probably having more fun. What was it about official dinners that gave everyone such long faces? They hadn't even finished the soup course yet, and the conversation had dwindled to nearly nothing while everyone picked at their food, if it was possible to pick at soup.

Maybe having a fancy dinner their first day there after taking a train through the night hadn't been the best idea. But time wasn't on their side. Tomorrow, they would launch straight into meetings and visiting Parliament.

Essie tapped her foot on the floor. Everyone in this room was family, at least to her. Even if they were going to talk about war and weapons and traitors later on, they didn't have to be stuffy now. "So...Mother and Paige. How has the new shampoo and conditioner been working?"

"I love it. My hair has never felt this good." Paige ran her fingers over her pinned curls. "No wonder elves wear their hair down all the time, if it feels like this."

Edmund swiped a hand over his short-cropped, brown hair. "It's done wonders for my hair. Can't you tell how sleek it is?"

Julien nudged Edmund and ran his fingers over his beard. "My beard has never felt this good."

Now this was the family banter Essie was used to.

Jalissa sniffed and set down her spoon, nudging her soup a little farther away from herself. "We elves do not wear our hair long for petty reasons."

And her family had managed to offend the elves. Already.

The serving staff whisked away their bowls of soup—both finished and unfinished—and replaced them with plates of steamed and seasoned vegetables.

Spices. Seasoning. Essie stuffed a bite in her mouth with only minimal blowing to cool it down first. She closed her eyes, savoring the burst of flavor on her tongue. How she'd missed seasonings like this. The elven dishes were flavored with little to no seasoning, making them plain and somewhat bland most of the time.

Beside her, Farrendel made a small choking sound. She glanced over at him in time to see him swallow, eyes watering, as if he'd just eaten one of the hot peppers that grew in the southern kingdoms.

These spices weren't that hot. They weren't even the spicy kind of spice. Just normal spice.

Unless...Essie eyed Jalissa as the elf tried to surreptitiously scrape the spices from the vegetables. Elves had sensitive hearing and smell. Why not sensitive taste as well? That would explain why their foods were so bland. They didn't taste bland to elves.

She leaned closer to Farrendel. "You don't have to eat it if you don't want to."

He breathed out a sigh and pushed the plate a little farther from him. Averett was glancing between Farrendel and Jalissa, as if he sensed something was wrong but didn't know what it was.

Essie pushed her chair from the table and stood. "I'll be back in just a moment." As she passed Averett, she whispered, "I'll take care of it."

Hopefully he understood what she meant and would relax instead of worry.

Essie hurried down the main corridor. It would've been quicker to take the servants' hall that connected the dining room directly with the kitchen, but it was narrow, and Essie didn't want to get in the servers' way. They were already working hard enough to put on this fancy meal without having their princess bumbling into them.

After hurrying down a short section of stairs, she pushed the door open into the kitchen. The clanging, bustling, whistling, hissing, shouting, sizzling clamor of the kitchen smacked into her along with a wave of heat and mouth-watering aromas.

"Princess Essie!"

Essie blinked away the cloud of steam in time to see Head Chef Figo barreling toward her. He was tall and lean as a whip, probably due to his habit of running to stay in shape. His hair streaked with gray at the temples, but the lines on his face were more from smiling than age.

He stopped short of hugging her and swept an elaborate bow instead. "Welcome back to my kitchen, princess."

"How I've missed your cooking." Essie resisted the urge to give him a hug.

"I've heard elven cooking leaves much to be desired." Chef Figo shook his head. "My servers tell me your elf husband doesn't seem to appreciate my cooking."

"That's why I'm here, actually." Essie tried to think of a polite way of phrasing it. She didn't want to offend Chef Figo or make the elves sound rude. "Elven food tends to be bland and use very little spices. I thought that was just how they preferred to cook, but I realized tonight that elves have a more sensitive sense of taste than we humans do. A little spice goes a long way for them. So what tastes good for us humans is overwhelming for them."

"Ah, I see." Chef Figo nodded, looking over at the pieces of steak, laid out in preparation for the main course. "I shall see their dishes as a challenge to create masterpieces without spices."

"Thank you. I know they will love your cooking once the level of spices is no longer overpowering for them." Essie breathed in a deep breath of the savory aromas filling the kitchen. "After tasting your cooking again, I'm going to miss it all the more when I return to Estyra."

"I will give you a list of spices to purchase." Chef Figo gave her a wink. "Perhaps you can teach the elves to cook properly."

"That would be wonderful. Even if I have to sprinkle the spices on once the plate is set before me, it will be worth it." Essie's mouth watered as another wave of delicious smells reached her.

Chef Figo flapped his hand at her. "Go. If you don't hurry back, you'll miss the next course."

Essie hurried back just in time to wolf down a few

more bites of vegetables before her plate was whisked away and replaced with a small salad. The dressing was served in small tureens with a spoon so they could ladle as much or as little dressing onto the greens as they liked.

"This one is very mild, if you want to try it. Or that one is more fruit based so it is also mild," Essie whispered to Farrendel in elvish.

Jalissa eyed them, so hopefully she would take a cue from Farrendel.

Farrendel dribbled a little bit of each on edges of his salad before choosing the raspberry dressing. Jalissa promptly choose that one as well.

Essie tried to relax. Hopefully now Jalissa and Farrendel could enjoy the rest of the meal. Still, it was exhausting trying to anticipate all the snags involved with introducing Farrendel to her culture. Had he been this worried with her? It wasn't as easy as he'd made it look.

When the main course arrived, Farrendel's steak was free of pepper and other seasonings while hers was topped with a pepper and mushroom sauce.

He glanced from his plate to hers, then met her gaze. "Linshi."

Elven for *thank you*.

"I didn't want you to be miserable trying to eat." Essie sliced into her steak. "Food is too delicious to waste."

SIX

F arrendel knelt on the pink rug in Essie's room and carefully retrieved the canvas-wrapped packages he had hidden among his belongings, trying to keep his hands from shaking. This was an important custom among his people, and something he would have done if he had courted Essie properly. In Tarenhiel, it would be a significant moment before a proposal.

He reached for another package, a throbbing starting at the back of his head. All this stone around him, pressing down on him. He willed the headache away, at least for now.

"What are those? I don't remember seeing you pack them." Essie halted at his side, peering over his shoulder. Unfailingly curious, as always.

After the formal dinner with her family, Essie had brought him back to her room, explaining they would be gathering with her family informally in her mother's sitting room, but they could take the time to change into comfortable clothes beforehand.

In Tarenhiel, this was not something done in comfortable clothes in an informal setting. But he would have to make allowances for their different customs here. He located the last package and set it on top. "An elven custom I must perform."

As he stood, the packages cradled against him, she nudged his arm. "You're being rather mysterious. Usually your brother is the one who likes to be cryptic."

In Tarenhiel, the prospective bride was not supposed to help. Yet these were unusual circumstances, both because Essie was human and because she and Farrendel were already married. She deserved to be courted properly. Marrying with such haste was not customary for his people, and he needed to prove to her family and, perhaps, to himself that for all the haste of their marriage, he did not take it lightly.

But Essie and her family would not know the significance of this tradition. Perhaps it would be better to enlist her help to make sure he adjusted for human traditions and did not accidentally offend them while he was trying to honor them.

Farrendel set the packages on the bed, then sat cross-legged beside them. How did he go about explaining this? "It is customary that when an elf asks his intended's family for their blessing for the match, he presents a gift to each of the family members."

Essie sat on the bed across from him and touched his arm. "You never mentioned this to me. I would've helped."

"I know." But that was the part of the tradition that

made it difficult, especially for him. "But I cannot have your help. The tradition is to show how well he knows her family, proving to her and her family that he seeks to honor them."

"So let me get this straight. You had to pick out gifts for my family without my help whatsoever." Her voice held a trace of laughter.

Farrendel stared down at the canvas-wrapped gifts. "Yes."

"I take it this would normally happen after a couple has been courting a while and he has presumably gotten to know her family in person very well. Making it rather tough for you, considering you only met most of my family briefly."

"You talk. A lot." He had also read everything Weylind's sources had collected on the royal family of Escarland several times. Once before that meeting to discuss a peace treaty and several times since finding himself married to Essie. As it was difficult for elven spies to infiltrate Escarland, the dossiers had not told him much beyond what Essie had revealed, except for a few suspicions about her brother Edmund's role in Escarland's Intelligence Office.

When he lifted his gaze to Essie, her eyes were sparkling, and her mouth tilted in a grin. "How you manage to pay attention to even half the stuff I say is beyond me. I usually forget most of what I've said within minutes of saying it. Now I'm very curious to see what you picked out for each of them based on my ramblings alone."

He had gone the simple route and had not personalized the items as much as would have traditionally been the case. Nor did he plan on giving speeches behind the meaning of the gifts, a part of the tradition he was more than happy to eliminate. Courtship rituals involved an excessive amount of talking and interacting with other people.

"I do not know how your family will react." He could not hold her gaze. "It breaks tradition, but I believe I need your help. I do not want to offend them."

"You won't. Not unless you picked out something super scandalous for some reason."

Unless an elf-made knife was considered scandalous here in Escarland, he did not think so. He shook his head.

"In that case, it would still probably be awkward if you just handed out gifts by yourself since this isn't a human custom. And tonight is probably already going to be awkward enough. So let's not add to it." Essie reached out and squeezed his hand. "But, it *is* customary for humans to give each other gifts after traveling or living somewhere new. I actually have gifts for my family as well. I wasn't sure if I should hand them out tonight and distract them from meeting you, but if you have gifts as well, we'll hand them out together."

Farrendel felt some of the tension release from his shoulders. He had been dreading going through with this tradition. Essie knew his intention, and that was all that mattered in the end.

"If we hand out gifts together, it'll be clear to my family that we are doing things together. The presence of two gifts, obviously one from each of us, will show them I didn't pick out the gifts solely by myself." Essie rested a hand on his cheek, lifting his gaze to hers. "I know it isn't exactly your elven tradition, but the result will be the same. You'll show my family you care, but in a way they'll understand by our traditions."

Now he was especially glad he had checked with Essie first. Observing her interacting with his culture did not teach him all there was to know about her culture. Nor was his study of the little that elves knew about humans turning out to be sufficient. Fighting a civilization was entirely different than marrying into it, and he had not even had the experience of fighting humans to draw from.

Essie spent a few minutes digging out her gifts for her family and tucking them underneath the strings holding his packages together so that they formed one gift with two wrapped parcels. As both were wrapped in the standard woven canvas used by all shops in Estyra, the gifts coordinated enough to look like one gift when Essie finished.

"Here. You can carry the gifts for my brothers, and I'll take Mother's and Paige's gifts. The ones for the nephews, too. They're young, so they might find being handed gifts by you a little intimidating. Sorry." Essie gathered her portion of the parcels and headed for the door.

He grabbed the remaining packages and hurried after her. She led the way down the hall to another oak door nearly identical to the one for her room. She swung it open without knocking and strode inside without missing a step.

Did he need another reminder of how much this place was not home? And that he might not belong here with her? The pounding behind his eyes throbbed more painfully. It was dull enough he could ignore it for now, but it would only grow worse the longer he stayed in this palace.

Bracing his shoulders, he stepped inside the room. All the chairs were already filled. Her brothers each had one of the padded chairs while her mother and Queen Paige had the settee.

Two small human offspring were tearing about the room. At the sight of Essie, they squealed and raced toward her, the taller of the two in the lead while the smaller one toddled with his fist jammed in his mouth.

Essie knelt in time to catch the older one in a hug. "Bertie. Finn."

"We missed you." The older one leaned back, his eyes widening as he focused on Farrendel standing behind Essie.

Farrendel shifted as the conversations in the room trailed off and all eyes swiveled toward him, the outsider in their midst.

"This is your Uncle Farrendel. You know how your mom and dad are married? Farrendel and I are married." Essie reached behind her and patted Farrendel's arm, her bright smile never wavering. "Farrendel, this is my three-year-old nephew Bertie, short for Albert, and one-year-old nephew Phineas, though we call him Finn for short."

The human custom of nicknames was still a mindboggling one for him. Why did the humans have this need to shorten perfectly acceptable names?

And yet, the nickname Essie fit her better than her full name of Elspeth. Bertie and Finn seemed more appropriate for the young ones. Perhaps humans used nicknames to fit personalities in a way their full names did not.

As Essie's nephews were still young, their human years were not that different from what their ages would have been if they were elves. While the human aging process was apparently constant, elves aged rapidly at the beginning and end of their lifespans while the middle years experienced very little aging.

Due to the heart bond with Essie, Farrendel was no longer sure what his life span would look like. He would probably start to notice aging at a more rapid rate, as the heart bond lengthened her lifespan and shortened his. Not something he was too concerned about. Until he met Essie, he had believed—and hoped—he would die young in battle. He had not had any reason to want to live a long life before her.

Bertie peered at Farrendel before he pointed. "Why does he have long hair? And funny ears?"

"He's an elf." Essie glanced at Farrendel, her eyes seeming to be asking something of him. What, he could not begin to guess.

The younger of the two scurried to King Averett, scrambled onto his lap, and buried his face against his shoulder.

Bertie turned to Essie. "He looks mean."

Farrendel winced. He had forgotten to smile. Essie had told him not to appear too scary with her family.

Essie tickled Bertie's stomach until the boy squirmed away from her. "He's just nervous about meeting all of you. You're scaring him."

Bertie crinkled his nose, still peeking at Farrendel warily.

Farrendel understood and did not fault the child. He himself was wary of all the people who were near strangers to him in this room. The weight of all the eyes focused on him made his headache throb harder. He probably should say something, but the words stuck in his throat. Why was it so difficult to talk in front of people?

Essie patted Bertie's back. "Why don't you go to your mama for a moment, all right? We have presents for everybody."

"Presents!" Bertie's face lit up, and he zipped across the room to Queen Paige.

She pulled him onto her lap. "You didn't have to get us anything. You've already been sending us the elven shampoo and conditioner."

"That isn't the same as giving you things in person." Essie rested a hand on Farrendel's arm, giving him a smile before she faced the room again. "We wanted to share a little bit of Tarenhiel with you."

How did Essie always say the right thing? He could not even manage a proper greeting to those in the room right now, and yet she was smiling as if in total ease, her words making it clear this was something from both of them.

He kept his gaze focused on her, since it was easier than looking at the others. When she glanced at him, smiling, he could not help but attempt a smile in return.

While Essie handed out the gifts to her mother and Queen Paige, Farrendel distributed the gifts to King Averett, Prince Julien, and Prince Edmund as quickly as possible, looking at the floor rather than at them.

Essie sank onto a seat on the floor next to the end of the settee where Queen Paige sat. Farrendel eased to the floor next to her. It meant King Averett occupied the padded armchair next to him, but it was not like Farrendel had much of a choice. His stomach churned.

Edmund inspected the package in his hands. "So, do

we all just tear into our packages? Or should we be more organized about this?"

Farrendel could not force himself to say anything else. At this point, he had fulfilled the tradition. He did not care what human tradition they had for opening gifts. It was a struggle just to sit there, head pounding, when all he wanted to do was bolt.

CHAPTER
SEVEN

E ssie took Farrendel's hand, his fingers cold in hers. He looked about ready to throw up from nerves. What was in those gifts? She couldn't imagine what Farrendel might have picked out for each of her family members. She squeezed his hand and whispered, "Well, I'm impressed."

At the very least, Farrendel had proven to her that he cared enough to follow through with this tradition, even when it was clearly painful for someone as shy as he was, even with her smoothing it over for him.

Averett waved to Mother and Paige. "Ladies first."

"All right." Paige grinned and untied the string holding Essie's gift first, since it was the one on top. Mother was only seconds behind her.

Both of them revealed jars filled with a thick, creamy substance.

"It's lotion. I picked the scents to match the shampoo and conditioner I sent earlier." A lavender and vanilla for her mother and lilac for Paige.

Paige opened her jar, sniffed it, then held it for Bertie to sniff when he asked, since he was still sitting in her lap. "It smells amazing. Thanks so much."

Then they were opening the packages from Farrendel, which had felt floppy and soft when Essie had been adding her part to the gift earlier. So it didn't surprise her when Mother and Paige revealed several yards of elven silk.

What did surprise Essie was how perfect the colors were for both of them.

Paige gasped and held up sapphire blue silk that would look stunning with her hair. "This is beautiful."

Mother ran her fingers over a forest green silk that was still muted enough to fit the dark wardrobe she wore to still mourn Essie's father. "Yes. Thank you, Essie. If the seamstress starts now, she may be able to finish dresses before the welcome ball."

Essie glanced at Farrendel, but as he had his shoulders hunched, his face mostly obscured by his hair, he didn't seem to want to claim this part of the gift as his. "If you'd like, I can send along one of my elven dresses so the seamstress can make you similar dresses. Or you can have overdresses made from this silk."

It was hard to tell since they were folded, but there did not seem to be enough fabric to make a human-style dress, not with the current fashion of massive skirts. As Farrendel had only seen Essie's wedding dress, he would not have realized that the width of that skirt was normal fashion for balls.

"I'd love an elven-style dress." Paige grinned as she carefully set her gifts out of range of Bertie, who was squirming and asking about his present.

As her brothers started unwrapping their gifts, Essie nudged Farrendel's arm, whispering, "Now I see what that early morning dress delivery was all about. My new dress was just a cover for their fabric, wasn't it? Sneaky."

Farrendel didn't manage a smile, but some of the green cast to his face faded.

"This is great." Averett held up Essie's gift. She'd gotten all of her brothers wooden fountain pens made of a dark wood and lacquered to a bright shine. He inspected the nib. "I suppose I'll have to use this next time I sign a treaty with the elves."

"Exactly." Essie hoped there would be a lot of need for treaties and trade agreements and such things in the future. "There's even a tiny secret compartment for extra ink or anything else small enough to fit." She glanced at Edmund.

Grinning, Edmund inspected his for a moment before he twisted the top, clicked a section, and revealed the hidden compartment. "This is going to come in handy."

She wasn't going to ask what spy-related items Edmund was already planning to smuggle.

Farrendel had straightened at her gift, inspecting Averett's pen from over the arm of the chair. "Is this Fingol's handiwork?"

"Yes. After Illyna's hair products have caught on so well, I'm hoping to introduce his work to Escarland next." Illyna was one of Farrendel's friends and had become Essie's first friend among the elves.

"So even our gifts are politically motivated." Averett shook both his head and his new pen at her. "Bad form, Essie. That's the kind of stunt only kings and Parliament members should pull."

Farrendel leaned back, as if he was decidedly uncomfortable sitting between her and Averett, even when they were only teasing each other. Essie grinned back at Averett, doing her best to put on her most innocent expression. "I'm a princess. I know how to play the game just as well as kings and Parliament members."

She said it as a joke, but it was either joke about it privately with her family or drown in the burden of it. Seriously, if she sneezed, the maker of her handkerchief would suddenly find themselves swamped with orders.

Across the room from Essie, Julien had gone ahead and opened Farrendel's part of the gift, revealing a flat, wooden box. He opened it and let out a low whistle that caught the attention of the others in the room. Glancing around, he picked something out of the box and held it up, revealing a gleaming, eight-inch-long dagger with an elegant, simple hilt. "This is going to go great with my historical weapons collection."

"What?" Edmund tore at the wrappings, opened the box, and revealed a matching dagger. "Whoa."

Essie nudged Farrendel. "You seriously gave my brothers daggers when you weren't even sure yet if they'd like you? Did you really think arming them was a good idea?"

Farrendel shrugged, his shoulders tense as he glanced between her three brothers. "Daggers do not pose a threat to me."

"Very true." Essie patted his shoulder. "Well done on the gifts."

Averett held his dagger out of reach of Finn on his lap. "Thank you, Essie." A pause. "Farrendel."

It was strange hearing her brother address Farrendel in such a casual, family setting. Essie knew and loved both of them, but they were still strangers to each other, for all she'd written letter after letter over the past three months.

Bertie finally squirmed out of Paige's grasp and off her lap. "My present?"

"Yes, it's time for presents for you and Finn." Essie set the two gifts on her lap and patted the space in front of her.

Averett set Finn on the ground, and both nephews hurried closer, though they halted just out of arm's reach, staring at Farrendel. He was a stranger to them, and they were wary of strangers. Especially one with long, flowing hair and pointed ears. At least he wasn't wearing his swords. That would just make him even more intimidating.

Essie gave them both a smile, trying to put them at ease. "It's all right. The presents are from both me and Uncle Farrendel."

Farrendel was sitting still, doing an admirable job of not looking too scary. If anything, his eyes had a soft, longing look to them. Did he perhaps like children? She'd never asked him. How much would he put up with? "His hair is very soft. And his ears feel just like our ears."

Farrendel glanced at her, his mouth tilted in a hint of his smile, and leaned forward, sweeping his hair behind his ear.

Essie held a hand out to Bertie. "Do you want to feel his ears and hair? He doesn't bite."

Now she was making Farrendel sound like an animal in a zoological park. But Farrendel seemed like he was going to oblige her nephews. At three and one, it would help them understand. Hopefully.

Bertie inched forward, still staring wide-eyed.

Essie touched her own ear. "Here, feel your ear."

Bertie patted his ear with his hand.

"Now touch his ear." Essie traced a finger over the point of Farrendel's ear. He froze. She tried to remain casual. "See, Bertie. Farrendel's ear might be shaped differently, but he's still a person like us."

The others in the room had taken to quietly talking about their gifts, though Essie could still feel plenty of gazes focused on them. She kept her focus on the nephews and Farrendel.

Bertie poked Farrendel's ear, then patted a lock of Farrendel's hair. "You are nice."

"Yes, he is. I like him very much." Essie patted Farrendel's arm, feeling him relax as he straightened. "Now would you like to open your gifts?"

"Yes!" Bertie plopped down and, as soon as Essie handed his gift over, yanked at the strings tying the canvas wrapping closed.

Essie held out a hand to Finn. "Do you want me to help you open your present?"

Finn gave Farrendel a wide berth before he plopped into Essie's lap. She tugged on the bow she'd tied back in Estyra. The string loosened and the wrapping fell apart, revealing a carved wooden figurine about two inches tall of an elf warrior that looked a lot like Farrendel, with two swords raised and his hair flying behind him. Finn snatched it up, grinning. "Army guy!"

"Yes, it's an army guy. An elf army guy."

Bertie glanced over at it, made a whining noise, and shook his package. He'd managed to get the string tangled, rather than loosed. He held the sad-looking bundle out to Farrendel. "Uncle Farrendel, can you do it?" Bertie stretched out Farrendel's name, as if trying to figure out exactly how to say it. It was an awful lot of syllables for a three-year-old to tackle in a single name.

Farrendel took the bundle and picked at the string, trying to untangle the knot Bertie had made.

After a moment, Averett held out his new dagger, gripping it by the blade with the hilt toward Farrendel. "Here. This will make it easier."

With a glance at Averett, Farrendel took the knife and sliced the string in a single swipe. Just how sharp were those daggers he'd gifted her brothers?

"Elf guy." Finn clutched the figurine in a fist, waving it about. He stood, as if to leave, but Essie reeled him back in, tugging him back onto her lap. "You still have another present."

She was just as curious as Finn was to find out what Farrendel might have decided to give her nephews. Hopefully nothing sharp. After untying the string, she unwrapped the canvas and revealed...a second figurine. This one looked like Essie. The figurine had a rifle strapped across her back, making her look warlike without being in a fighting pose.

Essie laughed and glanced at Farrendel. "Now I know why Fingol gave me such a strange look when I picked up my order. I thought it was because wooden figurine toys weren't something you had in Tarenhiel. But apparently, we had the same idea."

"I did not know what to give them, and he mentioned your gift. So I asked him to make another one." Farrendel returned the dagger to Averett as Bertie hopped to his feet, a figurine clutched in each fist, as he raced around the room to show everyone his new toys.

Finn joined him a moment later, waving around his own figurines. Once their new toys had been admired by everyone, the boys raced to the corner where they dumped out baskets filled with their toy soldiers.

"So, Farrendel..." Averett swiveled in his chair to face them better. "Essie has sent us a lot of letters, but I'd like to hear it from you. Tell us about yourself. What's your role in Tarenhiel? What sort of accommodations do you have in the elven palace?"

Farrendel shifted, staring at his hands.

Julien studied the dagger in his hands. "Do you have any hobbies? A large weapons collection?"

"And what about your magic?" Edmund's smirk told Essie this was his spy's intuition at work. "I've heard it's rather awe-inspiring."

Essie took one of Farrendel's hands, squeezing, feeling the heart bond warm between them. Talking to others was difficult for him, and her brothers hadn't earned Farrendel's trust enough for him to open up. It would take him time.

But she couldn't talk for him. Not in this case. He needed to answer for himself, however much or little he was comfortable saying.

Farrendel's shoulders were tight, his grip tighter still.

Paige rolled her eyes. "Stop interrogating him. Especially you, Avie. You remember how intimidating my father was."

At the time Averett started courting Paige, her father had been the captain of palace security, though he had since retired. Even though Averett was his king, he apparently hadn't been afraid to come down hard on him about his motives for courting the captain's only daughter.

76

"It's so much more fun being on this side of things." Averett stretched out in his chair, folding his hands over his chest.

Great. Her brothers were settling in for a long night.

Essie bit her lip, words building up in her throat. Hopefully Farrendel thought of something to say soon because she couldn't take much more of this.

Farrendel glanced at her, some of the stiffness easing from his posture, his mouth twitching with a smile. "You want to talk."

"Yes." The word came out with a whoosh of air. She'd been holding her breath in an effort to stop her chatter. "It's just so hard not to answer. Please, tell them something before I explode."

That tilted Farrendel's smile wider still. It faded quickly, though, as he raised his head and faced the room. "I am Laesornysh. It is my duty to protect Tarenhiel from the trolls."

And, he was back to hard and scary, his tone flat. When she'd first met him, Essie had found it intimidating. Now she saw it for what it was. A mask to protect the vulnerable, broken part of him.

But it probably wasn't the best route to go for reassuring her brothers. They had seen this side of Farrendel already at the wedding. This hard persona had caused them to worry for the past three months about what type of marriage they'd just handed their sister into.

By the way Averett, Julien, and Edmund stiffened, their jaws tightening, hands straying toward the new daggers they had just been given, Farrendel's mask had been a mistake. Essie wasn't sure what to do or say to ease the rising tension.

Mother leaned forward, spearing Avie, Julien, and Edmund with a look, before she gave Farrendel a soft smile. "Duty is something we understand very well in this family."

Farrendel's gaze lifted, and he studied Essie's mother for a long moment. "I have a whole branch in Ellonahshinel."

"That's equivalent to a wing of the palace to himself," Essie hurried to add. Not that a single main room and three connected bedrooms was really a whole wing, but it was as near as the elven palace had. Besides, she was going to run with the change in topic now that Farrendel had brought it up. "I wish I could show it to you. Ellonahshinel is huge."

Farrendel raised his hands, and a faint blue light began to flicker around his fingers. He glanced at her, as if asking her permission.

But for what? Essie sucked in a breath. What was he planning to do? Why had he activated his magic?

Her brothers started reaching for their daggers once again.

Farrendel's magic didn't build into the charged, crackling magic he'd used against the trolls. This was a soft, brilliant blue light tracing patterns in the air. He formed a picture of Ellonahshinel, its branches crackling magic instead of wood and leaves.

Both nephews left off with their playing in the corner and eased closer. Essie waved Bertie over. When he drew close enough, she pulled him onto her lap, and he settled against her without protesting. Finn crept closer, staring wide-eyed.

"Would you like to hear about the big treehouse where I live now?" When Bertie nodded, Essie described their home and how they had to walk across the branches like roads. Then she moved on to the town of Estyra with its shops nestled into the trees, connected with branches and rope bridges. All the while, Farrendel illustrated her stories with patterns drawn by his magic.

"Maybe you can all visit someday," Essie finished, giving Bertie a hug and reaching over to ruffle Finn's hair. She looked to her family watching them. "We mean it. Once the danger of this war is over, I'd love to host whoever wants to come in Estyra. We have a few guest rooms where you can stay."

"Yes." Farrendel met her gaze and tipped his head in a small nod. Letting her, and her everyone else know, that he was on board with her inviting her family.

"And the branches aren't that scary once you get used to them, though we might want to carry these guys." She poked Bertie's stomach.

"Hey." Bertie jumped off her lap, giving her an exaggerated scowl.

Farrendel's fingers flared with blue light again. He flicked his wrists, and magic burst in a starburst of sparkles like miniature fireworks popping inside the room. The blue sparkles hung in the air like fireflies. He glanced at her, then held out his palm to one of the sparkles. It winked out against his hand.

Essie reached out and let one of the floating sparkles land on her hand. It fizzled out with a faint tingle. Not a painful tingle. More a ticklish sensation. She laughed and reached for another one. She wasn't sure how to describe it. This was pure magic floating in the air.

A few of the sparkles landed on Bertie's head. He brushed at his hair, giggling. He jumped, smacking one of the magic sparkles between his hands. Laughing, he jumped for another.

His smile broader than it had been since before the trolls attacked on the trail from Lethorel, Farrendel sent up another burst of magic that had both nephews on their feet, swatting at sparkles and giggling with the fun.

Essie joined in, catching Farrendel's magic sparkles and the nephews in turn.

By the time they were done, she had Finn on her lap, and Bertie had collapsed onto Farrendel's lap.

Essie leaned her head against Farrendel's shoulder. "I didn't know your magic could do that." She said it so that no one but Farrendel could understand. Well, Farrendel and Edmund, but Edmund seemed to be deep in discussion with Mother.

"I used to do this for my niece and nephew. Before I became Laesornysh." By the tone in his voice, she could tell he'd forgotten how his magic could be beautiful and fun.

She took his hand in both of hers. "You're tired, aren't you?"

Farrendel leaned his head on top of hers. "Yes."

"Sorry. You're usually in bed by now. We can leave, if you'd like."

Farrendel straightened and squeezed her hand. "Stay with your family. I know you missed them."

"Are you sure? I don't mind going with you. Our guards only occasionally patrol this hall, but it might not be such a good idea if you were caught wandering the palace at night. They might be jumpy to come across an elf, even if they know you're supposed to be here." Essie hugged Finn.

"Do you want to leave?" Farrendel searched her face.

How could he possibly know her this well after only a few months? "Not really. But it's all right. I'll have other times to talk with my family."

"Then stay." Farrendel pushed a strand of her hair behind her ear.

Why was she even arguing against this? Even if she was tired, she wasn't ready to end the night yet.

"All right. I'll walk you to our room, then come back. It's only a few yards down the hall and back." Essie struggled to climb to her feet while holding Finn. The boy stirred but didn't wake.

Farrendel rose to his feet gracefully, even while hefting Bertie.

Essie turned to the rest of her family. "Farrendel's tired. I'm going to walk him to our room so the guards don't get nervous about him wandering by himself, then I'm going to come back."

Paige pushed off the settee. "Essie, you stay here. Looks like I need to put the boys to bed anyway." She gave Essie a conspiratorial smile.

Apparently, Paige was looking for a chance to chat with Farrendel. Her own, subtle way of making sure Farrendel was good enough for Essie.

Essie rolled her eyes at Paige and handed Finn over to her sister-in-law. "Be nice to him."

"Of course." Paige turned to Farrendel. "If you would be so kind as to carry Bertie for me, I'd appreciate it."

Farrendel nodded, adjusting his grip on Bertie. Essie's stomach did a tight, tingly flip at seeing Farrendel cradling a child.

Averett popped to his feet, eyeing Farrendel as if he wasn't sure about letting Farrendel go off alone with his wife and children. But he leaned forward and kissed Finn on the cheek, murmuring a goodnight the boy wouldn't hear while he slept. Then Averett whispered something to Paige and gave her a short kiss.

Farrendel's eyes widened. Essie covered her mouth to hide her grin. It was probably the first time Farrendel had ever seen a couple kiss in public. Terribly shocking to an elf, even if it had been nothing but a peck on the lips.

Essie rested her hand on Farrendel's arm, getting his attention. "Goodnight." Before Farrendel could react, Essie stood on her tiptoes and gave him a brief kiss.

Farrendel froze stock still, staring at her.

She smirked and said in elvish, "You're in Escarland. A quick kiss goodnight is perfectly proper for a married couple."

Farrendel's mouth tipped in the hint of a frown. "Humans are strange."

"We are more tolerant of public displays of affection. There are limits, of course. But we do allow much more than you elves." Essie kissed his cheek for good measure. The expression on his face was too priceless to resist.

Paige waited at the door. "Ready?"

Farrendel nodded and hurried toward her, Bertie still sleeping against his shoulder.

Essie sank onto the settee in Paige's place, sighing at the relief of sitting on the soft cushion. She could handle sitting on the floor for a while, but now her tailbone had gone to sleep. With a glance around the room, Essie braced for the questions. Mother, Averett, Julien, and Edmund were all focused on her.

Mother patted her knee. "You look happy."

"I am." Essie relaxed into the cushion. How she'd missed cushioned seats with backs. Elves tended to either have hard-backed chairs or cushions on the floor. Nothing in between.

Averett pushed off from the doorway and sat on the floor in front of her. "Should I be worried about sending my wife and children off alone with that elf husband of yours?"

"No, of course not." Essie blew out a breath. "You saw how gentle he was with the boys. I know it's going to take you a while to believe me, but he isn't as scary as the title Laesornysh makes him sound."

"Are you truly all right?" Averett's gaze lifted to hers, his eyes filled with the torment he'd been putting himself through the past three months.

"Avie, I'm fine. Please stop beating yourself up for the marriage alliance." Essie leaned forward, hoping her sincerity came through in her voice. "Farrendel might not be the person I would've picked to marry under normal circumstances, but he's the one I should've been looking for. He listens when I chatter and dotes on me to the point I'm pretty sure all the gossips in Estyra have been talking about it. You should've seen the way he stood up to his family for me several times."

Averett's forehead still furrowed. Julien rubbed at his palm. Mother looked about ready to hug Essie. Only Edmund remained relaxed. Thanks to the train ride, he'd had a few hours more of interaction with Farrendel. Not that those hours would count for much, especially since Edmund knew more of Farrendel's secrets than the rest of them.

She needed to be vulnerably honest to convince her family. "I love him, and he loves me. I know you probably don't believe me, but could you please try to be welcoming? We can't stay long, and I don't want to spend all of it filled with tension."

"We will." Mother sent a glare to each of Essie's brothers.

Edmund grinned. "We'll play nice."

Essie didn't believe that. Her brothers hadn't made their minds up about Farrendel yet. Things would be interesting until they did.

CHAPTER
EIGHT

His head pounding dully, Farrendel strode down the darkened hallway, carrying Essie's nephew and matching his stride to Queen Paige's. Was he supposed to say something? He tried to think of something, anything, but even if he could think of something, he would not be able to force it out.

At the far end of the hall, two guards paced back and forth. They stopped and glared at him, though they did not reach for their weapons. Probably due to Queen Paige's presence beside him.

"What do you like most about Essie?" Queen Paige glanced at him before focusing on the hallway ahead of them.

It was the best—and worst—question he had been asked all evening. It was rather personal, but it was also Essie. He could talk about Essie. "I like her smile. I like that she talks."

They paused outside of a door a few down from the sitting room they had been in, and Queen Paige opened it. "It's a good thing you like her chatter. I have always worried she would end up with someone who would want to stifle her."

Why would anyone wish to do that? Farrendel trailed after Queen Paige, holding Bertie steady as the young one shifted in his sleep. Essie was so...Essie. Vibrant and lively and so richly full of happiness. He could not imagine asking her to be anything less than who she was. "When she talks, I do not have to."

"I can see how you'd appreciate that." Queen Paige led the way across a darkened sitting room to one of the doors set in the walls. This must be a suite of rooms like his in Estyra. With this sitting room as a main room and the bedrooms branching off it.

Farrendel left both the door to the hallway and the door to the sitting room open as he followed Queen Paige inside. She laid Phineas in a small human bed with gates surrounding it. That must be what Essie meant when she said they added rails for their young ones.

Across the room, another similar bed was set against the wall with smaller rails. It must be the bed for the human child he carried. He set the child down on the mattress. There were blankets. Was he supposed to do something with them? He was not properly trained for something like this.

Queen Paige laughed, stepped around him, and tugged the blankets over Albert. "You are just like Essie described."

What did that mean? Farrendel stepped back. His head pounded harder. All he wanted to do was curl up in bed.

Yet his own bed was far away in Estyra. Here, everything was unfamiliar. He was surrounded by stone, and the magic he had done earlier that evening had worsened his headache. Now, even his joints were beginning to ache.

He could not think about it. This was Essie's home. For her sake, he would bear this.

"I'll stand in the doorway of the room until you reach your room. Just to reassure the guards. They looked a little on edge." Queen Paige bustled back into the sitting room. When she reached the door to the hallway, she turned. "Is there anything you'd like to know about Essie?"

That stopped him in his tracks in the center of the sitting room. Essie had learned a lot about him by asking his family, and he had been cowardly enough to be glad his family had explained certain secrets so that he did not have to.

But he had been unable to ask her family about her. What would he like to know about Essie that her family could tell him that she could not?

He glanced at Queen Paige, then focused on the floor. "How can you tell when her smile is happy and when it is a mask?"

Would she understand what he was asking?

When he dared look up, he found Queen Paige was smiling, arms crossed. "It's a good sign you've figured that out already. Yes, Essie will keep smiling even when she's sad or angry or hurting. But if she's unnaturally silent while smiling, then something's wrong. But, this is Essie. If you push her and ask, she will eventually tell you. Or she'll burst into tears, then tell you. And if she's really, really angry with you, trust me, you'll know."

That was good information to know. He always feared

that Essie would be miserable at Estyra, and he would be unable to recognize it.

"Linshi." He ducked his head. "Thank you."

He hurried past Queen Paige into the hallway, mentally counting the doors until he found the one belonging to Essie.

"Goodnight," Queen Paige called from behind him.

He nodded and entered Essie's room. Quickly, he crossed the sitting room and the bedroom, opened the nearest window, and leaned out. The cool breeze washed over him, shoving away some of the headache.

Now to keep Essie from seeing just how miserable he was here.

COLD WASHED over Essie a moment before the muffled cry jerked her all the way awake. Rubbing at her face, she forced her gritty eyes open.

By the faint light of the moon filtering through the windows, Farrendel's form shook, tangled in the blankets.

"Farrendel. Wake up." Essie touched his shoulder.

He flinched away, his movement stealing the last of the blankets from her feet.

"It's all right. Wake up." She reached out and gently shook him.

Farrendel stilled, sucking in a sharp breath. His face was hidden behind a curtain of his white-blond hair as he pushed onto his elbows, breathing hard.

Essie huffed out a breath of her own. A nightmare-free night had probably been too much to hope for, especially for their first night here. At least she'd managed to wake him before his nightmare progressed past moans into screams. The palace walls were thick, but not thick enough that the guards and her brothers wouldn't come running at the sound of screaming. "Are you all right?"

"Yes." The word came out tight. A pause. Farrendel's shoulders shook. "No."

Essie eased closer and gently rested a hand on his shoulder. This time, he didn't flinch away from her.

Instead, he rolled into a sitting position, dragging the blankets with him. He shuddered, as if freezing. "I am sorry I woke you."

"It's all right. Really. That's what I'm here for. It's been a rough couple of nights." She rescued a corner of the blanket and pulled it over herself. "The nightmares usually start to taper off by now."

Farrendel leaned his head against the carved headboard. "I do not believe the nightmares will stop while we are here."

"What do you mean?" Essie searched Farrendel's expression, but his face was turned away from her.

The silence dragged on long enough she wondered if he'd tell her. What was so wrong that he wasn't willing to share it with her?

Finally, Farrendel let out a breath and faced her. "What I am about to tell you must not be repeated. Your brothers cannot know, as it would give Escarland the means to defeat Tarenhiel if our kingdoms ever go to war again."

"The trolls know this big secret, don't they?" Essie found one of Farrendel's hands and clasped his fingers, hoping the connection of the heart bond steadied him. This couldn't be good, if Farrendel was taking so many words to get to the point.

"Yes." Farrendel's thumb rubbed along the back of her hand. "You have never asked me how the trolls managed to capture me."

It seemed like a random change of topic. Yet, why had Essie never thought to ask? She'd seen Farrendel use his magic. How had the trolls managed to capture him, much less keep him prisoner?

Fifteen years ago, he had still been the elf equivalent of a teenager. His magic might not have been as strong as it was now. But Farrendel would still have been formidable.

She had never dared ask much about the torture and the resulting scars. She figured he would tell her when he was ready.

The middle of the night after a nightmare didn't seem like the time she would've picked for this conversation, but if Farrendel wanted to talk now, she wasn't going to cut him off. She clasped his hands in both of hers. "What happened?"

He was trembling, as if trapped in a snowbank instead of blankets. "I was just coming into my magic, and with both my father and brother on the front lines fighting the trolls, I wanted to help. My father refused to have me fight directly, but he finally grew desperate enough to let me provide a shield. My magic was powerful enough it drew the attention of the trolls. One night, the trolls attacked our camp. While I provided a shield for my father and brother, a squad of trolls sneaked around our line and captured me."

Essie eased closer to Farrendel. How had the trolls managed to capture him? Was it something like that ambush? Did they surround him and finally train enough guns on him to break through his magical shield?

Farrendel stared at the wood beams of the ceiling above. "Somehow, the trolls had learned our weakness. Stone impedes elven magic. For most, like my sisters, it is just a faint dulling. But I am, apparently, very affected."

"Right now, in the palace, your magic isn't as strong? You did magic earlier for my nephews. Were you able to do it because it was just a few sparks?" Essie raised her gaze, searching his face to read his expression. For as vulnerable as his words were, his expression remained shuttered.

"Yes. I can still use a great deal of my magic, even here. It is painful, yet not impossible, even if I am touching the stone." Farrendel gave a shudder that traveled all the way down to his fingers clasped in hers. "But if the stone is laced with troll magic, it actively blocks my magic. The trolls can manipulate both rock and ice. The late troll king, and now his two sons, wielded a very potent form of their magic. It was the troll king who personally used his magic to keep me contained."

A sudden nausea churned through Essie's stomach. Surely, he couldn't mean...

He pushed up his sleeve, revealing the thin scars trailing up his arm. "He threaded rock beneath my skin so that I could not use my magic. When I was rescued, it took hours to remove all the stone."

His scars. Essie ran her fingers over one of the scars trailing up his arm. If using his magic with stone nearby hurt, how much did it hurt to have stone embedded beneath his skin?

"My father died rescuing me. I could not use my magic to defend us, and..." Farrendel drew his knees up, his head hanging. "My father died because of me."

That's what his nightmares were about. All this stone

dampening his magic reminded him too much of the torture he suffered and the moment his father was killed rescuing him. "Your father loved you. He willingly sacrificed himself to save you from torture. It's what any parent would do for their child."

"He should not have. Not for me."

"Yes, for you. You are his son. He loved you." Essie rested a hand on Farrendel's cheek, tipping his face toward her. "Don't lessen his love or downplay what he did. Love is a sacrifice. It's putting someone else's needs above your own. Your father did that for you."

Farrendel gave her a nod so slight she only felt it because she had her hand on his cheek. "I became Laesornysh after his death."

In Escarland, the rumors about the war between the trolls and the elves had been so vague the timeline had become mixed up. They hadn't known Laesornysh was just a grieving teenage elf with far too much power. She'd never pieced together that the troll king's death at Farrendel's hands must have come after Farrendel's father had been killed. It had been torture and pain and grief that had turned Farrendel into a warrior and an assassin.

She had seen a similar rage during the trolls' ambush. Even when he'd been hurt, Farrendel's magic had exploded with terrifying fury. "Is your magic fueled by emotions?"

Magic and emotions were tied. She had seen that at work with the heart bond that had formed between her and Farrendel. The deep emotion of love had melded with magic to bind them together.

Could anger and pain do something similar with Farrendel's magic?

"Yes, in a way." Farrendel turned away from her

again, pulling back from her touch. "The more I give in to an emotion, the less control I have over the magic. I am not sure what would happen if I ever completely lost control."

She loved Farrendel, but sometimes his magic could be downright terrifying. If he ever lost control of his magic, it might just destroy a kingdom, and himself along with it.

No wonder he didn't want her brothers to know all this. If they knew the extent of his magic, they might begin planning a way to neutralize him if they needed to. It was just practicality and politics.

Essie rested her head on Farrendel's shoulder. "Are you going to be all right, staying here? I didn't realize staying inside Winstead Palace would be so hard for you. Maybe you should have stayed in Tarenhiel."

Saying the words hurt deep inside her chest. She'd wanted him to love her family and to fit into her home the way she had into his. But she should've realized how much of an impossible dream that was. She might be flexible and adaptable, but Farrendel wasn't. It wasn't his fault. It was the way he was, and the damage from the torture and trauma only made it worse.

Farrendel leaned his head on top of hers. "This is your home. I will be fine."

He wasn't. He couldn't sleep because of nightmares. The stone was apparently physically and magically affecting him. That was far from fine.

What should she do? She couldn't ask Farrendel to continue to suffer like this. Even if she appreciated that he was willing to sacrifice for her, this wasn't the kind of sacrifice she should ask of him. "Farrendel..."

"I will be fine." His voice had something of a growl to

it this time. "You sacrificed much to move to Estyra. I have dealt with these nightmares for a long time. I can survive this."

That wasn't encouraging. She didn't want him just to survive.

But they might not have an option here. There would be more diplomatic meetings, a few parties, balls, and other things that would keep them inside the palace. For the sake of peace, they needed to be here.

Why did coming home have to be this difficult?

CHAPTER
NINE

E ssie woke to her husband literally bouncing off the walls. Well, bouncing might not be the right word, but he was ricocheting off the walls and even the ceiling in a way she hadn't thought possible until that moment.

Farrendel dashed across the room, launched himself from a chair with such grace the chair didn't so much as wiggle, much less tip, and ran partially up the wall before he flipped backwards and landed easily on his feet. With barely a pause, he spun, did a springing leap from the top of the bookshelf, pushed off the ceiling, and flipped once again before landing on the bedpost.

He must have noticed she was awake since he did a small flip and landed cross-legged on the end of the bed.

Essie sat up and pushed her hair out of her face. "Sorry. You should have gotten me up."

There was a wooded section on the grounds that would have done Farrendel some good, though he probably would have needed her to let the guards know that he was allowed there.

It hurt how little freedom Farrendel had here. In Estyra, Essie had been able to wander through the elven palace on a whim without an escort. No one had paid any attention to her.

Here, Farrendel didn't even dare wander the hall by himself without fear the guards would misinterpret his actions. What kind of message did that send? It was as if he was still an enemy, not her husband.

"What do you need? Do you want me to ask a guard to show you a place outside that has trees?" Essie rubbed at her eyes. She had gotten far too little sleep the past few nights.

Farrendel tipped his chin in his small nod and rocked back and forth. "Where do you find food in the morning? You do not have a cold cupboard."

As much as she wanted to lie in the warmth for a while longer, she had too much to do. She pushed off the covers and slid her feet over the edge of the bed. "We either have to ask a servant to fetch a breakfast tray or there is always a breakfast laid out in the dining room for my family to eat if we wish."

"Your servants make even your breakfast for you?" Farrendel still sat on the end of the bed, elbows on his knees.

"Human royalty is less self-sufficient than elven royalty." Essie yawned and tiptoed across the rugs to her wardrobe. The day would be packed with diplomatic meetings so she probably should wear a dress, not tunic and pants. That would scandalize a few people, and scandalizing the old fuddies in Parliament would not help their cause.

She pulled out her midnight blue elven-style dress and laid it out on the bed. "If you want to take a minute to wash up, we can go down to breakfast. If you'd prefer, I'll ask one of the servants to deliver a tray of food for you tomorrow morning so you don't have to wait so long for breakfast."

"Do not make more work for them on my account." Farrendel slid to his feet.

It wasn't much extra work for them to load some of the food they were already setting out in the dining room and bring the tray to their room. At least, she didn't think it would be, especially since they were probably making special, less-seasoned food for the elves anyway. She would ask Chef Figo next time she stopped by the kitchen.

Farrendel padded into the attached water closet, only to come back out a few seconds later. "You do not have a shower spigot."

"No, we humans just figured out running water a few years ago, so we only added a faucet to the bathtubs we were already using. Maybe eventually your elven showers will catch on here, but right now, everyone still bathes in a tub." A long soak in a tub. How she'd missed it over in Estyra.

Farrendel cocked his head, eyebrows scrunched together. "How do you wash your hair?"

Now Essie understood his puzzlement, beyond the cultural difference. His hair was just as long as hers, and, if she'd learned anything about elves in the past few months, their long hair was significant to them.

"Well, usually I wash my hair separately and sometimes have a maid help." Essie had to bite her lip to stop her grin, waiting for Farrendel's reaction.

The slight widening of his eyes, his raised eyebrows, and the half a step back was the most scandalized shock she'd ever seen on him. His nose even wrinkled a bit, as if in pure disgust at the thought of some random servant helping to wash his hair.

She could offer to help with his hair, but she didn't think they were quite there yet. They had just started sharing a room and a bed a few days ago. There were still personal space boundaries neither of them was ready to cross yet.

"Or"— Essie had to smother a laugh at the way his shoulders relaxed a fraction at just the thought of having another option— "I kneel next to the tub and stick my head under the faucet. Not as easy as your elven showers, but it works."

That wrinkle was back on his nose again. She might have to scandalize him more often if he looked this adorable doing it.

With a straightening of his shoulders as if going into battle, Farrendel disappeared into the water closet again.

Essie changed into the blue dress and took a seat behind her dressing table. In Estyra, she'd taken to wearing her hair down and loose in the elven style, but here in Winstead Palace, she probably should pin her hair up. Especially since they were going to face Parliament today.

Without a maid to help her, the style wouldn't be as elaborate as it could be. But Essie's personal maid had taken the opportunity of Essie's marriage to finally admit her feelings for a certain footman, and they'd gotten married only a week after Essie had. She wished her all the best and would have to send a wedding present.

Essie probably could've asked for another maid, but it

wouldn't be nice to temporarily promote someone to lady's maid, only to demote them once Essie returned to Estyra. Besides, Farrendel was already edgy. They didn't need a maid adding more to his discomfort.

Still, a maid's help would have been nice. Essie jabbed another pin into her hair, trying to get it to stay in place. One downside of the magical elven conditioner was that it made her hair so sleek and soft that it kept sliding right out of the pins instead of staying in place. She'd even skipped washing it the night before since dirty hair stayed in pins better.

She tried to ignore the splashing and thumping coming from the water closet. At least Essie knew Farrendel could swim. He wasn't likely to drown.

As she added what she hoped was the last pin to her hair, Farrendel trooped from the water closet, wearing his silver tunic and trousers. His hair lay washed and wet down his back.

"I see you didn't drown." Essie swiveled in her chair and stood, grinning.

"No." The scathing look he sent toward the bathtub suggested it had been a hard-fought battle. But when he glanced back at her, his gaze was soft, searching. "Is this what it was like for you in Estyra? Always…" he paused, as if unsure how to word what he was thinking and feeling, "…out of place?"

What should she say? She had been determined to adapt and claim Estyra as her home, and that had helped with some of the awkwardness. Farrendel didn't have the pressure to try to make Winstead Palace his new home. He knew he was just visiting for a short time. And he, at least, could understand the conversations around him.

Essie hadn't even had that when she'd first arrived in Estyra.

Essie joined him and threaded her fingers with his. "It was tough, at first. I was glad you were patient and helpful when I didn't know what was going on or even what everyone was saying. I just muddled through it and tried not to care what anyone thought. That's how I tackle most things in life, to be honest."

"I knew it was difficult for you, but I did not understand what it was like. I am sorry." Farrendel hesitated, then wrapped his arm around her in a stiff attempt at a quick hug.

"You helped a lot, answering all my endless questions. Don't be afraid to ask. I won't laugh. Much." Essie couldn't help but grin. He already had asked questions when confused by Escarlish culture. At least their relationship was at a point where they felt comfortable asking each other random questions without censure.

"If there is anything you wish to transport to Estyra to make it feel more like your home, then please do."

"Even a bathtub?" Her grin widened at his scowl.

"Yes. Though I do not understand why."

"They can be very relaxing, when you're not wrestling with them trying to wash your hair properly." Essie took a step toward the door. "Ready for breakfast?"

"Yes. Please." Farrendel sounded almost desperate.

She would need to make sure he had something to eat first thing in the morning. Or, maybe, by the end of this visit, the guards would relax enough that Farrendel could wander to the family dining room by himself.

The family dining room was in the same wing, but on the main floor instead of the second floor. They strolled down the center of the corridor and down the very middle of the stairs, something Essie understood better now that she knew the stone walls affected Farrendel's magic. She'd been wondering if he was just freaked out by having so many solid, non-living walls around him after growing up in the treehouse palace.

Was it wrong that she was somewhat relieved at having solid stone walls around her and firm stone stairs beneath her, even if they made Farrendel uncomfortable? And handrails. How she'd missed real, solid handrails and walking somewhere without that lingering fear of falling to her death always in the back of her mind.

She pushed open the door to the family dining room and drew in a deep breath of the savory smells of sausage and eggs and toast and pancakes. A hot breakfast. How she'd missed it.

She had missed more of life at Winstead Palace than she'd realized. As much as she loved her new life in Estyra, three months living there hadn't been long enough for the newness and excitement to fade. What would it be like once the adventure wore off? Once home-sickness for her family and familiar life settled in?

Perhaps she would take Farrendel up on his offer and make a list of what she'd like to bring back to Estyra. Maybe if she made her elven home in Estyra a little more human, she wouldn't end up feeling as out of place as Farrendel confessed to feeling here.

And, as long as she could prevent war between Escarland and Tarenhiel, she would always be able to come home to Winstead Palace to visit. Maybe even invite her family to Estyra.

Edmund was already in the breakfast room along with Mother, Jalissa, and Jalissa's guard whose name Essie had yet to hear. The elf guard took her job so seriously she didn't seem inclined toward idle chatter. Not that elves in general often indulged in idle chatter.

Jalissa had stationed herself at the far end of the room, something in her blank expression more forbidding than usual. Farrendel let go of Essie's hand and strolled across the room to his sister. With their heads bent together, they began talking softly in elvish.

Was that almost the hint of dark circles under Jalissa's eyes? It was hard to tell on Jalissa's perfectly smooth face, but her skin seemed too pale. Was staying in a stone palace affecting her just as it was Farrendel?

Perhaps this was why negotiations with elves had never gone that well. The elves didn't want to admit stone was their weakness, yet humans kept inviting them into stone palaces, stone forts, even stone islands in the middle of the river, to conduct peace talks.

Essie scooped eggs onto her plate, adding sausage and a pancake liberally doused with maple syrup, before she claimed a seat next to Edmund.

"You look tired." Edmund waved a bite of sausage at her, then at Jalissa and Farrendel across the room. "So do they."

Edmund's room shared a wall with hers. A thick wall, so he shouldn't have been able to hear Farrendel cry out in his sleep.

"I'm fine, really. It has just been a busy few days." So much had happened, it was hard to remember they'd been ambushed by trolls less than a week ago.

The door burst open, giving entrance to two nephews running full tilt while Paige scrambled to keep up behind them.

"Auntie Essie!" Both of them ran to give her hugs, as if they'd forgotten they'd just seen her the night before.

Still, she hugged them close, savoring the feel of their small arms wrapping tight. Hugs from the nephews would be few and far between with her living in Estyra. When she pulled back, she pointed at Farrendel. "Think you can give Uncle Farrendel a hug too?"

Finn looked at her with big, round eyes and shook his head. But Bertie dashed over and plowed into Farrendel's legs with enough force to make Farrendel sway under the impact. Bertie stopped just long enough to give Farrendel a squeezing hug around both legs before dashing back to Essie. "Can you play with us?"

"We need to eat breakfast first." Then they would hold diplomatic meetings with the general of the army and the owner of the largest gun manufacturer in Escarland, followed by attending the afternoon session of Parliament, which would last who knew how long. They wouldn't catch much of a break for relaxing.

As much as she wanted to relax and spend time with family, that wasn't her main purpose here. She had to remember that to the north in Tarenhiel, the elves were mobilizing to defend themselves. Essie wanted to push her brothers to secure Escarland's help against the trolls, but that would drag both kingdoms she loved into this war. Yet, if Escarland didn't help, would Tarenhiel fall this time?

She glanced at Farrendel, where he and Jalissa were now gathering plates and dishing themselves food. Without Escarland's help, the weight of defending Tarenhiel would fall squarely on Farrendel's shoulders.

It might break him. He was already so broken from all the torture and war and death he'd endured and inflicted. What would more do to him? He was a warrior, but a warrior who felt every life he was forced to take so very keenly. Even if he didn't die in this war, it could very well kill him from the inside out.

As Farrendel took the other seat next to Essie, Julien and Averett entered the room. Averett held a piece of paper in his hand, and he scanned the room a moment before his gaze focused on Farrendel. He strolled over and held out the paper. "Telegram from across the border."

Farrendel took it and read while Essie glanced from Averett to Farrendel. Had the trolls launched a large-scale invasion? Was Farrendel needed to be Laesornysh and defend his home? "Is your brother ordering you home?"

Farrendel set down the paper. "Not yet. But he believes I will only have a week before I need to return to Tarenhiel."

A week. They'd hoped to have more time. Two weeks. Maybe even three.

Essie swallowed back the hard lump, shoving it aside with a deep breath. "All right. I guess we need to make the most of our time while we are here."

"When I am called back to Tarenhiel, you do not have to return with me." Farrendel met her gaze, then reached out and rested his hand on hers. "If the negotiations are not finished, you and Jalissa will need to stay here to finish them. You will be safe here, whatever the war brings."

Behind her, Averett cleared his throat. "Bad news?"

Essie hadn't realized she and Farrendel had been speaking in elvish.

"It seems our new brother-in-law might only be able to stay a week. I guess it's a good thing you moved the meeting with Parliament to this afternoon and the other meetings to this morning." Edmund, of course, had understood every word. It was rather hard to have privacy when one of her brothers was a spy. When Essie glanced over her shoulder, Edmund's gaze switched from Averett to Farrendel, and he spoke in elvish. "She is our sister. We will make sure she is safe."

Farrendel held Edmund's gaze for a long moment, before he tipped his head in a small nod. Some sort of understanding acknowledged between him and Edmund.

Essie wanted to huff and roll her eyes at their over-protectiveness. As if she was something breakable to be passed between them, always surrounded by guards.

But this was war. It wasn't something to be laughed off flippantly. In wars, whole towns were overrun. Innocent people were slaughtered. Being able to use a musket to defend herself might not be enough. Not in a war fought as much with magic as with guns.

Nor did she truly want to be in that position to have to take a life yet again. She bit back the surge of bile at the memory of the jerk of the gun in her hand, the troll falling before her.

A part of her wished she was an elven warrior so that she could run into battle at Farrendel's back, protecting him while he protected her. She wanted to declare she'd carry her gun into battle at his side.

But her presence would distract him from doing what he needed to do. He couldn't go into battle worried for her.

Besides, she could do more good for all of the elves if she stayed here. Even if Escarland didn't go to war on Tarenhiel's side, it might be persuaded to offer aid. Perhaps food or supplies. Maybe a safe refuge for those fleeing the war.

Essie gave Farrendel a nod to let him know she understood.

Averett heaved a sigh. "This is worse than when you and Edmund made up a secret language so you could pass notes to each other the rest of us couldn't read."

"Oh, come now. At least they are talking out loud. That's less strange than when you and Paige do your whole eye and facial expression discussions." Julien tipped his chair back on two legs, which earned him a glare across the table from Mother.

As he set his chair back on all four legs, Paige gave him a swat on the arm for good measure.

One week. That's all the time they had before the reality of coming war came crashing down on them once again.

CHAPTER
TEN

Essie scraped the last of her cheesecake from her plate. Mostly because the cheesecake was excellent, and it would be a shame to waste even a crumb. But partly to delay the inevitable when this midmorning desert turned into a political discussion. It was the reason they had come. Still, it wouldn't be pleasant.

She, Farrendel, Jalissa, and all of Essie's brothers had assembled in one of the private council rooms around a large oak table.

Jalissa set down her fork and motioned. The Escarlish soldier at the door opened it. The elf guard stepped inside, holding a canvas-wrapped bundle.

Essie sighed and set down her own fork. She couldn't put this off any longer.

Jalissa stood and took the canvas-wrapped gun from her guard. "King Averett, would you care to explain this?" She placed the gun on the table and whipped off the canvas.

Averett pointed at the gun. "This is one of the Escarlish guns found after that ambush?"

Essie had wired her brother a short version of the story when she'd let him know she, Farrendel, and Jalissa would be coming, along with the purpose behind their visit. Though, she had downplayed just how much danger she had been in.

"The trolls that ambushed the royal family less than a week ago were using these guns as well as one of your advanced repeater guns." Jalissa's gaze was sharp, her voice hard, as she stared at Averett.

"It was not my doing, if that is what you are asking. Surely you've observed our family interactions enough even in the few hours since you have arrived to see I love my sister very much. I would never aid an ambush that would place her life in danger." Averett gestured to the gun. "This is the work of a traitor, and we have already started an investigation into the matter. Edmund, do you have anything you can add?"

Edmund stared at the gun, his face taut. "It's worrisome that I haven't heard anything about guns being traded to the trolls. Whoever these traitors are, they are very smart, very cautious, and well respected enough to be above scrutiny. I have, however, heard rumors about groups who aren't happy with our new treaty with Tarenhiel. Many still hold grudges from the war. I haven't heard anything to make me think any of the grumblers were organized enough to pull off something like this."

Julien picked up the gun, turning it over in his hands with the ease of someone used to handling weapons. "To get a hold of these guns, the traitors must be high in the army or work at the factory that makes them."

Averett nodded, as if this was exactly the comment he

had been waiting to hear. "That is why I have invited General Freilan, the top general in Escarland's army, here today to answer our questions. I have also asked Charles Hadley, the owner of the largest manufacturer of weapons for the Escarlish army, here as well once we have finished our discussion with the general."

Essie settled into a more comfortable position in her chair. She hadn't realized how much she'd missed watching her brothers tag-team a meeting.

Averett motioned, and the guard opened a different door, this time admitting General Freilan. He wore his dress uniform with rows of medals and gold braid dripping down each shoulder. He saluted Averett. "Your Majesty."

"Please inform the crown and the ambassador from Tarenhiel on the progress of your investigation into how Escarlish army weapons came to be in the hands of Kostarians attacking the Tarenhieli royal family."

Essie tried not to shift. She had gotten used to hearing the elves referring to kingdom to the north simply as the trolls. But here in this diplomatic meeting, Averett would use their kingdom name to refer to them to keep the tone of this meeting as official and detached as possible.

The general's gaze flicked only briefly to Jalissa and Farrendel before he focused on Averett, as he should when reporting to his king. "We have only just begun our investigation. An inventory of all outposts, forts, bases, and warehouses is being conducted as we speak, though it may take several weeks to be completed. I have stressed to everyone the seriousness of this inventory. If there is a traitor in our ranks, I will endeavor to find him with utmost speed."

"Thank you, General. I expect to see reports of your

progress on my desk every morning." Averett's gaze didn't waver, his tone firm. Not afraid to push hard when necessary. Essie imagined their father must have sounded a lot like Averett.

General Freilan saluted again and backed away a few steps before he spun smartly and left the room.

"Please send in Charles Hadley," Averett ordered, his posture regal and straight.

A man in his fifties strode into the room. His graying hair was cropped short and thinning while his rotund stomach bulged against his red linen shirt. Beside him, a young man in his early to mid-twenties strode next to him. The young man had brown, sandy hair long across his forehead. His jaw was chiseled, his eyes a clear blue.

"Your Majesty." Mr. Hadley bowed to Averett. When his gaze flicked to Jalissa, then Farrendel, his jaw knotted, his eyes going hard. He pointed at the young man next to him. "This is my son, Mark. He is the head of our day-to-day operations."

Averett gestured to the gun on the table. "Is this one of yours?"

Charles Hadley picked it up, turned it over in his hands, before focusing on a part of the metal stock. Essie had briefly seen the serial number stamped into that metal when she had handled the gun in Tarenhiel. After a second's consideration, Mr. Hadley returned the gun to the table. "Yes, this was manufactured in my factory."

"Can you explain how this gun came to be in the hands of the Kostarians?" Averett's voice remained steady, hard.

Jalissa's gaze was knife-sharp on Mr. Hadley. Beside Essie, Farrendel was still. Poised. Essie half-expected to feel the crackle of magic at any moment.

"I don't know." Mr. Hadley crossed his arms. "Check with the army. This gun was their responsibility."

"Did this gun ever reach the army?" Julien crossed his arms and stared right back. "That's why you're here."

"I am a loyal citizen of Escarland. I would never knowingly hand over one of my weapons into the hands of a potential enemy." Mr. Hadley looked about ready to pound the table. Beside him, his son shifted, as if he was worried he would have to restrain his father.

"Even if you knew the gun would be used against the elves?" Averett's voice was even icier.

"My firstborn son died fighting those pointy-eared monsters." Mr. Hadley jabbed a finger at Farrendel. Both Farrendel and Jalissa stiffened. Mr. Hadley's jaw worked. "Yes, I am more than happy when the trolls kill a few of them. But I would never betray my own kingdom to do it."

"My father is incredibly patriotic. He would never betray Escarland." Mark rested a hand on his father's arm, pushing him back from the table. "I assure you that we will investigate this issue thoroughly."

"I expect a report on my desk before the end of the week. Preferably earlier." Averett's gaze didn't waver.

Essie restrained herself from cheering. Her brother had never looked quite as kingly as he did just then. Hopefully, Jalissa and Farrendel could see how seriously Averett was taking this situation with the traitor.

As Charles and Mark Hadley were escorted from the room, Jalissa glanced between Essie's brothers, some of the hardness leaving her face.

"Do you have any more questions? I'm afraid I can't give you all the answers this moment, but I am taking this seriously. I want to find this traitor just as much as you do. Escarlish weapons in the hands of a kingdom with whom we do not have a treaty is concerning." Averett grimaced, some of the stiffness leaving his shoulders. "Believe me, that is not something I want any more than your kingdom does. We will find the traitor or traitors as soon as possible."

"With elves staying here at the castle, anyone who has a grudge against them may see this as an opportunity to attack." Edmund leaned his elbows on the table. "It may flush them into the open."

"We are here on a diplomatic meeting. We will not be turned into bait." If she hadn't been so regal, Jalissa would've crossed her arms. As it was, she glared at Edmund.

"As Edmund pointed out, it's a situation that will arise inevitably from your presence. We might as well nip it now rather than wait for the next time Essie and Prince Farrendel visit. Unless you are suggesting they never visit?" Averett crossed his arms.

Jalissa stiffened, her eyes flicking toward Farrendel. As if she was worried about protecting him.

Farrendel didn't need protecting. Though, he would be hesitant to use his magic here. Both because he wouldn't want to give away how powerful he was and because it wouldn't be good politically if Farrendel was forced to kill Escarlish citizens.

Still, Essie probably should calm things down. That was her role, after all.

"You will be well-protected while you are here, contrary to what my brothers may be planning." Essie gave each of her brothers a stern glare and patted Farrendel's arm. "I want you to feel at home here while you are visiting."

Farrendel tipped his head in a slight nod. As all through the interviews, he'd been quiet. What was wrong with him? Was it just the number of people? He didn't enjoy being around people the way Essie did. Perhaps he needed more alone time? Was the stone bothering him even worse than it had before?

Tomorrow she'd have to show him the gardens and the best way to get to them from her room. The gardens and grounds at Winstead Palace were extensive, taking up several city blocks and surrounded by a well-guarded wall. He should be safe to wander the grounds as he wished.

Edmund gestured toward the gun sitting on the table between them. "I wonder at the traitors' motives. What do they hope to gain by causing a rift in our new alliance with Tarenhiel? Do they want war between Tarenhiel and Escarland? Or do they simply want us to stay out of Tarenhiel's war with Kostaria?"

"Or perhaps they saw an opportunity to make a profit and don't have any wider political motives?" Julien shook his head. "It's hard to know without more evidence. This could be simply a few workers stealing weapons from the factory and pawning them off on trolls willing to pay for them."

"Will we join the war on Tarenhiel's side?" Essie tried to keep her tone casual. Six months ago, she wouldn't have cared if the elves were at war with the trolls again. It would have been just a news item in the paper that she would've read, filed away under world events it was probably good to be aware of, and moved on.

But, now, she cared about Tarenhiel. She didn't want to bring Escarland into another war. But Tarenhiel also held a place in her heart. And she saw more clearly now how, if the elves fell to the trolls, Escarland would be next.

Averett met her gaze, something in his expression almost sad. "Our alliance was to secure peace between our peoples. Nothing more. Taking our people to war against the trolls is something I will need to consider carefully."

Essie nodded. This wasn't a decision Averett could make lightly. Nor was it one he could make without Parliament's approval. And convincing them to go to war for the elves—a former enemy—would be difficult.

Averett turned to Jalissa. "It is something the elves will wish to consider as well. If we do this, even without a mutual defense treaty, it will set precedent. Are the elves willing to return the gesture and come to our defense should one of our neighboring kingdoms attack us? Are you even willing to have our armies march through Tarenhiel? We are more numerous with more advanced weaponry. While you have powerful magic, it may not be enough to stop us from overrunning you once we are inside your borders."

Essie clenched her fists under the table. Surely Averett wasn't suggesting Escarland would stab the elves in the back like that?

Jalissa eyed Averett coolly. "Surely you are not suggesting it is your plan to finish your father's work and conquer Tarenhiel?"

"No, that isn't my intention. But it will be something my advisors suggest, even with Essie's marriage to help dissuade them." Averett's gaze remained steady. Far steadier than he had been three months ago when negotiating her marriage to Farrendel. It seemed he had come more prepared for this meeting than he had that one. "If you want Escarland's help in this war, I will need a good reason to present to my advisors and generals as to why we want Tarenhiel to remain its own, sovereign nation and why it would be foolish for us to invade and restart my father's war."

Essie blew out a breath, forcing herself to relax. She could more clearly see the position the elves were in. Escarland hadn't known how close the elves had come to crumbling fifteen years ago. If not for her father's death that had halted the war, Escarland might have won. The elves had been caught between Escarland's armies from the south and the trolls in the north.

They were looking at the same scenario once again. But in those fifteen years, Escarland had gained another generation of people. The guns were more advanced. The army even stronger than it had been only two decades before. Yet, due to their long lives and tendency not to have many children, the elves had regained little of the population they had lost in those wars.

This situation would only continue to grow worse. How could the elves remain standing if the populations of the nations around them continued to outpace them? And their weaponry continued to advance past what the elves' magic could handle?

Maybe it wouldn't happen in this particular war. But what about a hundred years from now? Thanks to the heart bond between her and Farrendel, there was a good chance she might live to see that war, as long as both she and Farrendel survived this one. Farrendel would be called on to fight that war too.

It would be a war the elves wouldn't be able to win. Not unless something changed.

The elves needed a mutual defense alliance with

Escarland probably more than they wanted to admit. Now if only Essie could figure out a way to foster a friendship between the two nations instead of this shaky back-and-forth they currently had.

CHAPTER
ELEVEN

An underground tunnel connected Winstead Palace with Ellory Hall where Parliament met. Essie had never thought much of it, until a guard opened the large double doors to the stairs leading down into the tunnel and Farrendel came to such an abrupt halt Edmund bumped into him.

On Farrendel's other side from Essie, Jalissa's face went a shade of gray-green. Even Jalissa's guard had a flicker of emotion.

Essie should've realized taking this route was going to be a bad idea. Farrendel was already uneasy surrounded by the stones of Winstead Palace. Stepping into that underground tunnel would feel like someone was smothering him.

His hand, gripped in hers, squeezed tighter. She leaned closer. "Are you going to be all right?"

He stared at the tunnel and slowly shook his head.

At the top of the stairs, Averett turned. "Is something wrong?"

"Is there any way we can take the carriage to Parliament?" Essie forced herself to smile, as if nothing was wrong.

Averett shook his head. "One of the groups most vehemently anti-elf has camped out with a group of protestors on the steps of Ellory Hall. The captain of the guard recommended we take the back way in rather than risk our guests."

"I hadn't heard the protestors were that violent?" Essie glanced between Averett, Julien, and Edmund. What hadn't they been telling her? "I heard there was some protest about the closer alliance with the elves, but I didn't think it was widespread."

"It isn't. Wasn't. Not at first." Julien crossed his arms and glanced at Edmund, as if asking him to elaborate further since Edmund was probably the one with the most information, outside of Averett.

Edmund glanced around, then must have decided the guards in the vicinity were trustworthy, even if he lowered his voice. "Only a few people are truly angry about the alliance, but lately someone has been stirring them up and turning them violent. We don't know who the leader is yet but…"

"It's probably the same traitor who gave guns to the trolls and wants to start the war between Tarenhiel and Escarland again," Essie finished for him, squeezing Farrendel's hand.

"War is profitable for some people, especially those who don't have to fight in the war themselves." Averett grimaced and rubbed at the spot where his crown rested on his forehead. "We suspect the traitor is a member of Parliament or has high connections in Parliament."

Making it difficult even for Edmund's spies to ferret

them out. It would take a cartload of irrefutable evidence before anyone could do anything to stop the traitor.

"Then we had better head to Parliament before they start the meeting without us." Which they might. Parliament and the monarchy had a rather tense back-and-forth. For generations, Parliament had been working to undermine the throne's power in Escarland, while the kings and queens had fought back to retain as much power as possible. It was frustrating, at times, but it worked as a checks and balance system on both Parliament's power and the king's power.

Beside her, Farrendel had steadied, but his breathing was almost too deliberate and measured.

Essie lowered her voice, speaking in elvish, "Are you all right or do I have to insist we take a carriage?"

Farrendel squeezed his eyes shut for a moment before straightening his shoulders. "It will not help our cause if I am forced to defend us from an attack by your people. I will be fine."

He wouldn't be, and by the look on Jalissa's face, she wouldn't be either.

With her hand still firmly gripped in Farrendel's, Essie led the way down the stairs behind Averett and two of the guards. Farrendel, Jalissa, and Jalissa's elven guard huddled close on Essie's heels, staying as far from the stone walls as possible.

At the bottom of the stairs, a small train consisting of only one train car and two engines, one facing forward and the other backwards, waited on a thin set of rails. No steam puffed from the stacks, nor were there any coal cars attached to the engines.

Averett waved at it. "This is one of the few trains in Escarland powered by magical devices. The fumes of a traditional train would have been too much in this tunnel."

Farrendel had his mouth pressed together in a tight line and remained stiff as a statue. Jalissa managed a tiny nod.

As soon as they boarded the train, Farrendel turned sideways on the bench, pulled his knees up, and rested his head on his arms, breathing tight and strained. Essie squeezed into the space between him and the wall and rubbed his back.

Jalissa and her guard claimed the bench in front of Essie and Farrendel while Edmund sat behind them. Edmund leaned forward and said in elvish, "If you're going to throw up, you might want to do it out the window before we get to Parliament."

"Not going to," Farrendel bit out, though he didn't raise his head.

Averett sank onto the bench across the aisle from them. "Is everything all right?"

Essie rubbed Farrendel's back, feeling his slight trembling through her fingers. No, everything wasn't all right. But she couldn't explain to her brothers exactly what was going on. "Elves...don't like to be underground."

That was mostly true. She wanted to explain more why this might remind Farrendel of the torture he'd suffered at the hands of the trolls, but now wasn't the time or place.

Averett studied both Farrendel and Jalissa but didn't say anything as Julien and the guards claimed seats and the train started moving.

"I probably should warn you." Averett sat forward in his seat to better peer at Essie past Farrendel's hunched form. "Parliament wasn't too happy with your marriage alliance with the elves. It seems some of the old timers think I 'wasted' Escarland's one princess on the elves rather than bargain you away to some other, more important kingdom, to their eyes, anyway."

That made Farrendel stiffen and raise his head.

Jalissa raised her eyebrows. "Tarenhiel is not important to Escarland? Then what, I ask, are we doing here?" Her tone had a bite to it.

"Trade is all important to Parliament. They don't yet see the trade benefits of a stronger alliance with Tarenhiel, and they all too quickly forget how close we came to war before we signed this treaty." Averett rested his elbows on his knees, his head still held high to keep his crown perfectly balanced. "I am willing to consider the benefits to not just a peace treaty, but a closer alliance. But if you wish to convince Parliament, then you must prove to them today that Tarenhiel is still standing strong and an alliance will be beneficial to both Tarenhiel and Escarland."

"I see." Jalissa sat straighter, her head held higher despite her pallor. "You wish for my kingdom to become like yours, consumed by trade and greed. Our way of life would become nothing but something to be bartered."

"The world is changing. Better your kingdom figures out a way to adapt, thrive, and preserve your way of life rather than have it forcibly stolen from you." Averett straightened, but his gaze never left Jalissa's face. In that moment, he wasn't the sometimes-uncertain older brother Essie saw often, but the king he'd had to learn how to be when the crown landed on his head at age twelve. "I believe Tarenhiel has much to offer and can be a worthy ally to Escarland. I would not have pushed for this alliance nor agreed to my sister's marriage if I hadn't believed that."

Jalissa gave a nod.

Farrendel gestured between him and Essie. "Your Parliament thinks our marriage was a waste."

Of course that was the part he was still stuck on. Essie squeezed his shoulder. "Were they still pushing for a marriage alliance with Mongalia?"

"Yes. As if I would ever marry my little sister off to a widower over twice her age, even if he happens to be the crown prince likely to become king any day. I'd rather you be happy than a queen." Averett grimaced and eyed Farrendel, as if he still wasn't sure that particular marriage alliance was any better.

"And they wonder why I jumped at the chance to form a marriage alliance that actually sounded appealing to me." Essie leaned forward to kiss Farrendel, but since he was hunched over, all she could reach was his ear. She planted a kiss on the tip of his ear anyway. "It turned out even better than I hoped."

Farrendel rubbed his ear against his shoulder, as if completely embarrassed she would toss out all sense of elven propriety by kissing him, even his ear, in front of her brothers. At least his embarrassment brought some color back to his pale face.

Julien made a gagging sound. Edmund jabbed a thumb at the window next to him. "If you're going to turn all lovey-dovey, I'm throwing myself out of this train."

The comment broke the last lingering tension from a moment ago. Even Farrendel's mouth twitched in a hint of a smile. Perhaps some lighthearted banter would help distract him, though at this point they weren't far from the stop at Ellory Hall.

Essie met Averett's gaze over Farrendel's shoulder and mouthed, "Keep talking."

Averett held her gaze just long enough to be an acknowledgement. A smirk crossed his face, and he leaned back on his bench, resting an arm across its back. "What Parliament doesn't realize is that while I would never bargain away my only sister against her will, I would be more than happy to marry off a few brothers. I have plenty of those to spare."

Julien puffed out his chest, striking a pose. "We are rather handsome specimens. I'm sure you'll be able to bargain us for quite the trade deal. I hear Mongalia's crown prince has a daughter about the right age."

"Oh, come now, Julien. If Avie's going to go about this whole marriage alliance thing the right way, he would have to marry you off to Mongalia's crown prince's unmarried, forty-year-old sister. I hear uncomfortably large age gaps are the way it's supposed to be done." Edmund sprawled in his bench, his face too carefully straight and stoic.

"Leaving the younger princess for you, I suppose." Julien wagged a finger at him. "Tricky as always."

"Well, Mongalia isn't our only option." Averett turned to Jalissa. "You elves wouldn't want to take another of my siblings off my hands, would you? Kind of a marry one, get another one free deal?"

Jalissa glanced from Averett to Farrendel and then strangely enough toward Edmund, as if she wasn't sure how to go about answering this banter. Finally, she faced Averett with her perfectly composed expression. "I believe even free would be too expensive for the chaos it would cause."

Edmund grinned, and Julien plastered on a wide-eyed, horrified look. "Essie, just how much chaos did you manage to cause in Tarenhiel?"

Essie shrugged. "Not that much, I don't think."

Farrendel glanced at her. "You fell asleep on my shoulder. In public."

"It wasn't really public. It was just your family." Essie heaved an exaggerated sigh. "Elves have this weird thing against public displays of affection of any kind. Seriously. You can't even hold hands more than a couple of fingers. Not even in front of close family."

"That's it. I'm moving to Tarenhiel." Edmund clapped Farrendel on the shoulder. "You have an extra room where I can bunk down?"

"No touchy-feely stuff of any kind." Essie nudged Edmund's hand from Farrendel's shoulder. "Not even brotherly affection. Elves have large personal spaces."

Edmund grinned, as if she'd just given him the best weapon for brotherly teasing. That wasn't comforting. Edmund might be the youngest of the three brothers, but he was the sneakiest. She wasn't sure how he'd decide to use his new-found knowledge.

The train shuddered and screeched to a halt.

Averett pushed to his feet. "Looks like we're here."

Jalissa and her guard followed Averett from the train, almost tripping on his heels. Farrendel climbed to his feet slowly, as if any sudden moves could send his stomach lurching in directions he didn't want it to go. But he strode steadily from the train, marching up the stairs from the underground tunnel.

At the top, guards opened the reinforced doors, revealing a spacious corridor with black and white marble tiled floor and vaulted, arched ceilings soaring high overhead. Sunlight streamed into the hall from a bank of windows overlooking the broad expanse of the river with the other half of Aldon beyond while, on the other side of the corridor, a small atrium held a single tree and a few bushes.

Essie tugged Farrendel in the direction of the atrium. Not that it took much urging on her part. "Avie, while you check if Parliament is ready for us, Farrendel, Jalissa, and I are going to step into the atrium for a moment."

None of her family questioned her. Maybe, despite Jalissa's and Farrendel's best efforts to appear blank and forbidding, some of their desperation showed through the cracks.

As soon as they stepped inside the atrium, Farrendel let go of her hand and sank to the ground, his back to the tree. He closed his eyes, breathing slowly and deeply.

Jalissa glanced around, a hint of a wrinkle on her nose. She touched the tree, her hand glowing faintly green. Moments later, the tree's leaves brightened. More leaves thickened the canopy overhead while the bushes and grass below filled in to a strong, solid carpet.

Some of the tension left Farrendel's shoulders. "You humans live far too much indoors."

With their airy treehouses and pathways along the tree branches, the elves lived nearly always in the open air with nothing but the thick foliage of their forest above them. Coming to Winstead Palace must have been a shock. They hadn't stepped outside since the brief walk from the train to the palace.

It had been normal to go about her day often never leaving Winstead Palace. Forays outside were brief hours spent in the garden or walking Aldon's market or doing charity work. Stone walls surrounding her made her feel safe. They didn't bring panic attacks or dampen magic the way they did for Farrendel.

Edmund stepped into the atrium. "They are ready for you. Which, for Parliament, means they want you to sit in your seats feeling uncomfortable for another hour or so until they finally admit they want you."

Jalissa brushed off her skirt, even though she'd never sat in the dirt. "They will not keep us waiting." She swept from the atrium, head held high. Her guard, who had stationed herself at the door, fell into step behind her.

Essie grinned and held out a hand to Farrendel. "I guess if you make a grand enough entrance, no one keeps you waiting."

Farrendel glanced at her hand, as if he wasn't sure what to do with her gesture, and rose to his feet without her help. Essie couldn't put her finger on the exact moment, but sometime between sitting and standing, he had gone from vulnerable Farrendel to the elf warrior Laesornysh. His face hardened, his jaw set.

He held his arm out to her, and she rested her hand on his forearm in the elven manner rather than tuck her hand in the crook of his arm in the custom of Escarland.

She held her head high, her shoulders back. They were about to make an entrance, and she was going to look every inch a princess of both Escarland and Tarenhiel.

At the end of the hall, the guards opened the doors to Parliament's meeting hall, too in awe of Jalissa to argue.

Averett remained outside. As the king, Parliament's hall was considered off limits for him, though it wasn't for Julien, Edmund, or Essie. They all marched in after Jalissa.

Escarland's Parliament was arranged in several tiers in a half circle facing the center. A podium was in the center where members could address the rest. Unlike the elven council, with its quiet serenity, several Parliament members were already shouting at each other even before Jalissa marched into the room.

At their entrance, several Parliament members shot to their feet. It took a moment for their shouts to solidify into various forms of, "What is the meaning of this?"

Julien stepped onto the podium. "Esteemed Parliament members, the ambassador from Tarenhiel, Princess Jalissa, would like to address this assembly."

Lord Crelford, one of the lords who did not exactly like elves but did not hate them either, climbed to his feet. "We told you we'd let you in when we were ready."

Jalissa speared him with one of her looks. "I am ready now. I came here in good faith to bring the goodwill of my people to yours. But if you do not wish to hear what I have to say, then I will leave. I am sure Mongalia or Afristan will be more open to the trade deals I am prepared to present."

Oh, Jalissa was good. Essie struggled to keep her expression regal as she stood next to Farrendel off to the side.

Most of the Parliament members took their seats, pausing just long enough to pretend it had been their idea. Lord Crelford made a magnanimous motion with his hand. "Please make your case."

Not exactly the best invitation, but it was the best Jalissa was probably going to get.

Jalissa held her head high and faced the ranks of the members. "Six months ago, the incidents at the border between Escarland and Tarenhiel escalated to the point that citizens of both kingdoms were raiding across the border. Destruction and eventually deaths occurred. Your king and mine both decried these actions and took the unprecedented step to meet and sign a peace treaty, a peace treaty that was strengthened by the marriage of my brother Prince Farrendel Laesornysh to your Princess Elspeth."

When Jalissa gestured to Essie and Farrendel, Essie glanced up at Farrendel and smiled. It was for show for Parliament, but she hoped some of the true warmth of her feelings for Farrendel had shown through.

He, of course, remained cold and still as an ice statue.

"For three months, we have had peace." Jalissa's jaw tightened. "But, recently, the royal family of Tarenhiel was attacked by trolls using Escarlish weapons. Your king has assured me that this was caused by the actions of a few traitors in your midst and does not represent the view of most in Escarland."

That gained her some nods, but also some crossed arms. A few glares.

Lord Kranshaw shot to his feet. "You filthy elves would've had it coming."

Jalissa stiffened. Beside Essie, Farrendel's magic crackled beneath the surface. Essie felt it building, ready to be unleashed. She should've expected Lord Kranshaw to speak up. He was up there on her list of possible traitors in Parliament. He had enough hatred of the elves.

"Now, now." Lord Bletchly held his hands out, palms up. "No need to insult our guests."

Lord Bletchly. He had lost a son in the war, but he was one of the few who didn't seem to unequivocally hate elves because of it. He tended to be a voice of reason in Parliament.

A cane thumped on the floor, drawing everyone's attention to the white-haired lord sitting in his chair near the center of the room. Lord Fiskre was one of the oldest lords there, and one of the most respected. He cleared his throat in the silence. "I, for one, would like to hear what she has to say. I'm eighty-three-years young, and I remember a time when Tarenhiel and Escarland were at peace. I grew up on stories from a time when our kingdoms had more of a friendship than they do now. I would like to see where Princess Elspeth and her elf can take our two kingdoms."

Essie knew there was a reason she had always liked Lord Fiskre.

Jalissa gave a slight nod. "Thanks to Princess Elspeth and the actions of your King Averett, King Weylind, my brother, has gained a new respect for Escarland. We have seen the way the times are changing. No kingdom will be able to stand alone. We have seen the strength in Escarland. We are not offering a stronger alliance with Mongalia or Afristan. We are reaching to you as the kingdom with whom we wish to ally."

Several of the lords murmured. Some had louder discussions with each other. Lord Crelford huffed and crossed his arms. "Why should we ally with you? Why would we risk being drawn into your war with Kostaria? What do you have to offer Escarland?"

"Thanks to the traitor operating within your borders, you are already in this war, though you do not know it." Jalissa's mouth tilted into a sharp kind of smile. "Thanks to our healers, we can show you advances in your medical practices. We can offer magically infused products, like our shampoo and conditioners, that your magicians cannot manufacturer."

That had lords like Lord Bletchly nodding. Trade they could understand.

"And we can offer our magic." Jalissa gestured toward Farrendel.

A crackle built a moment before blue lightning swirled from Farrendel's palms and up his arms. He raised his hand and magic exploded in the air before it dissipated in a fizzle of sparks in a bigger, more powerful version of what he'd done for the nephews.

About half the Parliament members were now huddled on the floor by their chairs. Others had jumped to their feet, as if preparing to run.

Guards dashed into the room, but Julien held up his hand, holding them back.

Even Essie, knowing how powerful his magic was and that this was such a small demonstration of it, had found herself taking a step back.

"That is the kind of magic found in Tarenhiel. If you wish to beg for a defense alliance, I will be at Winstead Palace." Jalissa spun on her heel and marched from the podium.

Essie should be taking notes on how to make a dramatic exit. Jalissa sure knew how to make a statement.

CHAPTER
TWELVE

The scream yanked Essie from sleep. She bolted upright, heart racing, and peeled her gritty eyes open. After the train ride underground to Parliament and back, she'd expected nightmares tonight. Farrendel had paced long into the night, as if he'd hoped collapsing into bed from exhaustion would stave off the nightmares.

Farrendel curled in a tight ball beneath the blankets, shaking. He cried out again, his head sheltered beneath his arms.

"Farrendel. It's all right. Wake up." Essie touched his shoulder to shake him awake.

He whipped around, eyes wild. His forearm knocked her hand away. A crackle filled the air a moment before blue sparks exploded outward.

The prickle of magic raked across her skin, the hair on her arms standing on end. The lamp behind her shattered, glass pinging against the wall and oil spilling onto the nightstand. Thankfully the sparks of Farrendel's magic didn't ignite it.

"Farrendel?" Essie didn't dare move. In the hall outside her room, there came the sounds of doors slamming open, people shouting.

His eyes cleared, then widened. "No...no...Essie..." He scrambled backwards from her, but he'd already been pressed to the edge of the bed. He tumbled off, the back of his head thunking against the nightstand.

"Farrendel." Essie crawled across the bed and peered down at him. "Are you all right?"

He was sitting on the floor, a hand to the back of his head. He glanced up at her, his silver-blue eyes pained and still confused.

Her door banged open, and Julien burst inside, a knife in his hand, followed by Edmund and Averett. All three of them wore trousers and their night shirts.

Farrendel raised his free hand, a crackle filling the air again, expression wild.

"Essie, are you all right?" Averett stepped forward, fists clenched, as if he was convinced she wasn't.

Essie rolled from the bed, planting herself between Farrendel and her brothers, shielding him and hopefully giving him time and space to claw the rest of the way out of the nightmare. "I'm fine, Avie. I wasn't the one screaming."

Julien and Edmund lowered their knife and fists. But none of her brothers moved, still tensed for trouble, as if they didn't fully believe her. Behind them, Mother peered inside, tying the belt of her dressing gown around her waist.

Essie needed to get them out of the room. Farrendel needed space, not her brothers gawking at him. "Everyone, out. Get out." When they didn't move, she hurried forward and shoved Averett in the chest. "He needs space."

She bodily herded her brothers out the door into the sitting room. The way they were crossing their arms, glaring, said they wanted an explanation. But Farrendel was still huddled on the floor, struggling with the aftereffects of his nightmare.

Essie hesitated in the door between the bedroom and sitting room. Would her brothers wait while she calmed Farrendel down? She couldn't just leave Farrendel shaking and panicking as he was.

Mother touched Essie's shoulder. "Sort out your brothers. I'll sit with Farrendel."

"Are you sure?" Essie couldn't force herself to move, pulled in two directions.

"Yes. Go on."

At least her mother understood the situation, far more than her brothers did. Essie stepped aside. "Thank you."

Mother swept inside and softly closed the door behind her. Giving Farrendel space and giving Essie a chance to explain.

She turned back to her brothers. They were lined up, arms crossed, feet apart.

Ready to take on the world for her if she needed them to. Even if she didn't at the moment.

Farrendel gripped his knees, shaking and trying to fight through the last tatters of the nightmares. Pain lanced through his head as it pounded. His stomach churned until he thought he might vomit there on the floral rug.

Essie...what had he done? Caught in the tumble between the nightmare and waking, his memories of the last few minutes were splintered. Was it nightmare or reality that he had lashed out?

The door to the room clicked, and soft footsteps crossed the rugs. Not Essie's. These were slower, not as quick and bouncing.

His heart raced, his mouth drying, his magic crackling in his fingers even as he struggled to yank it back in. He forced himself to raise his head and look, trying to steady his breathing and swallow back the panic.

Essie's mother eased down onto the rug. She gave him a soft smile. "Sitting on the floor isn't as easy as it used to be."

He blinked at her. What was she doing here? After what had nearly happened, surely she would hate him. Or be wary, at the very least.

Her mother did not waver, and something in the expression reminded him of Essie. "I know you don't know me very well, yet. But I hope we will have a chance to get to know each other better."

"Why?" Farrendel lifted a shaking hand to rub at his temple. Sharp pain stabbed from the base of his skull all the way to behind his eyes. Why would Essie's mother want to know him? Surely she saw him as the person who had taken her daughter away to a foreign kingdom, rarely to return.

"Essie is special to me. She's my only daughter. But that also means you're special to me, too." Essie's mother was poised, as if she wanted to reach out and hug him. Something he only recognized thanks to Essie. "I have three sons, but you are my only son-in-law."

Something deep inside his chest ached. As a young

child, he had believed the late elf queen had been his mother, as she was for his siblings. He had hung on their stories about her, imaging how she would have loved him if she had lived.

Melantha had finally been the one to gather the courage to tell him the person the rest of his siblings called mother did not belong to him. The dream of her that he had built in his mind had never truly existed. How could it have hurt so much to lose someone who had never truly been his?

"I never had a mother." He did not know why he was telling Essie's mother that. She would assume, as the rest of Essie's family had, that the late queen had been his mother and he had never known her because of her death. He hoped they would never add up the dates and realize that the truth was much worse.

"You poor boy." Essie's mother met his gaze. "You have me now, if you want."

The next thing he knew, Essie's mother shifted so that she was next to him and pulled him in for a hug, as if he was a small child she was comforting.

He held himself stiffly. What was he supposed to do now? It was everything he had longed for when he was a child.

But he was no longer a child. He had not been a child from the moment the trolls had wrapped his arms with magic-laced stone and dragged him back to their base for torture while they lured his father into a trap.

Still, he forced himself to relax. This was the family Essie had grown up with. Her mother was the reason Essie was so warm and caring, even though she had been even younger than Farrendel when she had lost her father.

135

Perhaps he could get used to having a mother for the first time in his life.

Essie crossed her arms and glared back at her brothers.

Averett broke first and stepped forward, reaching for her as if intending to hug her. "Are you truly all right, Essie? You aren't just smiling and carrying on like you always do."

"I told you. I'm fine." She gritted her teeth. She was too tired to deal with their lingering suspicion of Farrendel. They had seen him come near breaking on the train to and from Parliament. They had almost seemed to be bonding. And now they were back to being suspicious. She was grateful for their concern, truly. But this was getting ridiculous. "That was Farrendel. He struggles with nightmares, all right? And staying here isn't helping things any. The stone..."

Essie bit off her words. She'd promised Farrendel she wouldn't tell her brothers the truth. She drew in a deep breath, trying to calm down. "The stone reminds him too much of being captured by the trolls. He was only the elf equivalent of sixteen, and they tortured him. I've seen his scars. What they did to him..."

Her voice broke. She was exhausted. All she wanted was a peaceful night's sleep. Something neither she nor Farrendel had had in a week, except for the night on the train here. She was far too emotional and worn out for this conversation.

"You really do love him." Edmund stepped closer, his posture relaxing.

"Yes." The word held more depth of feeling than

she'd intended, too tired to hold her heart back from her voice. "If I have been hiding anything, it's been this. He's been trying so hard to give me time to enjoy being back home, but it's torturing him. And I don't know what to do."

She blinked back tears and tried to pull herself together. She wasn't going to break down and cry in front of her brothers. That would just be embarrassing.

Julien sheathed his knife, the elven dagger Farrendel had given him, now that Essie got a good look at it. "All right. Then he can't stay here. Family camping night. I'll fetch the camping supplies." After a pat to Essie's shoulder, he headed for the door.

"I'll get the firewood." Edmund hurried out the door after Julien.

"I guess that leaves fetching the food for me." Averett gave her a side hug. "We'll figure out a better solution in the morning."

Essie rested her head on her brother's solid shoulder. He carried the weight of the kingdom, but he was still able to help her with her burdens as well. "Will you wake Paige and the boys?"

"I'll let Paige know, but I think it would be best if we left the boys sleeping. They'll just be crabby and grouchy if we haul them out into the woods in the middle of the night. You look like you need as much sleep as you can get." Averett patted her back, then stepped away. "We'll give you and Farrendel twenty minutes or so before we descend on the campsite."

"Thanks. He should be ready for people again by then." Hopefully. Essie turned and faced the door to her room, her stomach strangely tight. Had Farrendel calmed down? She hadn't heard any more crashes, so Mother probably hadn't startled Farrendel. With a deep breath, she pushed the door open.

She'd expected a lot of things, but the sight before her wasn't one of them.

Mother sat on the floor next to Farrendel. Somehow, she'd broken through all of Farrendel's elven personal space boundaries, quite the feat. Farrendel leaned his head on her shoulder with her arm around him. They were talking quietly.

At Essie's footsteps, Farrendel and Mother looked up. Farrendel straightened, pushing his hair from his face.

Essie jabbed a finger over her shoulder. "We're going to stay outdoors at the family camping spot for the rest of the night. Julien and Edmund are grabbing the equipment and Avie's fetching the food."

"I'll see if Avie needs help." Mother patted Farrendel's back and stood. After a moment's pause, she bent and kissed Farrendel's forehead, as she'd done for Essie and her brothers when they'd been children. "Sleep tight."

"Linshi, Mamasha." Farrendel gazed up at Essie's mother with such trusting, silver-blue eyes. Essie caught the glint of the little boy he'd once been, the one who had longed for the mother he'd never had.

Essie gave Mother a quick hug. "Thank you. Can you make sure Avie doesn't forget the hot chocolate? I've been promising Farrendel a mug of hot chocolate for months now. Apparently, elves don't have any."

"I'll see to it." Mother nodded and strode from the room.

Leaving Essie facing Farrendel and wondering exactly what she was going to say to him after what had happened.

CHAPTER
THIRTEEN

E ssie reached for him. She needed to reassure him. "Farrendel..."

Farrendel pushed to his feet, stepping out of her reach. His gaze flicked over Essie, as if searching for injuries. "Are you all right? I did not...my magic..."

"I'm fine. I wasn't hurt." Essie tried not to think what could have happened. She had seen Farrendel's magic incinerate bullets and kill with sizzling bolts of power.

How had she survived unscathed? She'd felt the crackle of his magic. Had it simply missed her? Had Farrendel been alert enough, even unconsciously, to keep his magic from hitting her? She would've thought the bolt underpowered, but it had shattered the lamp easily enough. It had been far stronger than the sparks Farrendel had shot into the air when playing with the nephews.

Was it possible that the heart bond had protected Essie? Could Farrendel's magic have sensed not to hurt her?

The only way to test that was to stick her hand into a bolt of Farrendel's magic, and that didn't seem like a good idea. Not if she wanted to keep her hand.

Farrendel stepped closer and cradled Essie's face in both of his hands. "My magic could have killed you. If I had hurt you..."

"You didn't." Essie wouldn't let herself fear Farrendel. He hadn't lashed out on purpose. He shouldn't bear guilt for this. She took both of his hands and laced her fingers through his. "You've never lashed out before. It only happened this time because you've been pushing yourself to stay here beyond what you could handle."

He hung his head, staring at the floor. "This is your home. I wanted to give you time here."

"But staying here is hurting you." She touched his cheek.

"I am sorry. I do not want to be this weak. I thought this was something I could sacrifice for you. You sacrificed so much for me."

Was that what he thought? In some ways, she had sacrificed a lot to marry him. In the beginning, it hadn't necessarily been for him, but for Escarland. But she'd given up her home here. Time with her family. Even her own culture.

Essie tipped Farrendel's face up, but he still wouldn't look at her. "Yes, love is sacrifice. But love doesn't demand sacrifices that hurt you mentally or physically or emotionally. Not like this is doing. This isn't healthy for you. I'm sorry I didn't insist on changing our sleeping quarters sooner. I'm getting better at learning what you can and can't handle, but I'm not going to be able to antic- ipate everything. I need you to be honest with me when you truly can't handle something. That way we can figure out a compromise that works for both of us before you're pushed to the breaking point like this."

And before she was pushed to hers.

Farrendel nodded. Then, slowly, he wrapped his arms around her. She leaned her head against his shoulder, embracing him. A few hot tears burned their way down her cheeks. She didn't want to cry. Not over this. No one had been hurt. Nothing broken but an easily replaced lamp.

But everything in her felt worn thin and faded. Broken and exhausted. In the week since the trolls' attack, she hadn't had a fully restful night.

Was this what Farrendel felt like all the time? No wonder he was so skittish when the slightest thing could send his careful balance tipping out of his control.

"Essie, I cannot risk hurting you." Farrendel's arms tightened around her, his head leaning against hers.

She felt him draw in a breath, and she hurried to speak before he suggested they go back to sleeping in separate rooms or something crazy like that. They'd only been sharing a room for a week—a week of little sleep— but even then, she didn't want to go back to so much distance between them. "I know. And, you're right. We need to be more cautious. I won't shake you awake anymore or make a loud noise or anything to startle you awake. I'll call your name or something. It may take longer to rouse you, but it's probably wiser."

"I do not need to be awakened from my nightmares. I will wake myself before they stretch too long. It is enough to know you will be there when I do wake," Farrendel murmured, his mouth only a few inches from her ear.

"All right." It ached inside her that she couldn't do anything to rescue him from his nightmares. But she had been too naïve to think that he would never lash out magically or otherwise when startled awake from nightmares of torture and death. She took a step back out of his embrace to meet his gaze. "But let's also do our best to keep you from having nightmares in the first place. We won't be able to stop them entirely, but avoiding things like sleeping in stone buildings, for example, will help."

Farrendel's mouth quirked at one corner, as if he was attempting—and failing—to smile. "Yes."

As much as Essie would've loved to stand there in Farrendel's arms, her brothers had only given her twenty minutes before they would descend on the campsite. And, even while they were standing there, the stones of Winstead Palace were pressing down on Farrendel, hurting him. The sooner she got him into the forest, the better.

She pulled away from him and strode to the foot of her bed. After pushing open the trunk there, she tugged out two wool blankets that still smelled faintly of smoke. She tossed the brown one to Farrendel, keeping the green one for herself. "That's why we're going to camp in the forest on the grounds. Well, I guess we call it a forest. You're probably going to find the trees a bit underwhelming after what you're used to. But it'll be better than staying here."

After lighting a lamp, Essie quickly packed a few items of clothing and other essentials she might want first thing in the morning, like a hairbrush, as did Farrendel. Then she wrapped her blanket over her shoulders, took Farrendel's hand, and led the way from her room, down the hallway and stairs, and to the end of the family wing that opened onto a terraced patio overlooking the formal gardens. In the darkness, the forest loomed as a dark mass against the star-studded sky. The perfect night for camping outside.

As they stepped outside, Farrendel drew in a deep breath, some of the tension of his grip on her hand relaxing. More of his tensed muscles released as they stepped from the stone terrace onto the graveled paths through the formal garden.

Lamp in hand, Essie navigated through the carefully maintained flowerbeds to the far side where the woods had been allowed to grow wild and virtually untamed in the center of the acres of grounds the palace claimed. Only a few dirt trails crisscrossed the forest, trails Essie knew by heart after years of exploring them with her brothers and by herself.

This was a section of woods untouched by logging, filled with oaks, maples, and beech that she and Farrendel together couldn't wrap their arms around, though they were still small compared to the giant trees found in the elven forests.

Still, Essie breathed deeply of the fresh, green scent of the forest, her own muscles relaxing. She hadn't realized how used to living in the peace and quiet of a forest she had become until now.

In the middle of the woods, a small circle had been cleared of trees. A fire pit surrounded by stones was in the center. Large, split log benches surrounded the fire pit.

After setting the lamp onto one of the benches, Essie tugged her blanket tighter around her shoulders and took a seat on one of the benches that had plenty of room for two people. "What do you think? Is this better?"

Farrendel paced around the campsite for several moments before he joined her on the bench. "Yes."

"My father used to take the family camping here. He

couldn't always get away to spend time at the summer palace, so this spot became the place he could spend time with the family even for a night. It's secluded, but the palace staff could fetch him quickly if he was needed. And, inside the palace grounds as it is, it is safe for the royal family to camp without guards patrolling close by." Essie stared at her hands, trying to piece together the hazy memories she had of back then.

This was a personal, vulnerable thing to share, but Farrendel needed to understand what this place meant to her family. What it meant that he was being included here. "I only have a few, hazy memories of camping with my father here before he went to war. I was too little to go more than a handful of times."

"I am sorry." Farrendel took her hand. The heart bond flared warmer inside her chest.

She leaned against him, thankful he didn't flinch away. "You didn't kill him."

"My people did."

"It was war. A war neither of our kingdoms wanted but felt was necessary for a variety of reasons." Essie rubbed her thumb across the back of Farrendel's hand, tracing the faint line of a scar. "After he died, Mother still took us camping here, even though staying out in the woods isn't her favorite thing to do. She did it anyway because she didn't want us to miss out on this. This is a special place for us. It's a family rule only to bring family here."

The extra loud stomping on the trail behind them gave plenty of warning before Edmund's voice called out, "And that means you're stuck with us."

Farrendel flinched, as if he intended to pull away from

her, but Essie kept her grip on his hand, though she raised her head from his shoulder.

It wasn't as if they had been caught kissing, just a little handholding and sitting close. Edmund and Julien might complain, but Averett couldn't. Not if he didn't want her complaining right back about him and Paige. Which was extra strange, since Essie had watched her best friend and her brother get all snuggly with each other.

Essie glanced over her shoulder. All three of her brothers trooped up the path, arms laden. Julien and Edmund each had heaps of bedrolls and blankets in their arms and sacks of supplies hanging from their shoulders. Averett held a steaming kettle in each hand with a sack slung over his back.

Julien deposited his bundle onto one of the benches. "If he's stuck with us, I guess we'd better give him the rite of initiation. What was it again?"

Edmund dropped his armload of supplies on the bench next to Julien's and knelt by the fire pit. "I believe he needs to stand on his head, squawk like a chicken, and solemnly declare that what happens at camp, stays at camp."

Beneath Essie's hand, Farrendel tensed, like he was prepared to actually perform her brothers' made-up initiation rite. "Don't believe a word they say. There's no such thing as an initiation to family camping. Not unless it's them hiding in the forest making growling noises trying to scare their little sister."

"Would we really do that?" Averett set down the kettles while giving Essie an expression far too wide-eyed as he attempted to look innocent.

"Yes, you would." Essie glared at them with exaggerated anger.

"We paid for that one. She kept sending us under her bed to check for wolves." Julien handed Edmund a wad of kindling.

Edmund tucked it into the center of the neat stack of firewood he'd built, lit a match, and worked to convince the kindling to light.

"If you got eaten, I'd know there were wolves under my bed. Besides, I had plenty of brothers if the wolves ate a few. It was very logical." Essie glanced at Farrendel and had to suppress her grin. His gaze flicked between her and her brothers as if he wasn't sure what to make of this easy banter after they had been about ready to beat him up earlier that night.

Perhaps she and Farrendel should help out instead of making her brothers do all the work. Keeping Farrendel's hands busy might make him feel less awkward.

She tugged on his hand as she stood. "Come on. Let's sort through all the bedrolls and move everything to the right spot."

Since Farrendel didn't know which bedroll belonged to each person or which spots around the campfire they normally picked, Essie sorted through the pile, handed whatever she'd extricated from the jumble on the bench to Farrendel, and pointed where it needed to go. Within a few minutes, Julien joined them, and between the three of them, they had the waterproof tarpaulins laid out on the ground, layered the blankets and bedrolls on top of them, then added another tarpaulin on top to keep off the dew.

By the time they finished, Edmund had the fire burning brightly, sparks snapping occasionally. He had a stack of firewood at his feet, ready to add more when needed.

Averett had laid out the food on the bench, set up a

tripod over one side of the fire, and was pouring hot chocolate and coffee in various mugs. He held up both kettles. "Farrendel, do you want coffee or hot chocolate?"

"Hot chocolate?" He glanced at Essie, as if checking that was the right answer.

"You haven't had either, have you?" Averett shook his head. "Essie will try to convince you hot chocolate is better. She's never become a coffee drinker. The rest of us love it. I'll pour a little in a mug, and you can see what you think."

Essie didn't think Farrendel would like coffee, but she didn't say it. He should try it out for himself, and, to be honest, she wanted to see the look on his face when he tasted it.

Averett poured a swish of coffee into a mug and held it out to Farrendel.

Farrendel took the mug, peering into it as if he expected the coffee was poisonous. After blowing on it and shifting beneath all of their stares, he sipped. His face twisted, as if he couldn't figure out an elven expression strong enough to convey his level of disgust. He thrust the mug back at Averett, shaking his head.

"Not a coffee drinker either. It's an acquired taste, I guess." Averett tossed the remains of the coffee into the fire where it hissed briefly before being swallowed by the flames. With a glance at Essie, probably knowing her thoughts on hot chocolate in a mug tainted with coffee, he rinsed the mug with water from a canteen and wiped it dry with a rag before filling it about half full of hot chocolate. "Try this."

While Farrendel cradled his mug and blew on the contents, Essie claimed her own mug of hot chocolate from Avie. She returned to her seat on the bench, pulled the blanket around her shoulders, and risked a sip of her hot chocolate. It still scalded too hot against her tongue, but the sweetness and warmth filled her down to her toes.

Farrendel sat next to her, still eying his hot chocolate as if he didn't dare take a sip after the whole coffee-tasting debacle. With a glance in her direction, he sipped. Swallowed. Sipped again.

The tension eased from his shoulders. That hint of a smile tiptoed at the corners of his mouth.

"It's so much better than coffee, right?" Essie nudged him gently with her elbow.

"Yes." Farrendel took another sip.

"See? I'm not so outnumbered anymore." Essie brandished her mug, as if making a toast. "Hot chocolate is better than coffee. Farrendel agrees with me."

Beside her, Farrendel froze, as if worried her brothers would call him out on his opinion. But her brothers laughed, rolled their eyes, and reached for more coffee.

Once the roasting sticks were distributed, they toasted apples, sugar-covered dough, and marshmallows over the fire. Eating the treats with his fingers instead of utensils seemed to go against Farrendel's sense of manners, and he kept glaring at the stickiness on his fingers as if it had personally offended him.

After an hour of stories and several mugs of hot chocolate, Farrendel was blinking wearily. Not that she blamed him. It was the middle of the night, and he hadn't downed several mugs of coffee the way her brothers had.

Essie took his mug and gave him a nudge toward the two bedrolls set up behind them. "Get some sleep."

With a bleary nod, he lurched from the bench, sank onto the bedroll, took off his boots, and curled between the layers of blankets and tarpaulin until only the top of his head and the ends of his hair were visible.

Essie yawned and stared into the fire. She probably should turn in as well, but the fire cast warmth onto her face and the palms she held out. The blanket kept the rest of her cozy, so warm and content she wasn't ready to move.

Averett leaned his elbows on his knees, also staring into the fire. "I'm glad things have worked out so well between you and Farrendel. I feared I'd bargained away your chance at happiness."

"Avie..." Essie rolled her eyes. How many times did she have to tell him everything had turned out fine?

"Just as long as you don't get too mushy about it." Julien scowled.

"It does make me wonder." The serious tone to Edmund's voice had Essie sitting straighter. Edmund met her gaze. "He's an elf. He loves you, that much is plain to see. But what will happen when you age so much faster than he does? You're going to be forty before he even reaches the elf equivalent of twenty-five."

Essie tensed, looking down at her hands rather than holding Edmund's gaze. She could feel Averett and Julien both staring at her, waiting for her answer.

This was an answer she had been dreading. Back in Estyra, it had been easy to accept what the heart bond with Farrendel might mean for her lifespan.

But here, sitting around the campfire with her brothers, a part of her ached. Would this closeness she had with her brothers fade if they aged faster than she did? Would her relationship with them start to look more like what Farrendel had with his much older siblings? A sibling relationship that almost verged on something parental?

"That probably isn't what's going to happen." Essie struggled to find the words. A weariness pressed down on her, and she didn't want to take the time to tell the whole story of Daesyn and Inara, the elf-human couple who had shared a heart bond long ago. "Elves have this magic heart bond that can sometimes occur. In an elf-human couple, heart bonds can have the effect that the human lives longer, as much as four hundred or five hundred years. And, well, Farrendel and I have already managed to form one. I don't know if it will give me a long life or not, but there's a good chance it will."

Silence stretched, broken only by the crackling, popping of the fire. When Essie gathered the courage to raise her head, her brothers were studying her.

Edmund's face quirked with a smile, even if it didn't reach his eyes. "Are you going to get pointed ears or something?"

"No, I don't think so." Essie scratched at her ear. Still rounded. "The thing is, if I end up with an extra-long life, Farrendel's life will be shortened. Apparently, that's how it works. He willingly gives his years to me or something like that."

"You think he will give up several hundred years for you?" Averett glanced into the darkness beyond Essie, though he wouldn't be able to see Farrendel from where he was sitting.

She didn't even have to think about her answer. "Yes."

FOURTEEN

"That shouldn't be possible."

"It definitely isn't normal."

Reluctantly, Essie poked her head out from beneath the tarpaulin and blankets. It had been rather warm and cozy, curled up in a bedroll only inches away from Farrendel. Far closer than the space they usually kept between them.

But now she was alone, though the blankets remained warm. Dew coated the tarpaulin, the morning air cool against her face and in her lungs. The ground ached against her shoulder and hip where she'd lain on the ground all night.

"What do you think the elf king will do to us if his brother breaks his neck on our palace grounds?"

This comment was Julien's and drew Essie's gaze. Averett knelt by the fire pit, stoking the coals and adding logs, both kettles on the bench next to him to be re-heated. Behind him, Essie could just make out Edmund and

Julien still sprawled on their bedrolls on the other side of the benches and fire pit.

She must have moved enough to draw Averett's notice because he glanced in her direction and pointed upward. "Is this normal? Or is he just showing off?"

She tilted back her head until she spotted Farrendel high above in the trees, running along branches, flipping in the air, and spinning in kicks. At home in Estyra, he practiced much higher in the air, but somehow this looked more dangerous with the ground within sight.

Though, Essie was almost disappointed to note, he wore his shirt this morning. Too shy and proper around her brothers.

"If he was showing off, he'd have his shirt off." Essie sat up, propped her elbows on her knees, and stared upward at Farrendel. He flipped in the air and landed gracefully on a branch that couldn't have been more than two inches wide. "He practices like this every morning."

Perhaps some of her breathlessness came through in her voice because Edmund snorted. "If you start drooling, I'm going to throw up."

Such dramatics. Seriously. She wasn't being that obnoxiously swoony over Farrendel. Locating the nearest stick, Essie chucked it at Edmund. Of course, with her throwing skills, the stick only made it as far as the fire where it bounced off a log and came to rest on one of the surrounding rocks.

She took a few minutes to brush her hair and braid it. When she was presentable, she crawled from her nice, warm bedroll and helped with breakfast. She fried the bacon in a pan while Julien added the eggs to his eggs-and-vegetable skillet. Averett prepared the coffee and hot chocolate while Edmund picked up their campsite.

Julien patted Essie's shoulder. "There's this pair of doctors—a husband and wife team—I've heard some of the men in the army talk about. They specialize in dealing with trauma, or so I've heard."

There were doctors who specialized in that kind of thing? Essie glanced up to where Farrendel flipped back and forth between the tree branches. Could they help Farrendel? Though, surely if there was anything that could be done, the elves, with their skill in healing, would have done it already.

Still, it would be something to look into. "I don't think we'll have the time on this visit, but I'd be interested if you got their names."

"I'll look into them. Talk to those they've claimed they've helped to make sure they're on the up and up." Julien stirred the eggs one last time, then took the pan from the fire.

"Thanks." Essie couldn't put enough feeling into that word to convey how much Julien's care for both her and Farrendel met.

Nodding and straightening, Julien stuck his fingers into his mouth and gave a shrill whistle.

Essie rolled her eyes. "He's not a pet to be called with a whistle."

Julien shrugged. "It's the same whistle I use for the army recruits I'm training. Besides, it worked."

Above them, Farrendel halted what he was doing. Essie waved. "Breakfast is ready."

He jumped easily from branch to lower branch until he was about twenty feet in the air where he ran out of branches. Hopping from the branch, he flipped in the air and landed on the ground in a crouch, straightening fluidly as if the jump hadn't been anything impressive.

Julien nudged Essie. "Are you sure he isn't part cat?

She elbowed Julien back. Her brothers had gone straight from suspicion to welcoming him into the family with little brother teasing. "Be nice. I want him to like coming to visit the family."

Julien just smirked as Farrendel approached the campfire. His shirt and face only held a few traces of sweat so he must not have worked out as long as normal. Between his exhaustion making him sleep later and the outdoor air making her get up earlier, it had shortened his time.

She put an arm around his waist and kissed his cheek, speaking quietly. "Did you sleep well?"

"Yes." After a moment's hesitation, Farrendel gave her the tiniest peck on her temple, the tips of his ears turning pink, as if that much pushing of the no-displays-of-affection-in-front-of-people rule was already too embarrassing for him.

"Come on, lovebirds. Have some bacon." Averett pointed at the plates he had set in a row on one of the benches, the pieces of bacon carefully distributed so that everyone got an equal number.

After claiming plates, Essie and Farrendel took seats on their bench, and everyone dished out their own portions of the eggs and vegetables sprinkled with cheese.

Essie picked up her bacon with her fingers while Farrendel cut his bacon into bite-sized pieces and ate it with his fork.

When he caught her looking, he shifted and held up his hand. "My fingers are not greasy. It is more sanitary."

"Probably. But less fun." Edmund licked the grease from his fingers.

Farrendel's nose wrinkled, and he went back to eating his bacon with his fork.

"After breakfast, how would you like to join us at the training yard for a while? We usually practice with heavy cavalry swords, but you can use whatever you prefer." Averett's tone was almost too casual. After Farrendel's display of his athleticism that morning, her brothers had to be wondering what he could do. Their king, tactician, and spy mindsets would want to take Farrendel's measure.

Earlier, she'd worried about pitting Farrendel and her brothers on the training yard. But that was before everyone had seemingly bonded so well. Now, a little sword practice would bond them further.

Farrendel glanced at her and spoke in elvish. "Do you think it is a good idea?"

Essie smirked at him, answering in Escarlish so that all her brothers would understand. "I think it's a great idea."

ESSIE HELD the pair of practice swords Farrendel had chosen while he tightened a leather bracer on his forearm. When he struggled to tie the ends one-handed, she leaned the swords against the fence that surrounded the dusty, gravel covered training yard. "Here, let me."

Farrendel remained still while she tied the laces, then moved on to his right arm to tighten that bracer and tie it off for him.

A few feet away, her brothers were drawing straws to see who would fight Farrendel first. On the far side the training field, a few soldiers marched in formation for drill. Their commander might as well call a halt now. His carefully disciplined troops were about to be thoroughly distracted.

Farrendel picked up the iron practice swords, moving them up and down as if testing their weight and balance. They were shaped like the swords the army carried for hand-to-hand combat, slightly longer than the swords Farrendel normally used, but single-bladed instead of double. The practice swords had their edges rounded instead of sharpened. They could still break bone if swung hard enough, but they wouldn't cut or stab.

Farrendel glanced at the huddle of her brothers, where Julien triumphantly held up the short stick, before turning back to her. "How much should I hold back? Should I let him win?"

It was adorable—if a little heartbreakingly sad—how much Farrendel wanted her brothers to like him.

Essie patted his chest. "Don't you dare let him win. They'll respect you far more if you beat them fair and square than let them take a cheap victory."

"You do not mind if I beat them?" Farrendel tested the swords' weights again, something in his stance sliding into the cold grace of a prowling cat.

"I'm counting on it." Essie kissed his cheek. "Just don't humiliate them too badly, all right?"

Farrendel's answering smile held a dangerous glint. He lightly bounded up and over the fence surrounding the training yard and faced her brothers. "To make this a fair fight, I will face all three of you."

Julien raised his eyebrows. "You have a very poor opinion of our skills."

"If he wants to fight all three of us, I say let him." Edmund swung his practice sword through an arc.

Averett glanced at Essie and met her gaze. She nodded, then smirked. How long was it going to take Farrendel to disarm all three of them? Two minutes? One?

"Essie's smirking. We probably should be worried." Averett turned back to the others. "All right then, the rules."

He went over the rules, which were mostly that an opponent was defeated once he was disarmed and a few other miscellaneous rules about what to shout to surrender and stuff like that. One of the guards was called over to make sure everything was done by the book.

Averett, Julien, and Edmund spread out, practice swords in one hand. Farrendel waited, a sword in each hand, crouched but not tense.

Essie leaned against the fence. Her brothers weren't going to know what hit them.

The guard blew the whistle. Farrendel leapt forward, straight at Averett. Averett stumbled backwards, raising his sword. Farrendel parried Averett's sword, kicked up from the ground, and used Averett's chest as a springboard into the air.

Averett tumbled backwards, his sword flicked from his hand by one of Farrendel's swords.

Flipping in the air, Farrendel ripped Edmund's sword from his grasp with his twin swords and kicked Edmund solidly in the chest. The momentum sent Edmund toppling toward the ground while Farrendel landed in a crouch.

Julien backed away, putting distance between him and Farrendel. Of Essie's three brothers, he was the best with the cavalry sword. Thanks to modern weaponry, sword-fighting was quickly going out of style for everything but practice fights and dueling in the various human kingdoms. The hand-to-hand fighting taught by the army now focused more on the use of the bayonet, knives, and fists as a last resort.

That put Julien at a disadvantage when fighting Farrendel, who had trained not only more extensively with swords but also in a style humans couldn't match.

Farrendel stalked after Julien, not giving him space or time. Farrendel struck, first with one sword, then with the other. Julien parried the first few strikes, but with his one sword to Farrendel's two, he couldn't block indefinitely.

On his next strike, Farrendel followed Julien's parry and brought his other sword up, trapping Julien's sword. With a spinning kick, Farrendel swept Julien's legs out from under him while ripping his sword from his hands.

Julien landed on his back in the dirt.

Thirty seconds. Even shorter than Essie had guessed.

For a moment, Farrendel stood tense and battle ready. Then, he slowly straightened, lowering his swords to his sides, his gaze wary, as if he expected Essie's brothers to be mad at him for defeating them so quickly.

Surely they wouldn't be, would they? Essie tensed as well. All three of her brothers still sat or lay where they had fallen, having been defeated too fast for any of them to climb to their feet yet.

Then Edmund started to laugh. Within moments, Julien had joined him, followed by Averett sitting upright and chuckling in a more dignified manner.

Edmund rolled to his feet, still laughing. "That was spectacular."

"Told you Essie's smirk should have warned us." Averett held out his hand, probably to have Edmund pull him to his feet.

Julien stuck out his hand to Farrendel. Farrendel

stared, unmoving. Julien grinned and waggled his fingers. "You're supposed to take my hand and pull me to my feet."

"Like this." Edmund yanked Averett upright so fast he stumbled.

Averett shoved Edmund. "More gently than that."

Moving warily, Farrendel transferred both swords to one hand, gripped Julien's offered hand, and awkwardly helped Julien upright. As soon as Julien let go, Farrendel swiped his hand on his trousers.

Edmund slung an arm over Farrendel's shoulders as best he could since he stood several inches shorter. He grinned in Essie's direction. "You're right, Essie. He's a keeper."

"Told you." Essie's grin widened at the faint tinge of pink on the tips of Farrendel's ears. He wasn't used to being the center of attention quite like this.

Julien draped an arm across Farrendel's shoulders from the other side. "What do you say? Think we should make it a more interesting fight this time?"

Farrendel had his elbows pulled tight to his sides, as if trying to put as much space between them as he could while being in the center of a brother-hug sandwich. "Yes?"

Averett rested an elbow on Edmund's shoulder. "What did you have in mind?"

Julien swiveled all four of them to face the crowd of soldiers that had gathered at the far end of the training field. He raised his free arm, still gripping his training sword. "All right, boys! What do you think? Who would like to challenge the four royal brothers of Escarland? The more the merrier!"

Some of the soldiers roared and hopped the fence to

enter the training field. Others glanced at each other, as if unsure, while a few glared at Farrendel as if they wanted to fight him, but not in practice.

Essie straightened. What did Julien think he was doing? Yes, it had been fun to see Farrendel take out her brothers so quickly, but to pit him against a horde of Escarland soldiers? That was too much like a real fight, wasn't it? "Avie?"

Averett said something to Julien, then herded Edmund and Farrendel toward Essie. Julien marched toward the other side of the training yard, still shouting and waving to get more soldiers to join the group forming in the yard.

When Averett, Edmund, and Farrendel were close enough, Essie gestured from them to Julien. "Do you really think this is a good idea? There are probably a few soldiers there who would love the chance to get revenge on an elf."

"All the better to let them attempt it with practice swords than with real ones." Edmund jabbed his thumb at Farrendel. "Besides, do you really think they'll have a chance at hurting him?"

"Well, no..." Essie tried to meet Farrendel's gaze, but he had gone hard, his gaze focused over his shoulder on the soldiers massing at the far end of the training yard.

"This isn't exactly what I had in mind, but I think this could be your opportunity to remind everyone why we made this alliance with the elves." Averett's lowered tone brought Farrendel's gaze around. "Word of what happens here will spread. Half the city will hear about it before the end of the day, mark my words. If you want to remind everyone why Escarland might want to consider making Tarenhiel an ally beyond the simple ceasefire we currently have, then this would be it."

Across the training field, word must have been spreading. Soldiers were piling out of the barracks, and even from here, Essie could spot the shoulder bars of a few officers keeping order. Not all the soldiers were volunteering to fight. Most were simply curious and eager to watch.

But a good fifty soldiers now gathered in the ring, including a few officers, who would keep them organized and provide more strategy than a leaderless horde of men would have.

Could Farrendel take on that many? Without guns shooting at him, he could kill that many with his magic far too easily. But this wasn't a fight to the death.

Farrendel turned to Essie, lowering his tone and speaking in elvish. "Should I use my magic?"

"Can you use only a little bit of your magic? Like you did with the nephews?" Essie also spoke in elvish. Though, the only person they were really excluding from this conversation was Averett. Edmund could understand them just fine, annoying brother that he was.

Farrendel nodded. "Yes."

"Then do it." Edmund clapped Farrendel on the shoulder, speaking in elvish as well. "Prove that Essie made the right choice in marrying you."

That straightened Farrendel's shoulders and added a hardness to his expression.

As he looked about ready to march across the field and take on the whole pack of soldiers by himself, Essie leaned forward and kissed Farrendel's chin. "A kiss for luck."

The corner of his mouth quirked for a moment before he spun on his heels and marched across the training yard, hefting his pair of training swords.

With a grin, Edmund followed on Farrendel's heels.

Averett crossed his arms. "What did Edmund say to him?"

"More or less told him to prove to everyone that he's worthy of me." Essie leaned against the fence, trying to relax. This would be fine. Her brothers wouldn't let anything happen to Farrendel.

"That explains it." Averett turned toward the others. "Looks like I'd better get over there before they start without me."

As he strolled to the center of the training field, Paige leaned against the fence next to Essie. "What's going on? The servants were chatting that something was going on at the training field."

That didn't take long. Essie waved at the gathered soldiers. "Avie, Julien, Edmund, and Farrendel are practice-fighting that crowd of soldiers."

"All of them? At once?" Paige raised her eyebrows.

"Yes." Essie gripped the top rail of the fence.

In the center of the training field, her brothers and Farrendel gathered in a circle, probably planning their strategy. The soldiers were also gathered in a larger circle, the four lieutenants who had volunteered for the practice fight organizing them into groups.

A whistle blew. The signal for the pack of around fifty soldiers to face off against her three brothers and Farrendel. The soldiers formed four squads, each led by a lieutenant.

Averett and Julien stood in the center with Farrendel and Edmund slightly behind and to either side. What was their plan? Essie would've expected Farrendel to be in front, the way he had been when fighting the trolls.

The whistle sounded again. Two of the four squads of soldiers rushed forward, coming at her brothers from either side.

When they were only a few yards away, a crackle filled the air a moment before a wall of blue lightning flared between the soldiers and her brothers with only a narrow gap left in the center for only a few soldiers to come at them at a time.

Farrendel had told her he'd started like this, simply providing a shield. Interesting first move on her brothers' part.

"That's Farrendel's magic?" Paige had gone still, staring.

"It's impressive, isn't it?" Essie had been using that word too often, but she couldn't think of what else to call his magic. Scary, perhaps, but she didn't want to give the wrong impression.

His magic was scary. It might be awe-inspiring now, but she had seen how easily it could turn deadly. Even though she trusted Farrendel to stay in control of his magic, it was still uncomfortable standing there, watching his magic get all too close to her brothers and her people's soldiers.

The groups of soldiers staggered back a step, staring ahead and upward at Farrendel's shield of blue lightning.

Averett and Julien pressed forward, taking on two of the soldiers at a time. For several minutes, they fought, disarming the soldiers one at a time with Edmund providing aid when needed.

At this rate, the soldiers would eventually overwhelm Averett and Julien when they tired. Not to mention, this fight would last far longer than Essie had been expecting.

Then Julien shouted something Essie couldn't make out above the clash of weapons and the crackle of Farrendel's magic. Edmund crouched. Farrendel leapt, using Edmund's back as a springboard. Edmund stood in time with Farrendel's leap, giving him an extra boost into the air.

Farrendel somersaulted in the air above Averett's and Julien's heads. As he straightened, a bolt of his magic lashed out, touching the swords of the nearest soldiers.

The soldiers jumped and dropped their swords. Farrendel landed lightly on his feet in the cleared space in front of Averett and Julien, the two training swords ready. After only a moment's pause, Farrendel stepped into the pack, the blue lightning bolts of his magic trailing down each of his blades.

After an initial pause, the lieutenants urged their squads of soldiers to move forward. They rushed Farrendel, probably trying to overwhelm him with numbers.

Farrendel met them with whirling swords and crackling magic. His hair whipped around him, and yet, when the soldiers tried to grab the strands, they never seemed to be able to touch it. It was as if Farrendel sensed the movement or the stirring of the air through his hair and spun in time.

Perhaps elven hair really was magic. If it started glowing when he sang, she wouldn't be surprised at this point. Not that she could picture Farrendel singing.

Essie's brothers pressed close behind Farrendel, far closer than the elves had during that ambush. They spread out, taking on any of the soldiers that made it past Farrendel, though Essie suspected Farrendel was letting a few get past him so that her brothers felt useful.

Farrendel, Averett, Julien, and Edmund fought their way to the far side of the training field. Only about fifteen of the soldiers facing them were left still holding weapons.

Averett waved toward them. "Well?"

Farrendel's mouth quirked. He flicked his hand. Bolts of magic flared, leaping from training sword to training sword, knocking them from the soldiers' grips. Magic exploded outward. Dust flew. Even standing yards away, Essie couldn't breathe for a moment.

Then Farrendel's magic winked out. The dust slowly drifted back to the ground, revealing all the soldiers knocked to the ground.

Were they all right? Essie dug her fingers into the wooden railing.

One of the soldiers sat up with a groan, quickly followed by the others.

Essie's breath whooshed out. They were bruised but fine.

Edmund pumped his fist in the air and whooped. Julien slapped Farrendel's back so hard Farrendel stumbled forward.

Averett patted Farrendel's shoulder and faced the watching crowd of soldiers. "That was quite the display of elven power. I, for one, am glad he's on our side, thanks to my sister's marriage."

The soldiers laughed. Just like that, the defeated soldiers were lining up to shake hands with Farrendel. For his part, Farrendel tolerated all the hand shaking, putting on his hard, impassive warrior face for it. Maybe not the friendliest expression, but at least he didn't show how freaked out he was.

Some of the soldiers who had watched the first time called for another round, but Averett bowed out with all the diplomacy of the king he was. He steered Farrendel toward where Essie stood along the fence, Julien and Edmund trailing behind as they extricated themselves from all the backslapping.

When Farrendel was close enough, Essie leaned forward and took one of his hands. "You did great."

His hard expression cracked, a hint of a smile blooming.

"What do you think, Avie?" Edmund strolled up, swinging his practice sword. "Can you clear your schedule? I think it's time we hung out as brothers with our new brother-in-law."

"I'll see to it. Enjoy your brother time." Paige kissed Averett's cheek before she nudged Essie. "It's been too long since we've had girl talk."

Essie had missed her long chats with her sister-in-law. But she glanced at Farrendel. She didn't want him to think she was just abandoning him to the mercies of her brothers.

Julien reached over the fence and ruffled her hair like he used to do when she was little. "We'll take care of him."

Farrendel was a grown elf. Essie didn't need to hover the entire time they were here. He needed to stand on his own two feet with her family just as she had with his, and that would only happen if she wasn't there watching over his shoulder.

Still, she squeezed his hand and switched to elvish. "Are you all right with this?"

Farrendel glanced at her three brothers. He straightened his shoulders, much as he had when facing the fifty Escarlish soldiers minutes ago. "I will be fine."

"All right." Essie kissed his cheek.

This would be fine. Her brothers seemed to like Farrendel. They just wanted to get to know him better. Hopefully Farrendel would relax enough to let them.

CHAPTER
FIFTEEN

F arrendel stood to the side as Essie's brothers let the Escarlish soldiers know that the practice fights with the elf were over for the day. It was mildly amusing to see how disappointed the soldiers were. As if getting thrown about by his magic had been entertaining.

Averett and Julien strode up to him, their shirts soaked with sweat. Farrendel had not prolonged the fight long enough to perspire, but the morning sun already beat down on the courtyard. Without the shade of the trees and being farther south, Escarland's late summer was far warmer than Tarenhiel.

Edmund jogged to join them. He grinned. "The pond?"

Averett flapped his shirt away from his skin. "Good plan. Though..." He turned to Farrendel. "You can swim, right?"

"Yes." Of course he could swim. It was a basic skill

taught to every young one at an early age. Did humans not think it a necessary life skill?

He found himself herded down a path into the forested part of the grounds once again. It was futile to try to resist Essie's pack of brothers.

The trees opened up to a pond with a dock jutting into it. The pond appeared to be fed by a creek that flowed out the other side to connect to the Fyne River on the other side of the tall wall. This spot was sheltered between the river and the forest, reminding him somewhat of Lethorel, the retreat for elven royalty where he had spent much of his growing up years.

Edmund gave a whoop and broke into a run, peeling off his shirt as he went. He hopped on each foot as he pulled off his boots at the edge of the pond. Julien was only steps behind him, dropping his boots next to Edmund's.

With another undignified shout, Edmund raced the length of the dock and jumped from the end, tucking up his knees in the move Essie had called a *cannonball*. A massive splash sent water into the air and waves across the pond.

When he popped to the surface, he gestured. "Come on, Julien! Can you do better than that?"

"Easily!" Julien sprinted the length of the dock and launched himself into the air. His cannonball came down with a tremendous splash that sent a wave over the end of the dock.

Averett dumped his boots and shirt on the pile. With a whoop, he jumped in as well.

Farrendel grimaced, slowly pulling off his boots. He had not mentally prepared for this. Would Essie's brothers question him if he jumped in with his shirt on? It

169

seemed Essie had been correct that swimming only half-dressed was customary for human males.

"Come on." Julien was the one gesturing now. All three of Essie's brothers had popped to the surface, treading water in the center of the pond.

Edmund grinned. "If you don't jump in, we'll go over there and throw you in."

Somehow, Farrendel did not think they were bluffing.

He added his boots to the pile, along with his belt. Then, as quickly as he could, before he could think himself out of it, he yanked off his tunic and shirt. As he did not know how deep the pond was, he would need to emulate the human version of entering the water and attempt a cannonball of his own.

He dashed to the end of the dock and jumped outward. He gripped his knees. The moment of hanging in the air as he fell seemed longer than it did for a dive.

His back smacked into the water, then the cold closed over him. Water rushed up his nose, not something he had anticipated with this unusual method for entering the water. He blew the water out as he sank deeper into the water, not wanting to come up coughing and sputtering.

Uncurling, he shoved from the bottom and pushed to the surface. He broke into the air, shaking water and hair from his face.

Essie's brothers cheered, though it turned into chuckles. Edmund laughed. "I have never seen someone do a cannonball so solemnly."

"Like it was a serious endeavor." Julien splashed Edmund.

"Be nice to our brother-in-law." Averett shoved a wave of water at both Edmund and Julien.

The water fight quickly devolved into a bunch of

dunking and thrashing. Though, they left Farrendel out of it. They might feel comfortable lightly teasing him, but they were being careful not to push him farther than he was comfortable going.

A part of him was grateful. But another part, the larger part, wanted to belong to this family. Could he be one of them in a way he had never managed with his own family?

His family had always been distant, and not just because he was illegitimate. He was much younger than the rest of his siblings. His brother had already been married by the time Farrendel had been born, with Farrendel's nephew Ryfon born only fifteen years after Farrendel was.

It was not an uncommon problem among elves to have siblings so strung apart that they never managed to be close. And yet, Farrendel had not managed to be close to his nephew and niece either.

Perhaps this was his chance to do things again and be a part of a family.

Diving beneath the water, he hugged the bottom, coming up beneath Edmund. Grabbing his ankle, Farrendel yanked him underwater before darting out of reach.

He popped to the surface a few seconds before Edmund, bracing himself for the reaction.

Edmund came up with a big grin. "Well done, little brother. I didn't realize you could be that sneaky."

Was that a smile he felt tugging on his face? Farrendel splashed a wave of water at Edmund.

Somehow, the water fight turned into him and Averett against Julien and Edmund. Until Farrendel had met

Essie, and then her family, he had forgotten how to have fun like this.

When he finally climbed from the water, he wrung the water from his hair, then reached for his shirt, intending to pull it on as quickly as possible.

Footsteps crunched on the bank and halted behind Farrendel. "Essie mentioned you had scars."

Edmund. Farrendel gripped his shirt, knuckles whitening, skin crawling. Feeling those stares. Imagining their judgment.

"Pretty impressive." Julien's voice and tone had Farrendel glancing up. Julien pointed to a scar down the length of his arm. "I got pushed from a tree."

"You fell. Not my fault." Edmund strolled into Farrendel's line of sight. He pointed at a scar that ran across his stomach. "A little argument with some border guards."

He did not say which border and whose guards. Farrendel did not dare ask, though a scar like that was done with a bladed weapon, not a gun.

Averett tapped the scar of a bullet wound to his shoulder. "Assassination attempt."

"We all have our scars." Julien shrugged. "They aren't a big deal."

They did not care? He had caught his own family talking about his scars once, saying how it was a shame he was so scarred. How they needed to make sure they kept loving him since it was doubtful anyone else would.

But Essie had. And, maybe, her family too.

Still, Farrendel breathed a sigh when he had his shirt on, more relaxed with his scars covered.

Edmund halted with his shirt halfway on, one arm in, one arm still wedged trying to get into the arm hole. "I have an idea."

"That sounds ominous." Julien tugged his shirt over his head.

Edmund's grin widened. "No, this is a great idea. I think you'll like this one."

When Edmund's gaze focused on him, Farrendel's stomach sank. Julien might like this idea, but would he?

"YOUR FARRENDEL IS A SWEETHEART." Paige smirked, strolling along the path next to Essie.

"He is." Essie resisted the urge to glance over her shoulder.

Paige giggled. "I've never seen you look so swoony."

Essie's cheeks hurt from her grinning. "Well, he is very easy to swoon over."

They shared another giggle. Then Paige's smile faded. "Are you happy? Truly?"

"Yes. I really am. I can't wait until you visit Estyra. It's the most beautiful city I've ever seen, and the elven palace is lovely. There's something so peaceful about it. It's like camping, but a much more luxury version, all the time."

As they neared the palace, Paige steered Essie down a side path in the garden. "I have a surprise to show you. Actually, it's Averett's and your mother's surprise, but I was sent to fetch you."

"What is it?" Essie asked, even though she didn't really expect Paige to answer.

Paige just grinned and led the way under a trellis arch. They exited onto a broader path that connected the main Winstead Palace with Buckmore Cottage, the place traditionally reserved for the Queen Mother, if she was still living when her son assumed the throne.

"Wait, are we going to Buckmore?" Essie hadn't stepped foot inside in three years, not since her grandmother had passed away. At that time, her mother could have moved into the cottage, but Essie had been still seventeen, and Averett hadn't wanted to break up their family. Thankfully, Paige and Mother had never needed the distance that some young queens wanted from their mothers-in-law.

"It's built of wood, not stone." Paige gestured as the first glimpses became visible between the trees.

How had Essie forgotten about that? She hurried forward, stepping from the shadowed path into the garden of Buckmore Cottage. This garden was less formal, left wild with large maple trees growing so close to the cottage their branches had to be periodically trimmed back by the castle staff.

Mother stood at the back door, directing servants in opening windows, cleaning rugs, and hauling out a mountain of outdated, ugly furniture.

"But…" Essie halted next to Mother, tucked against the wall to stay out of the way. "You're loaning it to me?"

"Actually, Avie is giving it to you. As much as the crown can gift anything, that is." Paige waved at it. "It can function as a sort of elven embassy when you aren't using it. Don't think I haven't noticed how your Farrendel isn't the only one uncomfortable at Winstead Palace. His sister Princess Jalissa also doesn't seem to be faring well either. This way, you can see to making Buckmore Cottage a place elves are comfortable visiting, something that should be necessary with this new peace and hopefully stronger alliance."

"You're both all right with this? Mother? This is supposed to be your home if you want it." Essie wasn't sure why she was arguing. The cottage was wood, except for the stone foundation. It was within easy walking distance along the path that connected it to Winstead Palace. It would be within sight, if it weren't for the screening pine trees.

The surrounding pines, oaks, and maples gave it a cozy, private feeling. Something Farrendel would love. He would have easy access to the forest each morning without worrying about guards constantly patrolling the corridors.

The front of Buckmore Cottage faced the street, so she and Farrendel could go into town if they wished. Yet it was still enclosed behind the stone wall that surrounded the entire Winstead Palace complex and grounds, along with a guarded gate, making Buckmore Cottage nearly as secure as the palace itself.

Mother shook her head. "You need this place far more than I do. Besides, Winstead Palace has been my home since I married your father. I'm not ready to be shunted off into my dotage just yet. As long as Paige doesn't mind having me around, I'll stay at the palace."

"I love having a babysitter around so that I can leave the children with you rather than a nanny." Paige smirked. "Besides, it won't be too much longer before you will be dividing your time between grandchildren in Escarland and grandchildren in Tarenhiel."

"Eventually." Essie huffed. She and Farrendel had been married for all of three months. They were still working toward being closer, much less thinking about children.

"All in good time." Mother patted Essie's arm. "Let's get this place cleaned out and organized."

It took the rest of the morning and into the afternoon to help a horde of servants haul all the clutter and extra furniture from Buckmore Cottage. It had become something of a dumping ground for unwanted, mostly ugly furniture over the years.

While the servants finished cleaning the cottage, Essie returned to the palace. She would need to pack her and Farrendel's things and decide what from her old room she would like moved to the cottage. On her way to her room, she let Jalissa know to start packing for a move to a new place. Jalissa's tight expression relaxed somewhat, the only sign she was relieved to be leaving all the stone behind.

In her old room, Essie set her travel sack on the bed and began stuffing the dresses, shirts, and tunics she'd taken with her from Tarenhiel.

The door opened and closed behind her. Moments later, Farrendel perched on the end of the bed, sitting cross-legged. "Why are you packing? Did my brother send another message?"

"No, nothing like that. It's a surprise. A good surprise." Essie placed the last dress inside her bag. "Did you have a good time with my brothers?"

"Yes." Farrendel's smile crossed his face. "I like your family."

"I'm glad." Essie leaned over and kissed his forehead. Even though she was curious, she didn't ask what her brothers and Farrendel had done all morning. He wasn't likely to tell her. It was brother code, after all. "If you want to pack your things, I can show you your surprise."

Farrendel raised his eyebrow at her, but he set to work packing.

As soon as he was packed, Essie led him from the palace, collecting Jalissa and her guard along the way.

Essie held Farrendel's hand as they strolled down the path connecting Winstead Palace with Buckmore Cottage. Farrendel didn't ask her where they were going with their bags slung over their shoulders.

The trees cleared, and Buckmore Cottage appeared before them. A turret formed one of the corners while gingerbread molding stood out white against the light blue paint. White trimmed all the windows and doors.

"Welcome to Buckmore Cottage." Essie tugged Farrendel forward. "It's the dower cottage for the Queen Mother, but Mother and Averett both agreed and gifted it to me. It will be our home while we are here, and the elven embassy when needed."

Jalissa joined them, standing on Farrendel's other side. "This will be adequate."

"It's mine, Jalissa. Averett gave me permission to renovate it however I want. And I want to make this as comfortable for visiting elves as possible." Essie waved to the cottage.

"I see. In that case..." Jalissa glided forward and rested a hand on the doorpost. A faint green light glowed around her hand, then flowed into the wood. Moments later, saplings sprang from the earth. Vines climbed the cottage. Branches and leaves even grew from some of the formerly dead wood of the doorways and window frames.

The green glow ended, and Jalissa pulled her hand from the wood.

Essie forced her smile to stay in place. "It's beautiful, Jalissa."

It wasn't. The cottage now looked like the forest was trying to eat it, but perhaps with time the elven magic would transform the cottage into a more cohesive union of Escarlish and Tarenhieli architecture.

"It will do for now." Jalissa eyed her handiwork, her mouth pressed in a line as if she wasn't exactly happy with the result either.

"Come on. Let me show you the inside. I've claimed the turret room for Farrendel and myself, but you can have any of the other rooms." Essie stepped around Jalissa and reached for the door, dragging Farrendel by the hand behind her. Farrendel gave his sister something of an elven shrug as he was hauled past.

Essie gave Farrendel and Jalissa a tour of the cottage, starting with the main floor, including the kitchen.

"We won't have any servants staying here. A few of the maids will drop by during the day to clean, but that will be it. So feel free to wander however you like." Essie waved at the cozy kitchen with a rustic table with a thick, butcher block top dominating the center of the room. "I had the ice box and pantry stocked, so there will be breakfast here whenever you want it."

Jalissa nodded as if the announcement was a grave matter, but Farrendel gave Essie his small smile.

The tour continued on the second floor. While Jalissa left to wander through the rooms to pick her favorite, Essie pulled Farrendel to the last door at the end of the corridor. It opened onto the round turret room facing the forested grounds.

Five windows were set into each of the turret's walls while the sixth wall held the door. Gauzy white curtains were pulled back against the blue and white patterned wallpaper. Most of the furniture had been removed, leaving only an oak armoire for their clothes, a settee beneath one of the windows, a small bookshelf, an ivory-painted dressing table, and the bed pushed along one of the walls below a window. All the rugs had been removed except for a dark blue one patterned with white flowers next to the bed.

Essie crossed the room and pointed toward one of the windows. One of the thick branches from the nearby oak tree passed within three feet of the windowsill. "I think you can jump from here to the tree, if you don't want to go all the way downstairs to get outside."

Farrendel halted next to her, unlatched the window, and pushed the leaded panes open, letting in the breeze, laden with scents of city mixed with woodsy smells. He leaned out the window, his hair falling over his shoulders.

But he wasn't saying anything. Was that a good sign or a bad? Essie shifted from foot to foot. "Well, what do you think? Is this better? Do you like it?"

Farrendel pulled back into the room and faced her. He lightly touched her cheek, brow wrinkling. "I do not want to make you lose your home yet again."

It was so sweet of him to worry. He needed to stay here for his sanity. He didn't have a choice. He could have simply accepted the cottage and new room without thinking about her.

She wrapped her arms around her waist. "I'm excited. I have Buckmore Cottage to redecorate and make it mine in a way I couldn't do even with my rooms in Winstead Palace. I didn't realize how used to having my own place I'd become in Estyra. I'm glad to have a bit of space. Besides, my family is a short walk away."

Compared to the long walk across the tree branches that led to Farrendel's out-of-the-way rooms in the elven palace, the nice, flat path to Winstead Palace was a dream come true.

Essie leaned into Farrendel's hand, hugging him closer. "Truly. I'm happy with this. Neither of us could relax at Winstead Palace, and I think this will be good for us."

"Then, yes. This is better." Farrendel closed the distance between them. His kiss was soft, gentle.

Essie kissed him back, tingles in her stomach, lightness in her head.

Yes, Buckmore Cottage was exactly what they needed.

CHAPTER
SIXTEEN

The birds were singing. The sunlight splashed across the bed, warm and cozy. Essie stretched, truly refreshed and relaxed for the first time in a week. A nightmare-free night for both her and Farrendel. She wouldn't take it for granted again.

As expected, Farrendel's side of the bed was empty. She propped herself onto her elbows and peered out the nearest window. About a hundred feet away, barely visible in the foliage, Farrendel's silver-blond hair flashed in the morning sunlight as he back flipped from one branch to another.

The perfect morning. As nice as it would be to linger, she needed to be ready when Farrendel returned. After rolling out of bed, she picked out clothing from the armoire. Elven tunic and trousers with a human-style skirt on top. Her people probably weren't ready for a woman in trousers strolling through their capital city just yet. It would be enough of a shock to see elves.

As she sat at the dressing table in front of the mirror,

Farrendel swung through the window, landing lightly on his feet. With barely a pause, he crossed the room and kissed her temple.

"You seem happy this morning." Essie tried to smile up at him while her hands were filled with her partially braided hair. This was the Farrendel she'd begun to see at the elven retreat of Lethorel. Not to mention, it must be a good sign of his relaxation that he wasn't wearing his shirt. He'd felt secure enough here that he hadn't covered his scars.

"Yes." Farrendel sat cross-legged on the floor next to her. "What are we doing today?"

Essie hurried to finish her braid. It was hard to appreciate Farrendel's muscles while watching what she was doing to her hair. "I was thinking it would be a good day to visit the market in Aldon. If we drop in unannounced, we shouldn't have problems with protestors. I have several places I'd like to take you. And after the market, we can exit the far side of the city and take the horses for a run. I arranged with the palace maintenance staff to install shower spigots in Buckmore Cottage while we're gone, and I figured you wouldn't want to be here for the bustling. I think they understood what I was asking them to do. We'll see when we get back, I guess."

Farrendel was giving her his *look*. The far-too-blank expression that said he was internally laughing at her while she rambled on.

Essie would've shaken her head, but she was gripping the end of her braid. She picked up a hair ribbon to tie it off, but it would be easier if she had both hands free. She held out the end of her braid to Farrendel. "Can you hold this?"

His expression didn't so much as flicker as he pinched

her braid just below her fingers. With Farrendel holding her braid, she tied the green ribbon tightly.

"Thanks for your help." She smiled, her head still cocked as Farrendel gripped her braid.

He gave her hair a slight tug, his mouth tipping into something almost like a smirk.

"Don't you start! You spent too long with my brothers yesterday." Essie leaned closer, intending to tug his hair in return. But the move put her face only inches from Farrendel's. Her breath caught with his nearness. Even if he was sweaty after his morning routine. Sweaty, and still shirtless.

He closed the distance, his kiss starting gentle before deepening. His hand traced across her cheek into her hair. Her hands found their way into his long, silky hair, her thumb skimming the top of his pointed ear.

She should've thought to move to Buckmore Cottage before. No brothers to interrupt. No servants to barge in. Only Jalissa somewhere down the hall, and she had far too much sense to come charging in.

When he pulled back, she leaned her forehead against his and said the first thing that came to mind. "You're all sweaty and gross."

"Sorry." Farrendel's smile didn't look all that sorry. He snatched one more kiss before he stood.

"The water closet is down the hall." Essie turned back to the mirror and grimaced. "You messed up my braid."

Farrendel gave her that almost smirk again as he grabbed clothes and strolled from their room.

Essie tucked her hair back into place as best she could without redoing the braid. She didn't want to undo the ribbon Farrendel had helped her tie.

Once both she and Farrendel were presentable, she

organized their trip to the market. Jalissa accepted her invitation to go along. Avie couldn't come. He couldn't manage two days off in a row. Nor could Julien. But Edmund decided to tag along. Probably to spend time with Jalissa more than Essie, but at least that would leave Essie free to focus on Farrendel.

Of course, an escort of guards had to come as well. By the time they were done, they had a party of nearly twenty headed into Aldon. A far cry from the relaxed stroll just she and Farrendel had taken through Estyra.

Compared to the elven capitol city, Aldon was a massive, sprawling thing bustling with nearly as many people as the entire population of Tarenhiel. Aldon wasn't the type of city that royalty could just stroll through without some preparation.

By the time they rode through the gate in front of Buckmore Cottage, Farrendel was getting his restless, slightly grumpy look that meant he needed breakfast soon.

The guards obligingly cleared the way to the market. As they rode through the streets, Farrendel and Jalissa glanced around, crowding their horses close to Essie and Edmund.

As they waited for a wagon to rumble by, Jalissa leaned closer to Farrendel and whispered in elvish, "The humans breed like rabbits."

Edmund snorted, and his voice lowered as he also spoke in elvish. "I don't think we're as bad as all that."

Jalissa's nose wrinkled in a delicate line as she gazed around them with raised eyebrows. Except for the small bubble of space provided by their cordon of guards, the streets were choked with people on foot, on horseback, and riding in carriages. Gawkers stopping to stare at the elves further snared the traffic. Jalissa gave a sniff. "No, you are worse than rabbits."

Edmund smirked. The wagon cleared from their path, and they nudged their horses forward once again, ending the conversation.

Farrendel's gaze flicked around at their surroundings, his face blank, his shoulders stiff.

Essie reached out and touched his arm. "Relax. The guards will keep us safe. Besides, most people are friendly."

"Are you certain?" Farrendel edged his horse closer to Essie on the mare he had given her in Tarenhiel.

"Yes. You'll see." Essie patted his arm again. She had to remind herself how foreign this was to him. She'd grown up in this city. She was used to the bustle, the smells, and the noise in a way he wasn't.

A few of the people hustling along the boardwalks stopped and waved. Essie waved back, doing her best to keep her waves slow and regal instead of wildly exuberant as was her tendency. People called her name, prompting more waving. Even some cheering.

Essie leaned closer to Farrendel. "Do your best to smile. Maybe even wave. Try to be a friendly elf. Not an angry elf."

Farrendel's hard expression cracked with a twitch of his mouth that might have been a smile. Or a grimace. Essie couldn't tell. He gave a flick of his hand in something like a wave at a few people.

"That's it." Essie rested her hand on his arm again.

When he glanced at her, his expression—definitely a smile this time—softened. He looked like he wanted to kiss her, something she wasn't sure they could manage while riding.

In the distance, she heard her name called again. More than a few cheers now. She hadn't meant for her and Farrendel's look to be anything but a mushy look between the two of them, but at least the witnesses in the crowd around them could see they loved each other. It would help with the tide of popular opinion.

Their guards led them down another broad street. Ahead, a huge building of brick and glass stretched for an entire city block. A massive wooden sign proclaiming *Aldon Market* hung over the double doors.

"I figured we would wander the market. We could go from street to street, but that would take all day. Most of the shops in the city have a small booth here with their more specialty items. It's a good way to browse the whole selection, then track down any shops that catch your interest." Essie halted Ashenifela in front of the market. "It's a fun place to wander."

Edmund swung down from his horse, then turned to Jalissa. "If it would be acceptable to you, Princess Jalissa, I would be happy to escort you through the market."

Jalissa stared down her nose at Edmund for a few seconds, just long enough for it to get uncomfortable, before she gave a sharp nod. "Very well. I suspect my brother and Elspetha will wish to have time to themselves."

Essie grinned. Jalissa had them pegged. She slid from Ashenifela and grabbed Farrendel's hand the moment he was on solid ground. "The guards will take care of our horses. Come on. I have so much I want to show you."

She tugged Farrendel toward the entrance. All right, it was more like dragged. But this was one of her favorite places in Aldon. The market was always changing with new items and new booths. A whole balcony area was dedicated to booths where artists could display and sell their work.

As they stepped through the doors, the echoing noise of the enclosed market slammed into her almost like a familiar hug. The smells of spices and cooking food and fancy soap and floral candles filled the air. Essie drank in a deep breath.

Only when she tried to take a step forward and got yanked back by her grip on Farrendel's hand did she notice his hesitation. She glanced over her shoulder.

He'd backed up, as if considering bolting through the doors.

"Are you all right?" Essie backtracked and lowered her voice. "Is it the brick?"

"Yes. No." Farrendel shook his head, his hair gliding across his shoulders in silver-blond strands. "There are a lot of people in an enclosed space."

Essie squeezed his hand. "Do you want to keep going or do you need to leave?"

Farrendel drew in a deep breath, straightening his shoulders. "I will be fine."

"Don't be afraid to tell me if you need to leave, all right?" Essie kissed his cheek, then she set out once again, at a slower pace this time.

Farrendel fell into step with her, even if he remained stiff and tense. As they weaved into the crowded aisle, he pressed closer to her. Essie couldn't tell if it was because he wanted to protect her or wanted her to protect him from all the humans.

"Let's get food first. What sounds good? There are egg wraps or egg sandwiches or there's a small café in the corner where we can sit down and eat. Do you have a preference?"

"Food." Farrendel quirked a smile.

"Got it. Let's sample a bunch of stuff." Essie led him to the booth with the egg and sausage sandwiches and ordered two of the smallest sandwiches. The woman behind the counter bobbed a curtsy to Essie and sneaked glances at Farrendel as she took Essie's payment.

Farrendel wrapped his sandwich in a napkin so that he could eat it without touching the food with his fingers. He wolfed the sandwich down in just a few bites.

Essie stopped at a booth with egg and spinach wraps, then a booth with stir fried vegetables and potatoes topped with cheese, eaten out of a bowl with a fork, much to Farrendel's appreciation.

Essie dumped their bowls and forks in the tub the booth had set out for the dishes. "Come on. Now we need to get dessert. My favorite bakery always has a booth in the market."

Farrendel followed her without protest as she threaded her way between the people, who usually stepped out of her way with slight curtsies and sideways glances at Farrendel.

Essie tried to see this market as Farrendel saw it. Brick walls surrounded them with glass windows set high in the walls. Steel sheets covered most of the roof, but parts were made with steel frames and glass panels, giving more light. Rows of booths filled the space while people bustled, carrying bags and parcels and food.

They turned a corner, and the warm smell of cinnamon and yeast and baking bread wafted in the air. The Sixth Street Bakery's booth was tucked into the end of a row, a pipe connecting the oven to a large, central chimney that served several of the food booths in this section of the market.

The white-haired woman beside the oven set down a tray and bustled toward them. "Princess Essie! It is so good to have you home!"

"It's good to be back in Aldon. I've missed your cinnamon rolls." Essie resisted the urge to give Mrs. Burke a hug. Essie was close to her, but not that close. A princess did not distribute hugs to people in the marketplace. "Please tell me you have some still warm."

"I just spread the frosting on these." Mrs. Burke pulled out a tray. The cinnamon rolls lined up, the frosting melting in white, gooey pools.

Essie reached into her pocket for coins, but Mrs. Burke shook her head. "No need to pay. These are gifts. For your wedding."

It was always tricky accepting gifts as a princess. People often gave gifts, hoping to eventually get a favor in return. But Essie had spent enough money at this bakery over the years and her patronage of the place was well-known. It was unlikely that Mrs. Burke was angling for a favor; she was simply offering a gift out of the kindness of her heart.

"Thank you. Farrendel and I appreciate it." Essie smiled up at Farrendel. He was attempting to appear friendly, which was mostly him lurking at her side with his mouth occasionally twitching with something that might have been a smile or a muscle spasm. It was hard to tell.

Mrs. Burke slid two of the cinnamon rolls onto napkins. She leaned closer as she handed them over. "Your elf husband is the silent type, I see."

Essie stifled a snort. "He's quiet but sweet. And, he understands Escarlish."

"Oh." Mrs. Burke covered her mouth. "I apologize, Prince Farrendel. No offense meant."

His ears tipped a shade pink, Farrendel glanced at Essie, as if asking her what he was supposed to say next. Essie gave him what she hoped was an encouraging wave. She had to be careful not to keep answering for him in situations like this.

He gave a small sound in the back of his throat. "It was a pleasure to meet you."

Mrs. Burke smiled. "Oh, you're a dear."

"Yes, he is." Essie handed one of the cinnamon rolls to Farrendel. Mrs. Burke was Essie's secret weapon when it came to public opinion. Mrs. Burke's bakery was a favorite among the elite, and she'd tell everyone how Farrendel was a sweetheart and he and Essie were very much in love. It might not sway the hardened, but some would listen.

With a final wave at Mrs. Burke, Essie strolled back into the crowd. She bit into her cinnamon roll, closing her eyes for a moment at the sweetness. She'd missed these so much in Estyra.

She tried to savor it. She really did. But somehow the cinnamon roll disappeared in only a few warm, gooey bites.

As Essie licked the last of the frosting from her fingers, she couldn't help but laugh at the glare Farrendel was giving his own sticky hands. She bumped into him. "Just lick your fingers."

Farrendel frowned. "Humans are..."

"Sticky? Gross? Unmannerly?" Essie nudged him with her elbow.

"Unsanitary. Do you eat everything with your fingers?"

"No. After all, it would be hard to eat soup that way." Essie held out her hand to him. "Come on. Let's find a faucet so we can wash our hands."

Farrendel shook his head, leaning away from her. "No hand-holding until you wash your hands."

"My hands? Your hands are the ones still sticky with frosting." Essie headed for the nearest corner, where a public water closet would have a sink.

"You licked yours."

"You've kissed me. You didn't find my saliva disgusting then." At least, she didn't think he did. He seemed to enjoy kissing her well enough. But elves were apparently persnickety about things.

"It is supposed to be in your mouth. Not on your fingers." Farrendel's expression remained blank.

She had better cut off this line of thinking and fast. If she gave Farrendel too much time to think about it, he might never want to kiss her again. Kissing was something that only sounded good if one didn't think about it too logically.

But then she finally noticed the twinkle in his eye.

He was joking with her. This joking, absurd side wasn't something she saw in Farrendel often, and it had taken her a moment to recognize that's what he was doing.

This was love. Not just the kissing and attraction, though that certainly was nice. But simply the fact that she enjoyed his company. This moment, walking through the market with him, was special and fun and different than anything she'd experienced with anyone else. When times got hard, this was what she'd choose to dwell on. Laughing with him. Smiling. Having fun together.

They only had a few more days. She drew in a breath

at the pang deep in her chest. In two or three days, he had to return to Tarenhiel and go to war. Until that war was over, there would be very few days like this one.

The smile dropped from Farrendel's face. "What is wrong?"

"I don't want today to end. You're going to be leaving for war, and…" She couldn't finish. She didn't want to lose this. Lose him. Not when they were building something real and deep and precious between them.

"Do not think about it." Sticky hands and all, Farrendel stepped closer, though he didn't touch her. "Do not let tomorrow spoil today."

Wise words. She could usually push aside what-ifs. But this seemed bigger. Harder. The hurt deeper.

"All right." She smiled and shoved away the worries. He was right. She would savor today. "Let's sanitize our sticky fingers."

SEVENTEEN

After Essie and Farrendel washed their hands, they browsed a few more aisles. They briefly stopped at the merchant selling Illyna's elven shampoo and conditioner. The merchant was already nearly out and hoping for a new shipment to arrive quickly.

Next to that booth, Essie found one of the local coffee shops that had a booth with a selection of coffee, hot chocolate, tea, and mugs.

"We should pick out mugs we can take back to Estyra for hot chocolate there." Essie dragged Farrendel into the booth to the mug display. "What one would you like?"

She already knew which one he'd pick. It was a deep blue fading to black at the rim, made of a thick ceramic.

Farrendel considered the mugs for a moment, before he gently picked up the dark blue mug she'd spotted. "We do not have a way to heat hot chocolate in our rooms in Estyra."

"I have a plan for that." Essie claimed a deep green ceramic mug that matched Farrendel's blue one. "A small camp stove should do the trick until we can convince either an elf or human inventor to come up with a compact, magically-powered stove. If they can power trains through magic, surely someone can figure out how to power a small heating device. Lance Marion is the human inventor I was probably going to ask. He has a shop at the edge of Aldon, and he has worked with the Crown before. We can stop there before or after our ride since we probably want to have him start right away, considering you elves have a thing against fires in your treetops."

"Yes." Farrendel's mouth twitched.

Great. He was laughing at her again. Essie gave him a fake glare before she turned to the girl running the shop. She couldn't be more than fifteen or sixteen, and she was staring rather unabashedly at Farrendel. Essie wasn't sure if it was because Farrendel was an elf or because he was good-looking.

Essie turned on her brightest, professional princess smile. "Do you offer samples we can taste before we make our purchases?"

The girl blinked, started, then swiveled so quickly that she nearly toppled from her stool behind a small countertop. "Oh, right, yes." The girl took a deep breath, and a professional mask settled over her face. "We offer samples of all our coffees, teas, and hot chocolate varieties. What would you like to try, Your Highness?"

"What would you recommend for the hot chocolates?" Essie softened her smile, hoping to put the girl at ease. This had always been her job as a princess. As king, Averett couldn't mingle with the people the way she could and, when he did, he needed to keep an extra layer of regal professionalism in place. Edmund and Julien could be charming when they wanted to be, but they didn't love mingling with people the way Essie did.

As the youngest, Essie had more freedom. She could be the approachable princess who felt more like one of the people than the rest of her siblings.

The set to the girl's shoulders relaxed, and she smiled. "The double chocolate supreme is my favorite, though a lot of people also like the dark chocolate delight and caramel chocolate craving."

"We'd like to try all three, if it wouldn't be too much trouble."

After tasting the samples with lots of chatter on Essie's part and nods from Farrendel, they settled on two packages of the double chocolate and one of the dark chocolate. As they paid, Farrendel eyed the shelf with the packages of hot chocolate, as if he wasn't sure three would be enough.

Essie leaned closer and whispered in elvish, "We'll get more at another booth."

The furrow between his brows disappeared, and he nodded.

This was the reason she was glad she'd married another member of royalty. She didn't have to explain to him that they needed to spread their patronage out between shops.

They left the shop with Farrendel hugging his paper-wrapped mug to his chest like it was the most precious gift he'd ever been given. She took his free hand, swinging their clasped hands slightly as they weaved into the traffic in the aisle.

It was getting more crowded, and Farrendel's fingers tightened on hers, his shoulders tensing.

He was probably nearing his people limit by this

TARA GRAYCE

point. He'd put up with a lot of noise and bustle for her. It was probably time she found him a little peace and quiet.

She steered him toward the stairs to the loft section that stretched across the far side of the space. "There's a full coffee shop in the loft by the artists' booths. We can get a table by the railing in a quiet corner, sit for a moment, and look for Edmund and Jalissa. Once we've found them, we can leave the market and go for our ride."

Farrendel gave a large nod. "Yes."

He must be ready to be done with people. Together, they climbed the stairs and strolled to the coffee shop in the far corner. This shop was busier and didn't offer the free samples nor did it have as many specialty items. But it had a good, creamy hot chocolate that Farrendel and Essie savored while they searched the crowd from the balcony.

"I don't see them." Essie scanned the crowd bustling back and forth below. Jalissa's long, dark brown hair should have been easy to spot, flowing down her back as it was instead of pinned up. Plus, there should have been a cleared space in the crowd where the people gave her brother and Jalissa room.

"They are not down there." Farrendel's tone was calm, not worried. As if he knew something she didn't.

When she glanced at him, he pointed past her. She turned to see Edmund and Jalissa strolling toward them from an aisle between the artists' booths up here.

She should've guessed Jalissa would prefer strolling the art gallery rather than the bustle of the booths below.

Edmund flopped into the chair near Essie. "Well, that was an enjoyable morning."

"It was tolerable." Jalissa perched gracefully in a chair

near Farrendel. Her gaze swept over him, as if making sure he was all right.

He smiled and tipped his head as if to reassure her.

Essie held out her mug of hot chocolate. "Do you want a sip of hot chocolate?"

Jalissa's nose wrinkled, as if the thought of sharing Essie's mug disgusted her. But she took the mug and delicately sipped. Her eyebrows arched. "This is good."

"Would you like your own?" Edmund started to push himself to his feet.

"No, but thank you." Jalissa swung her gaze from Edmund to Essie. "Are we done here?"

"Yes. We'd like to leave for our ride, if that sounds good to you." Essie reclaimed her mug and gulped down the rest of her cooling hot chocolate.

Jalissa nodded. "That is acceptable."

When they returned to the market's entrance, their horses and patient guards were waiting. A small crowd had also gathered. They waved, and Essie waved back as regally as she could manage.

It took nearly half an hour to reach the far side of Aldon to the stretch of rolling hills perfect for running the horses. The guards they'd sent ahead met them, letting them know it was safe.

Essie tightened her grip on Ashenifela's reins and grinned at Farrendel. "Ready?"

Farrendel flashed a quick smile before he kicked his horse into a gallop.

"Hey! That's cheating!" Essie laughed and urged Ashenifela forward. The mare leapt into a gallop.

The wind tore fingers through Essie's hair. She laughed harder and leaned low over Ashenifela's neck. By Farrendel's grin when he glanced over his shoulder, his hair whipping around him, this was his favorite part of the day.

AFTER SPENDING OVER AN HOUR RIDING, they needed to return. The shadows lengthened across the hills. The breeze swept cool from the west.

At the edge of town, they split their group in two. Edmund and Jalissa took half the guards to return straight to Winstead Palace. Essie and Farrendel, surrounded by the rest of the guards, headed for Lance Marion's workshop.

Lance's workshop was a large, brick building near the outskirts of town, at the edge of the manufacturing district. The rolling door was thrown wide open.

Essie dismounted and handed Ashenifela's reins to a guard. "Wait out here for us, please."

The guard nodded as Farrendel dismounted and entrusted the reins of his horse to another guard.

Essie took Farrendel's hand and strode toward the open door. "You'll like this place. There is always so much to look at. Lance is part master magician, part inventor. He's a bit eccentric, to be honest. But nice."

Farrendel eyed her but followed.

As they stepped into the building, they had to dodge around tables with various metal devices laid out in different states of completion. Essie could only guess at what all the items were. Along the wall, tools hung from a peg board.

As they took another step into the building, a piercing shriek split the air. Farrendel flinched, a blue light flickering along his palms. A crackle of magic tingled against Essie's skin.

The shriek just wailed louder. Deeper in the building, falling metal clattered, followed by a man's voice muttering.

Footsteps pounded a moment before a young man with goggles pushed into his light brown hair raced around a stack of metal barrels. He clutched some kind of device in his hands. The wailing buzz came from the device while a needle set in some kind of dial was pressed all the way into the red zone.

"I have never seen readings like this." The young man circled the two of them, the device pointed in their direction. "Do you have a magical device in your pocket? But I can't think of any device that could contain this much power."

"Lance. It's me. Princess Essie."

Lance flapped his hand vaguely in her direction as he narrowed his circle around Farrendel. "No, it's not in your pocket. The magic is radiating from you. How is that even possible? I've never seen a person with this much magic."

Farrendel stayed stock still, hands pressed over his ears. He glanced at Essie, as if begging for help.

"Lance." Essie snapped her fingers in front of his face. "He's an elf. He has magic."

Lance started and glanced up. He blinked at Farrendel, cocking his head. "Oh, right. I should have noticed the ears. I guess that explains it. I have never used my magic sensor on elves before. Tell me. Do you have an average amount of magic for an elf or more than the average amount? Stand still while I perform a few tests."

"Lance, you can study my husband's magic later. Can

you please turn off that device? You're hurting our ears." Essie reached over and tugged on the device.

"Oh, of course." Lance flipped a switch. The shrieking mercifully cut off. "It wasn't doing any good anyway. I will need to build a sensor with a larger range to properly study your magic. Do you know its extent? Some direction would help me know how large a range to build into the detector."

"Lance." Essie clenched her fingers to keep from shaking him. He was usually absent-minded, but this was more than normal. She should have guessed Farrendel's magic would distract him.

Lance blinked at her. "Princess Essie! When did you get here?"

"Several minutes ago. This is Prince Farrendel, my husband. And, no, he's not going to be turned into one of your lab subjects." Essie wrapped her arm around Farrendel's, tugging him closer to her. He didn't resist, as if this young scientist with his shrieking device scared him far more than a pack of trolls.

"Oh, sorry about that. I can get a little carried away at times." Lance set the device on a nearby table, then gave a bow to Farrendel. "Though, if you ever wish to study your magic more in depth, please consider me an option. I would be greatly interested to learn more about how elven magic works. We humans have some theories, but without studying elven magic directly, all we can do is hypothesize."

"You are not scared of my magic?" Farrendel eyed Lance.

"Why would I be scared?" Lance glanced at the magical sensor again, his fingers twitching as if itching to pick it back up.

"I am Laesornysh." Farrendel said it slowly. Not a proud statement, but almost a question.

Lance just stared back for several seconds. "Is that supposed to mean something to me?"

"For someone inventing for the army, you really don't pay enough attention to the news." Essie clasped Farrendel's hand. How much would he want her to tell? She trusted Lance. Well, as much as Lance could be trusted. He wasn't malicious. He just might accidentally say something without thinking. "Farrendel is the elves' foremost warrior because of his magic. It is rather destructive."

"Really?" Lance clasped his hands behind his back, rocking on his heels. "How so? I was under the impression elven magic tended toward healing and growing. I suppose growing things can be destructive in their own way, but your magic sounds like it is something unusual, even for an elf. Fascinating. Are you sure you don't have time for me to run a few tests?"

Essie opened her mouth to protest but stopped. For all his distraction over magic, Lance was the first person all day who had talked to Farrendel rather than simply talking to Essie about Farrendel while Farrendel stood right there. She glanced up at Farrendel and spoke in elvish. "It's up to you. We have time, if you wish to put up with him."

"Will he be able to tell me more about my magic?" Farrendel also spoke in elvish, and in his tone was a depth of longing and hurt.

His magic had been both a blessing and a curse to him. It made him Laesornysh, earning him the respect of his fellow elves when his illegitimate birth would've kept him an outcast. Yet it was also the reason the trolls had captured and tortured him. It was yet another thing that made him different from other elves, wielding this wild, destructive magic that killed instead of healed.

"I'm not sure he will be able to give you many answers, especially today. He probably won't be able to tell you exactly why you have your type of magic, but he may, eventually, be able to figure out its limits and all of its potential uses. Testing takes time and lots of experimentation. A few tests today will help Lance figure out where to start, and he will probably want you to do more tests to determine more specifics later. That's how the scientific process works." Essie shrugged. "I can't say for certain what answers Lance may find, given enough time and experimentation. In the end, you will probably have a better idea of how your magic works, even if you don't know why."

Farrendel faced Lance, his fingers tightening on Essie's. "What would I have to do?"

"Excellent! Don't worry. This shouldn't hurt. Follow me to the back." Lance snatched his magical sensor, spun on his heel, and waved over his shoulder. "Oh, and Princess Essie, you might as well come too."

He scurried through the piles of metal scrap and half-finished devices so quickly Essie had to trot to keep up, though Farrendel had no trouble with his longer strides.

In the back, a large space had been cleared of junk. In the center, a magical power cell, nothing more than an empty canister with wires attached, rested within a mechanical device with more wires and dials. Essie had seen it before on trips to Lance's workshop.

Here, Escarlish magicians worked with Lance to channel their magic to power the device. It was a melding of magic and machine that Essie didn't fully understand

and wasn't about to ask Lance for an explanation. She'd made that mistake only once.

The device was surrounded by a shield of tempered glass and a waist-high wall of brick. Just in case something went wrong and the magician lost control or the magical device exploded, as often happened when working with finnicky magic and touchy mechanics. A smaller shield of tempered glass stood between the magical device and the place where the magician would stand, marginal protection for him in case of an explosion.

Essie claimed a seat at an iron workbench behind the outer wall of glass and brick while Lance directed Farrendel to stand behind the smaller wall.

Lance retreated behind the large wall to a bank of dials and switches near Essie. Adjusting his goggles over his eyes, he flipped a few on, creating a low hum of noise. "All right, Prince Farrendel. Please produce a small amount of your magic. Don't do anything with it yet. I would just like to observe how your magic manifests."

The blue glow surrounded Farrendel's hands, a crackle filling the air as the hum from the machinery grew louder. The magic grew into bolts of lightning curling around Farrendel, his hair rising from his shoulders.

The humming built into a shriek. Lance slapped a few more switches and pounded a few buttons. "Whoa, whoa, whoa! I said a small amount!"

The magic around Farrendel's hands died until it was just a whisper of sparks that he'd used around her nephews.

"That's good. Thanks. You can stop now for a minute." Lance leaned against his machinery for a moment before he turned to Essie, his eyes wide even inside the goggles. "Just how powerful is he?"

"I'm pretty sure he could level this building if he wanted to." Essie rolled one of Lance's pencils across the desktop. She had seen Farrendel kill with his magic. That's how powerful it was. "He doesn't even know his own limits. He's never let it get that uncontrolled."

"A good thing for all of us." Lance faced Farrendel again. "Let's try that again, but this time touch your magic to that wire there over your head. Just a little bit, as gently as you can manage."

Farrendel nodded. The blue sparks filled the space around him again.

"Just in case, close your eyes for a moment." Lance's voice was low, only for Essie to hear.

She squeezed her eyes shut. A moment later, a brilliant flash lit the space, bright even with her eyes closed. A zapping sound puffed out in a mini explosion.

When she dared crack her eyes open, white smoke puffed from the magical device. The wire that had once run to it was now completely gone.

Behind his protective barrier, Farrendel was blinking and rubbing at his ears, but he seemed unharmed.

"I was afraid of that." Lance flipped off his switches, the humming sound dying. He strode around the wall toward his ruined machine. "Your magic is too powerful for this device. It might even be a problem with the compatibility of a device made for human magic and your elven magic. Let's swap out the wire and a few of the mechanics and try again."

Essie shook her head and searched the desk for a piece of paper. Lance would be at this for a while. She might as well sketch out what she'd had in mind for a heating device while she waited.

She drew a horrible sketch, then worked to refine it

into something recognizable while Lance replaced parts and Farrendel blew up a few more magical devices. As he worked, Lance explained to Farrendel what he was doing, and Farrendel leaned close for a better look, occasionally asking questions. Somewhere along the way, Farrendel's questions turned into full sentences.

Interesting. Lance wasn't the person she would've expected Farrendel to bond with, but his excitement over Farrendel's magic had won him over.

As Essie added the finishing touches to her sketch, Lance let out a whoop. She glanced up. The magical device whirred, blue light swirling inside it.

Farrendel strolled around the protective shield, and Lance clapped him on the shoulder and gave him an exuberant shake.

Footsteps drew Essie's gaze. One of the guards marched into the workshop. "Princess? A crowd is gathering outside, and it doesn't look like they will remain peaceful. We should go."

"Of course. Thank you for staying alert." Essie pushed up from the worktable. "Farrendel. Lance. The guards think it's best if we head back to the palace."

"Good timing. With this magical device, I will be able to perform tests." Lance glanced back to the device, as if he itched to return to his experiments.

"Before you get wrapped up in studying Farrendel's magic, could you look at this sketch?" Essie waved the sketch at him. "It's the reason we came here today."

"Right. Of course." Lance took the paper from her.

She quickly explained what she wanted the machine to do. Lance nodded along, somewhat absently. She wasn't sure if that was because his brain was spinning with ideas for the heating machine or if he was still distracted by Farrendel's magic.

She didn't care. If learning more about his magic could help Farrendel feel more in control, then she would support him all the way.

EIGHTEEN

For the first time all day, Farrendel did not want to leave. Lance was a unique individual. He seemed to find Farrendel's magic fascinating rather than dangerous or unnatural. No wonder he was a friend of Essie's. Essie was one of the few other people who did not fear Farrendel because of his magic, even with everything she had seen of it.

When he had come with Essie to Escarland, all he had hoped was that her family would tolerate him. He had not expected to enjoy his time here once they had moved to Buckmore Cottage. He had especially not expected to discover that his magic worked better with human machines than it did with elven growing forests.

Elven magic and technology worked by growing and healing. By encouraging the forest to grow in the way they wished it to grow. His magic was such that his fellow elves could not envision a way to harness it in any manner other than death and destruction.

But if this Lance Marion could figure out a way to

direct Farrendel's magic to power something good and useful and nondestructive...

He could hardly imagine such an outcome. It meant his magic was meant for more than killing. That he was meant for more.

Essie slipped her hand into his as they strode through the heaps of metal and human machinery that filled the workshop, headed for the door.

As they stepped outside following the guard, Farrendel swept a gaze around the restless crowd growing around the entrance, only barely kept back by a small cordon of guards. A few shouts came from the back of the crowd. Something in a harsh tone about pointy-eared elves and a few other worse slurs that Farrendel wished he did not know even in Escarlish.

It was past time to leave. The crowd could turn ugly in a moment.

He had seen crowds like this before. His cheek throbbed with the memory of the results of one such mob. He had been the center of that one as well, for all that the insults had been in elvish as his own people turned on him.

He tensed, every muscle poised to react. His magic crackled beneath his skin, and he barely tamed it from exploding from his fingers. He could not use his magic on an Escarlish crowd. Essie's friend Lance might find it fascinating, but the Escarlish citizens would not take it kindly if some of their own were attacked by an elf.

As Essie reached for Ashenifela's bridle, a louder shout came from the crowd. A tomato whipped out of the mass of people, and it took all his discipline to do nothing but ease out of its path so that it sailed past his shoulder and splattered against the brick wall behind him. Bright red drooled like blood on the brick.

"Your Highnesses, please mount up." The guard shoved Farrendel toward his horse, hands hard against the small of Farrendel's back.

Farrendel dug his heels in, a hint of a crackle filling the air. He fought his instincts that wanted to lash out at the Escarlish guard shoving him.

"Farrendel, we need to go." Essie touched his arm.

He suppressed his magic. With a nod, he took his horse's reins from the guard.

They swung onto their horses. Two of the guards led the way, forcing their horses into the crowd. The other guards clustered tightly around Essie and Farrendel, so tightly he would not be able to use his magic even if he wanted to for fear of taking out those nearest him.

The shouting. The jostling. It prickled against Farrendel's skin, and he scanned the crowd. Too much danger here.

The guards led the way through the parting mob, turning the corner from the small side street where Lance's workshop was located to one of the broader streets. Some human women with young ones bustled between the shops selling various small magical devices and mechanical devices, but human men outnumbered the women.

Behind them, some of the crowd from the alley spilled into this street. In minutes, the crowd grew dense and seething. Shouts filled the air.

Not good. Not good at all. Farrendel kept his horse tucked close to Essie on Ashenifela. If something bad were about to happen, it would happen soon.

Several rotten vegetables flew in their direction. The

women tried to hurry their children from the boardwalk. With the street so crowded, many of the women and children had nowhere to go, trapped in corners without shops to duck into for safety.

A prickle across his scalp. He whirled, flaring his magic around them so abruptly all the horses snorted and shied, except for the two elven horses. A rock bounced from the shield of his magic.

But his instincts still screamed. Movement caught the corner of his eye.

Down. He needed to get Essie down and safe.

He launched himself from his horse and tackled Essie, cradling her against his chest. She gave a tiny squeak as they fell. He twisted and landed in a crouch, Essie pressed to his chest to keep her from slamming into the cobblestones.

A man stepped from the crowd, lifting a gun even as the crowd jostled him. A gunshot cracked, but the muzzle was not pointed at Farrendel or Essie.

Dropping Essie, Farrendel spun on his heel and flung himself forward, putting himself between the bullet and the unintentional targets. His magic flared and crackled around him, and something sparked into the smell of sulfur and heated metal.

He gritted his teeth at the screams behind him. A human woman hunched over her daughter. Did she understand that he was protecting her? Or did she think that Farrendel was the one attacking?

The gun lifted again. He could not allow the man with the gun to fire it again into this volatile crowd.

With a flick of his wrist, Farrendel sent a shaft of magic forward, latching it around the gun.

The man howled, both his hand and gun wrapped in

glowing, blue magic. The howl could not be pain, as Farrendel kept most of the power out of the magic to keep from hurting the Escarlish man, for all he had attacked royalty.

Two of the Escarlish guards rushed to the man. As soon as they gripped his arms, Farrendel released his magic, letting it disappear into sparks.

Behind him, the human woman and child were still sobbing. How much would he be able to reassure them?

He knelt, facing them. "I am sorry you were frightened."

Essie rested a hand on his shoulder, her voice warm. "Are either of you hurt? I'm sorry you were caught in that."

"We're fine." The woman swiped at her face, straightening. Her hands remained clenched on her daughter's shoulders. "Was…was that a gunshot?"

The daughter peeked up at Farrendel before focusing on the ground once again.

"Yes. Sorry. But don't worry. This is my husband, Prince Farrendel. He stopped the bullet with his magic." Essie's hand squeezed Farrendel's shoulder, and he did not have to look up to see her smile.

Farrendel was not sure how to comport his face to portray reassurance. With Essie's soothing tone, the best option was probably for him just to sit still and attempt a smile.

"Thank you. Your Highnesses." The woman tilted her head, her grip on her daughter relaxing as she bobbed an abbreviated version of the Escarlish curtsy.

The daughter peeked at Farrendel again. This time, she studied him, probably taking in his long hair and tapered ears that would appear strange to her.

Essie's nephews had found the sparks he could make with his magic fascinating. Perhaps this human girl would as well. He would hate to leave the terror of his crackling, fully powered magic as the only memory she had of elven magic. He might not be able to change the minds of the adults in Escarland, but perhaps the children would grow up with a different view of elves.

He held out his palm, flat, as if offering a gift. A flare of sparks swirled into the air, forming a flower. A moment later, it burst, raining down onto the hand the little girl stuck out. The girl's sniffing turned into a giggle.

It was enough. Farrendel eased to his feet and stepped back.

The woman bobbed another curtsy, first to Farrendel, then to Essie. "Your Highnesses." She hurried into the crowd, ushering her daughter along.

The gunshot could have turned the people from an anxious crowd into a rioting mob. But they stood still and silent, as if stunned. He could not read the crowd well enough to know what they might be thinking about the gunshot, his magic, or his actions.

No matter the reason, the silence persisted as they remounted. The crowd parted, letting them head home toward Buckmore Cottage.

CHAPTER

NINETEEN

ESSIE HELD Farrendel's hand as they strolled from the graveled drive to the front doors of Buckmore Cottage. "Today was a good day, despite the scare on the way back. I had a good time, though I'm glad we're home."

She meant it. Even though they had only spent a night there, Buckmore already felt like home. With Winstead Palace, and Ellonahshinel in Estyra, she was starting to collect a lot of homes.

"Yes." Farrendel halted and tugged her closer.

He said it with all the fervor of someone who didn't have many good days. She leaned her head against his shoulder. "I'm glad you enjoyed it. Even if there were too many people."

He pressed a kiss into her hair. "You like people and the market. I like to see you happy."

They were standing on the front step where anyone passing by could peek through the gate and see them. But

Essie didn't care. She turned her face and kissed him, trailing her fingers through the ends of his hair.

His hand cupped her cheek as he kissed her in return. Slow and gentle, deepening and lingering.

When he pulled back, Essie tucked her head against his shoulder again, trying not to think about the days passing far too quickly until he would leave. "Let's skip dinner with my family tonight and just stay in. Maybe read books. Make some of our new hot chocolate and drink from our new mugs."

Farrendel stepped back, but his mouth was tipped in a smile. She took his hand again, and he opened the door to the cottage.

As the door shut behind them and her eyes adjusted to the shade inside, movement drew her gaze. Next to her Farrendel stiffened, though the crackle of his magic didn't fill the air.

"Essie. Farrendel. I'm glad you've returned." Averett's voice came from the doorway to the parlor. His tone was low. Serious.

"Did you hear about the attack in the streets? It was scary, but Farrendel stopped the bullet. And I didn't think we'd caused too much of an incident for the royal image." Essie tightened her grip on Farrendel's hand. She didn't want to think about what might have happened if Farrendel hadn't been quick enough to incinerate the bullet.

"What about an attack? This is the first I've heard of it." Averett glanced between her and Farrendel. "I take it no one was hurt?"

"We're fine." Essie shrugged. "A mob gathered, and a protestor shot at Farrendel."

"I see." Averett's tone said he was making a mental

note to follow up with the palace guards for more details. "I'm here for something else."

That couldn't be good. Essie gestured to the parlor behind Averett with her free hand. "Is this a sit-down type of discussion?"

"Probably." Averett led the way back into the parlor. Inside the room, both Edmund and Julien lounged on the padded chairs.

This definitely wasn't good if all three of her brothers were waiting for them.

Essie sank onto a seat on the couch, leaving enough space for Farrendel to claim a seat next to her. He did, but slowly, as if he would have preferred the floor. Essie glanced between each of her brothers before focusing on Averett. "What's going on? Why do I feel like you're about to interrogate us?"

"Nothing like that." Averett dropped into a seat facing them. "General Freilan completed his audit of the army's records and inventory of all bases and warehouses. Julien and I have gone over all the reports and agree with his findings. The main army base and warehouse showed they had far fewer rifles, ammunition, and repeater guns than they should according to the paperwork."

"So someone in the army is the traitor." Essie's stomach tightened. "But how would someone manage to sneak that many weapons off one of the most secure places in all of Escarland? That base has better security than we have at Winstead Palace."

Her brothers all stared back at her, far too serious.

"We don't know yet." Julien rubbed the back of his neck. "You're right. It wouldn't be feasible for someone, even with a lot of help, to steal weapons to this scale. General Freilan believes the only way this could have happened is if those weapons never reached the army in the first place."

"He is investigating if someone at the army's warehouse has been helping to fudge the paperwork to cover up the missing weapons." Averett leaned his elbows on his knees. "Either way, that traitor or traitors in the army aren't the ones behind all of this. The real traitor is the person at the factory who is routing the weapons to Kostaria instead of the army."

Essie's stomach twisted. Those weapons had been meant for Escarland's army. That meant Escarland's people had paid for them through taxes. And instead of dealing honestly, this traitor had sold them to Kostaria, greedily getting paid twice for the same weapons. "Which factory? Do you know?"

"As we suspected, the missing weapons are all from the factories owned by Charles Hadley." Julien slouched in his seat. "But, besides the fact that he hates elves and the missing weapons came from his factory, we don't have any evidence to convict him specifically as the traitor. I interviewed him again this afternoon at his factory. He still flatly denies any involvement."

"While he was shouting at Julien, I took advantage of the distraction and snooped through the books." Edmund's smirk was short-lived. "The books appeared to be all in order, as if those weapons had been delivered to the army as promised."

"Could the weapons have been stolen en route?" Essie glanced between her brothers. Beside her, Farrendel was stiff and far too silent. He was fully Laesornysh as he absorbed this news. "Maybe when the train stopped for coal and water, the traitors could quickly slip some of the weapons off without anyone noticing."

"We thought of that. There have been no reports of train robberies, and unless the conductor is part of this gang of traitors, I would highly doubt the traitors could get away with that method on this scale." Averett shook his head. "Besides, Charles Hadley doesn't ship the weapons on the regular cargo trains. He purchased three trains of his own five years ago. Being able to ship via secured trains that carried nothing but the weapons for the army was one of the things that gained him the army contract in the first place. Last year, he upgraded all three trains to run fully on magical devices so that they don't have to stop."

"So it has to be specifically delivered to the border for the trolls straight from the factory." Essie grimaced. She wanted to reach for Farrendel's hand, but he was far too stiff and cold at that moment. "I don't see how Charles Hadley can be anything but involved."

"It gets worse." Edmund's voice dropped into a tone grimmer than she had ever heard from him. "There was something off about how many weapons the books are saying were produced versus the amount of raw materials that they have been ordering. If I were to guess, that factory has been producing far more weapons than the records show. If those weapons aren't being sold to the Escarlish army, then, my guess is, they have been sold to the trolls. The traitors probably only started skimming from the army weapons recently, once the demand from Kostaria grew higher than what they could produce on the side."

"How many?" Farrendel's voice was tight.

"We don't have an exact figure." Averett met Farrendel's gaze without flinching. "But, a lot. Enough to outfit a moderately-sized army, at the very least."

That was very, very bad. It meant this had been going on far longer and on a greater scale than it had first appeared.

The trolls didn't have just a few Escarlish weapons. They had enough to wipe out Tarenhiel even with Farrendel's magic fighting against them. He had been brought down with a single repeater gun. What would happen if he faced several all at once?

He'd die. That's what would happen.

"Isn't there anything we can do? Surely this is enough reason to help Tarenhiel against Kostaria?" Essie's chest tightened, all of her aching with the pain of what might happen to Farrendel, to her new elven family, to the home in Estyra she'd come to love.

"Until I can prove that Kostaria had an active part in this, I can't declare war on them. As far as Parliament will be concerned, this is a matter of traitors inside Escarland and nothing more. But if we can find the true books or get a confession that shows concretely that Kostaria has been actively seeking Escarlish weapons and aiding the Escarlish traitors, I might be able to make a case for more active help. Maybe."

"But these are our weapons. Tarenhiel is in danger because of traitors in our kingdom giving the trolls our weapons. Isn't there something we can do to make this right?" It felt all kinds of wrong that they were this helpless. Averett was the king. Surely there was something he could do.

"We need more proof. I'm sorry, Essie. I don't like it either. Believe me, I don't. If it were up to me, I'd march the army to Kostaria and wrest our weapons from their hands myself if I had to. But it doesn't work that way. Thousands of Escarlish soldiers would die. I need—and the kingdom needs—a very good reason before I give that order."

She nodded. She understood that. Of course she did. And after Father's war with the elves that was, afterwards, portrayed as hasty and costly, Averett would be doubly cautious. He didn't have a choice.

Averett turned to Farrendel. "We reported this to Jalissa earlier this afternoon. I also wired an abbreviated version to your brother, and he would like you to return to Tarenhiel as soon as you can. If possible, I want you to stay through tomorrow night. Officially presenting you to the Escarlish court as Essie's husband might be more essential than ever if I'm to convince Parliament that we should aid Tarenhiel."

Farrendel nodded. Essie swallowed back the lump in her throat. Just two nights and a single full day. Then Farrendel would leave.

Would she ever see him again? He was powerful, but he would be one elf against an army with firepower unlike anything the elves had ever fought before.

It would be a slaughter.

"But don't give up hope just yet." Julien crossed his arms. "There will be a raid on Charles Hadley's factory and office while he's at the ball tomorrow night."

"While that happens, the rest of us are going to keep an eye on those Charles Hadley interacts with. We have already been looking into his contacts and business associates, but we may observe something in person he hasn't committed to paper." Edmund glanced between them. His gaze was sharp, his tone professional. This was Edmund, the spy.

"If Charles Hadley is the traitor, then he's most likely behind the protestors. He won't want Farrendel's official presentation to the court to go smoothly." Averett huffed a sigh. "We don't know what he has planned. I'd prefer to arrest him right now, but he would just use a premature arrest to his advantage. So we will all need to be alert and prepared for anything."

"It still probably isn't considered proper for Farrendel to walk around with his swords strapped to his back." Essie grimaced. Even if he'd still have his magic, she'd prefer to have him armed.

"Nor would it be proper for you to try to stuff a rifle down the back of your dress." Edmund smirked.

"I was thinking a nice leather carrying sheath, matching Farrendel's for his swords. We could be a matched set." Essie grinned up at Farrendel. His hard expression didn't so much as twitch.

Averett coughed. "No swords or rifles. But if you have any knives or pistols you can hide out of sight, then do it. Essie, you still have that derringer we gave you when you were twelve, right?"

"Yes, I still have it. I'll wear it." Essie preferred her rifle to the small pistol, but she'd rather be armed if the traitor decided to try to kill Farrendel.

"If you need any knives or pistols, the royal armory is at your disposal, Farrendel." Julien patted his ankle, where he kept a derringer hidden. "Seriously, if you need anything, just name it. We don't want to lose our favorite brother-in-law now that we have him."

"I have a knife." Farrendel shrugged, a small lift to his shoulders. "And I have my magic. I will be fine."

His magic was their best protection. Unless the traitors managed to haul a repeater gun into the palace's ball-room, Farrendel could hold off whatever the traitors had planned.

As her brothers stood to leave, Averett rested a hand on her shoulder. "Sorry to bring bad news."

"At least we have some idea who one of the traitors might be. That's the main thing." Essie stood and hugged Averett. "We're going to stay in tonight since tomorrow will be busy. It's my second to last night with Farrendel before he leaves."

"I understand." Averett patted her back. "Julien and I are going to review the security at the palace again to make sure we're ready. We'll keep him safe."

"Thanks." Essie walked her brothers to the door, shutting it behind Edmund. She turned to find Farrendel had followed her. She wrapped her arms around his waist and leaned against him. "What do you want to do for the rest of the evening?"

Farrendel held her for a moment. Then he stepped out of her embrace. "I will be back. I need...space for a while."

"Oh. All right." Essie tried to keep her smile pasted on her face as Farrendel slipped out the door. She stayed in the doorway, watching as he dashed to a tree with a low-hanging branch and swung himself onto it. Within seconds, he disappeared into the upper branches.

After shutting the door, she leaned against it. She shouldn't feel this sinking feeling in her chest. He'd spent most of the day surrounded by far too many people, and now even being around her was too much for him. She didn't understand it, exactly. She needed people around her in a way Farrendel didn't. And he needed space and quiet in a way she didn't.

Still, even knowing that about him didn't make it easy to sit by herself while he went off to do his thing.

She gave herself a good shake. No reason to sit around

moping. She hadn't done that in Estyra, and she certainly wasn't going to do it in Buckmore Cottage.

Since she wasn't much of a cook, she tracked down a servant to bring them some of the food from Winstead Palace's kitchen. She checked on Jalissa. It seemed Farrendel's sister also needed space after a day in Aldon's market, so Essie left her to her book.

As Essie started the milk heating for hot chocolate, she heard a soft thump above her head. Moments later, the door to the water closet closed, and water started rushing through the pipes.

Essie smiled, though it felt small and weary after the long day. She'd checked, and the castle staff had finished installing the new water spigot while she and Farrendel were at the market. Farrendel would appreciate being able to wash his hair without hunching over the bathtub.

Just as she was pouring the hot chocolate into her and Farrendel's new and freshly washed mugs, arms wrapped around her from behind. She breathed in the minty scent of Farrendel's shampoo and conditioner, extra strong after his wash. She leaned back against him. "How does the new spigot work?"

"Much better." Farrendel rested his head against the top of hers. A strand of his wet hair brushed against her cheek.

Essie held up her filled mug. "I'm thinking a picnic and hot chocolate in the back garden. I left a pile of blankets by the door. If we're lucky, we'll have a clear night, and we'll be able to star-gaze."

"Perfect." Farrendel reached over her to claim his mug.

Between the two of them, they carried the picnic basket, the blankets, and their mugs of hot chocolate to the garden. Snuggling on a bench, they ate their supper, sipped their hot chocolate, and lingered there as twilight faded into a star-speckled night.

Warm and wrapped in blankets, Essie fell asleep curled against Farrendel's chest.

CHAPTER
TWENTY

E ssie sat at the small dressing table in their turret room, pinning up her hair. She'd been tempted to ask a maid to walk to Buckmore Cottage for tonight to help with her hair, but, in the end, she'd gotten used to making do. Besides, this was her and Farrendel's last night before he left for Tarenhiel. It wouldn't be fair to the poor maid to get stuck in potentially awkward situations.

After pinning another lock of her hair into the chignon at the back of her head, she smoothed the skirt of her deep green dress and considered her reflection in the mirror. It was strange seeing the human hair style with her elven dress. But it was, perhaps, a good strange. Right, somehow.

One more lock of hair stuck out at the nape of her neck. She tucked it into place and stuck in a pin to hold it there. Finally, she picked up the elven circlet that matched Farrendel's and tucked it into her hair. Perfect.

She picked up the pair of elbow-length silk gloves

she'd set to the side and pulled them on. There. She might not have the massive skirt in the style that was fashionable in Escarland, but with this mix of elven and Escarlish fashion, no one could mistake her for anything other than a princess.

What was taking Farrendel so long? He'd retreated to the water closet to get ready for the ball tonight and had yet to return. What was he doing in there? It wasn't like he had to spend hours doing his hair. He would wear it down like he always did, and, thanks to elven shampoo and conditioner, he didn't have to worry about frizz.

She turned back to her mirror. Was her circlet resting slightly crooked on her head?

She adjusted her hair. As she straightened the circlet, the door to their room opened and shut behind her. Due to the angle, she couldn't see the door in her mirror. "I was starting to worry about you. You usually don't take that long to…"

She trailed off as she turned around. Farrendel stood a few feet into the room, his gaze flicking from her to the floor, as if uncertain of her reaction. Instead of his usual elven tunic and trousers, he wore gray, Escarlish breeches tucked into his tall elven boots. He had a crisp white shirt underneath a gray waistcoat and a tight, black tailcoat that fit his shoulders and waist too exactly to be anything other than tailored for him. To complete the outfit, a white neckcloth lay just a fraction askew.

He motioned at it. "I could not get this right. It seems I did not practice long enough."

Essie slid to her feet, still gaping. She squeezed her eyes shut. She must be seeing things.

Nope. Farrendel still stood there in full Escarlish finery.

"You're dressed in...where did you even get those clothes?" Essie tiptoed closer, as if he would disappear if she made any sudden moves. If she'd been strange with her Escarlish hairstyle and elven dress, then he was stranger still with his silver-blond hair flowing across the finely tailored shoulders of his tailcoat.

"Your brothers helped." Farrendel's gaze swung to the floor, looking for all the world like he wanted to scuff his boot against the floor, though he remained stock still. "You adopted my people's manner of dress even here. I could do no less."

It was a strategic political move and wouldn't go unnoticed at the ball. Her, a human princess, dressed as an elf. Him, an elven prince, dressed as a human.

But he hadn't done this for politics. At least, not only for politics. He'd done this for her. To show her that he was just as willing to embrace her people as she had been to embrace his.

She closed the remaining distance between them, something sizzling in the air. She didn't know where to put her hands and settled for straightening the neckcloth. "You look very dashing."

The tight and tailored fashion in Escarland accentuated the slimness of his waist, the line of his shoulders. Even through the layers of shirt and tailcoat, her fingers felt his warmth. His strength.

She was leaning into him, her face tipped up to meet his gaze. "Farrendel..." His name whispered out on a breath.

Then she was kissing him. How much did they really need to attend the ball tonight?

Farrendel eased the kiss from her mouth to her cheek. "You are messing up my hair."

She laughed, tucking her head against his neckcloth. His hands were on her back, and, as far as she could tell without a mirror, he had nicely kept from messing up the hairstyle she'd spent nearly an hour perfecting. How he'd managed to have that much presence of mind, she didn't know.

It took immense self-control, but she forced herself to ease back from him. If she didn't, they'd end up late for the banquet being held in their honor.

When she inspected the damage her fingers had done to Farrendel's hair, she huffed. "You have, maybe, one hair out of place. Is it even possible to mess up your hair?"

She ruffled a section of his hair. He ducked away from her hand, grimacing. His hair floated back into place. Yep, definitely magical hair or conditioner or both.

"Nope. Apparently, it's impossible for your hair to look anything but perfect." This time when she reached out, she ran her fingers through his hair, smoothing the two strands that were out of place. As his hair trailed over her hand, it sparked a thought. "You sense what's around you with your hair, right? The air drafts or something like that, as far as I can figure out. How much would it bother you to have your hair tied back for an evening? Short hair is currently the fashion in Escarland, but long hair used to be fashionable about a hundred years ago. Not quite this long. More shoulder length for men. Anyway, the men would tie it back. It would give your hair a more human hairstyle. But you don't have to, if you don't want to."

Farrendel went still beneath her hand. After several moments, he tipped his head. "While I will need to be alert, my senses will be confused with so many people

227

pressed close. If you think that tying back my hair will help tonight, then I will."

How were her knees going this weak and mushy over something like a hairstyle? But it said a lot, that he was willing to tie back his hair for her.

"Just for tonight. You can go back to wearing it loose just as soon as the ball is over. Come on." Essie tugged him toward her dressing table and nudged him into her chair. "Let me."

He held himself stiff, back straight, in her chair. She reached for her hairbrush but stopped. If he could sense air stirring behind him, then either his hair or his scalp was rather sensitive. The hairbrush would probably hurt.

Not that his hair needed the aid of a hairbrush to detangle it. It glided over her fingers as she finger-combed from his scalp to the ends of his long, split-end free strands. As she gathered his hair, his shoulders relaxed, his spine melting back against the chair. Apparently, having one's hair played with relaxed elves just as much as it did humans.

She could see it all too clearly. Farrendel sitting on the floor, a crowd of nieces around him, braiding his hair, adding bows and ribbons and sparkling hair pieces while he willingly let them.

Or, maybe not nieces. Maybe daughters. Daughters with pointed ears like his and auburn hair like Essie's brother Averett. Not her own flaming red hair. She didn't yet love her hair color enough to wish it on daughters, even if Farrendel liked it.

Her fingers stilled. They'd been so focused on building their relationship in the here and now that long-term future plans hadn't come up. It was hard to plan that far ahead with the war looming over them.

She cleared her throat, hoping Farrendel couldn't tell how pink her face must be if he glanced up at the mirror. After locating a black ribbon, she tied it around his hair in a manly knot, making sure it wasn't too tight. "How's that? Does it hurt, at all? Don't be afraid to tell me. Believe me, I know the headache you can get from having your hair slicked back too tight or a hairpin jabbed into your scalp."

He cocked his head, his gaze focused on the mirror. With his hair tied back, the tapered points of his ears were even more obvious. Perhaps tying his hair back wouldn't make him look more human after all, though it did complete the overall look. Finally, his gaze lifted to meet hers in the mirror. "It does not hurt."

By his tone, she couldn't tell if he liked it or hated it. The fact that he had gone blank and flat-toned probably meant he didn't like it all that much.

She rested her elbows on his shoulders, wrapping her arms around his neck. "It's all right to say if you don't like it. Don't feel like you have to change your appearance for me. Not your hair or your clothes or anything, all right?"

His eyes widened, and he twisted to look at her rather than the mirror. "Is that how you felt in Estyra?"

The horror in his voice brought a smile. "No. I was more than happy to ditch my Escarlish clothes for Tarenhieli ones. Your women wear trousers, and no one thinks anything of it. And I can just let my hair stay down and loose without spending nearly an hour each day pinning it up. I was more than happy to change my style of hair and dress."

"I am happy to change tonight." He glanced back at himself in the mirror. "But I think only for tonight."

"Well, I think you'll be the most dashing man there no matter what you're wearing." She traced his ear with a finger, her head close to his as she leaned against his shoulders.

"Essie…" His voice had a tight, almost strained note to it she'd never heard before. "I think if you want to arrive on time, then we had better leave."

When he turned to face her, his expression was the soft, yearning one he got right before he kissed her. But he didn't close the distance. She didn't either.

The attraction she felt for him now was different than it had been. Yes, she loved his muscles. His scars. His looks. But, deeper than that, she loved his heart. She loved his protective fierceness that gained him those muscles and scars. She loved the vulnerability in his eyes when he admitted something personal to her. The shy look he had when attempting to flirt. The gaping wonder when he tried hot chocolate for the first time, and the way he smiled when she prattled on about nonsense.

Love was a choice. But it was also a deep companionship. A sacrifice. A moving emotion far less fleeting than a mere feeling. And it was choosing again and again to focus on the companionship and love rather than whatever anger or annoyance that arose between two people stuck together for any length of time.

And, perhaps, because love was all those things, that's what made it so complicated and hard at times.

With him looking at her like that, it took all of her will power to straighten and smile her most oblivious, perky smile. Picking up his crown from the end of her dressing table, she set it on his hair. "Well, then. I guess we'd better go."

He glided to his feet and held out his arm. Instead of

resting her hand on his forearm in the elven style, Essie tucked her hand around his upper arm, her fingers against his bicep. Honestly, the reason for the elven style was making much more sense. It was much easier to concentrate on walking with her hand lightly on his forearm rather than pressed against his muscle. Seriously distracting.

"Here." Essie nudged his elbow so that he didn't hold his arm out so far. "You can relax your arm. Let it stay almost loose at your side. That's it."

With his arm relaxed instead of tensed, the feel of his muscles beneath his shirt and tailcoat were much less distracting.

He took a step toward the door, but she halted him. She had one last thing she needed to say before they stepped out of the safety of this room and faced the front lines that was Escarland's court. When he glanced back at her, she touched his cheek. "Before my elven wedding to you, Jalissa told me to hold my head high and never let them make me feel ashamed for being human. The same goes for you now. Hold your head high tonight and please don't let anyone make you feel ashamed for being an elf."

Farrendel tipped his head in a nod. Then, together, they left their room and took the staircase down to the main foyer.

Jalissa already waited there in a green dress a few shades lighter than Essie's. Her guard waited a few paces behind her, hands clasped behind her back. Essie had yet to convince the elf guard to say a single word to her.

At Essie and Farrendel's approach, Jalissa cocked an eyebrow. "You are late."

Essie patted Farrendel's arm. "I was distracting him."

When she glanced up at him, the tips of his ears were flushing pink, something that was rather noticeable with his hair tied back.

Jalissa gave a ladylike sigh that was the elven equivalent of a snort and a roll of her eyes. With a tip of her head, Jalissa swept toward the back doors. Her guard fell into step behind her.

Farrendel and Essie followed out the double doors to the garden, then along the path that led from Buckmore Cottage to the garden of Winstead Palace. From the garden, they entered the double doors at the end of the family wing and found her family gathering there.

Her family turned as they entered. Edmund strode forward and gave Farrendel a slap on the back that had him stumbling a step. "Looking good, little brother."

That was the moment Essie noticed all three of her brothers were dressed identically to Farrendel in gray breeches, gray waistcoat, black tailcoat, white shirt, and white neckcloth. Granted, it was a standard ballroom clothing, but the fact that they were all matching wasn't a coincidence.

It melted a part of her to know her brothers were willing to work this hard to make sure Farrendel felt included in the family. From the moment they'd decided to accept him as one of their own, they hadn't held back.

Mother and Paige were both dressed in flowing elven dresses made from the fabric Farrendel brought for them with diamond-studded tiaras in their hair.

Whatever political statement the royal family was making tonight about this marriage alliance and what it meant for broader political relations between Escarland and Tarenhiel, they were making it together as a united front.

If she hadn't been all done up for a ball, Essie would've hugged all of them.

This was what she'd wanted from her marriage when she'd agreed to it. A peaceful alliance between their kingdoms. To have gotten it and fallen in love with her elf prince was a dream beyond what she could've imagined.

Averett's mouth tightened into a line, his eyes serious as he glanced between them. "Do you all have your weapons?"

Essie patted her upper calf. Her derringer was strapped to the inside of her leg just below her knee, the only place she could think of where it wouldn't show even while she was dancing while still being somewhat easy to grab without hiking her skirt to her waist. Mother and Paige both patted their calves.

Julien and Edmund nodded, though Essie wasn't sure where they could have hidden guns or knives or whatever weapons they were carrying. Their tight, finely tailored clothes didn't have any more hiding places than her flowing dress did.

"Do you have the extra knives I sent over?" Julien glanced at Farrendel. "I figured a few extra wouldn't hurt. And you did conveniently gift us with a few elven daggers, so we had spares."

"Yes." Farrendel tipped his head in his slight nod, though he didn't give any indication of where he might have hidden the knives.

"Now that we are fashionably on time, let's make our grand entrance." Paige smiled in her practiced, queenly way as she wrapped her hand around Averett's elbow.

Julien escorted Mother, and Edmund looked cat-with-cream happy over holding out his elbow for Jalissa, even if her guard fell into step behind them looking like she was prepared to behead Edmund on the spot if necessary.

Essie took Farrendel's elbow once again, pasting on her practiced smile. "Ready?"

His expression hardened into an impassive mask before his mouth twisted. An attempt to remember to appear friendly. Well, stoically friendly wasn't exactly working.

She kissed his cheek, making his expression soften. There. Now he was ready.

CHAPTER
TWENTY-ONE

E ssie stood at the top of the stairs leading into the ballroom, waiting while each of her family members were announced by a footman with a particularly booming voice.

"Princess Elspeth of Escarland and her husband, Prince Farrendel of Tarenhiel."

Essie gave her regal wave, grateful when Farrendel copied her a moment later. After a single wave, Essie gave Farrendel a subtle nudge, and they descended the stairs together.

In the ballroom, people were mingling and chatting, sipping from glasses of the punch and champagne and nibbling on the selection of appetizers to tide them over until the formal banquet.

This would be one of the hardest parts of the night. Small talk wasn't Farrendel's favorite thing to do, and they desperately needed him to make a good impression tonight.

"Princess Elspeth!" One of the young ladies around

Essie's age hurried toward Essie with a gaggle of other young ladies trailing behind her.

Essie stifled her groan behind her perfect princess smile. Lady Fristly. She was nice enough, when on her own. But at court functions, she tended to cling to Essie and pretend she was Essie's best friend.

Next to her, Farrendel had dropped his attempt at friendliness and had gone fully hard and stoic.

"We missed you so terribly when you left. You were so brave, marrying an elf you'd never met. I would never be able to do something so brave." Lady Fristly's brow puckered. "I feel so sorry for you, Princess Elspeth. It must be so terrible to have to be in a loveless marriage to someone who can't understand you, for a political alliance. I am here for you if you ever need to talk."

Essie wasn't sure what to correct first. There was so much wrong with that statement. "It isn't like that, Lady Fristly. Farrendel..." Essie trailed off. What should she say?

Farrendel caught her gaze, and his expression softened with the hint of a smile. "I do not think you should bother explaining." He spoke in elvish, and his smile took on a mischievous tilt. "I think this will work better."

He tugged her closer and pressed a kiss to Essie's temple, causing a peal of giggles from Lady Fristly and her gaggle of ladies.

Lady Fristly glanced at Farrendel and batted her eyes. Full on batted her eyes and gave a small giggle. "Oh, I see. The rumors are wrong. He's so handsome." She dragged out the last two words, adding a few more eyelash bats.

Essie wrapped both hands around Farrendel's arm, tilting her left hand so that her ring was clearly visible.

Just to make sure Lady Fristly got the hint that Farrendel was taken. Very, very taken. "Thank you for your best wishes on my marriage. Please excuse us. I need to introduce Farrendel to a few more members of the court."

"Oh, of course." Lady Fristly dissolved into more giggling and batting her eyes. It was so overdone that it was just to get attention.

It made Essie almost feel sorry for Lady Fristly. It must be a hard life to feel like a person needed to pretend to be empty-headed to be noticed.

As Essie tugged Farrendel away, she would've bumped into someone if Farrendel hadn't halted her in time.

The offended harrumph told her the person's identity before she looked up. Charles Hadley stood with his arms crossed.

Farrendel tensed, shifting to place his shoulder partially in front of Essie.

Behind him, Essie clenched her fists, resisting the urge to reach for her derringer. They weren't supposed to let Charles Hadley know they suspected him, yet her skin crawled being so close when he could be plotting to kill Farrendel that night.

Mr. Hadley glared at Farrendel and muttered something under his breath about pointed ears and a few other words not fit for polite society.

Next to him, his son Mark nudged him. "Please, Father. Be polite." Turning, Mark grinned and held out a hand to Farrendel. "Nice to meet you again."

Farrendel solemnly shook his hand. After all the practice he'd had during his visit to Escarland, he managed not to flinch.

Essie held out her hand for Mark to bow over. "I hope

you have a pleasant evening tonight. You as well, Mr. Hadley."

Mr. Hadley's scowl remained in place. "Awful waste of resources, to celebrate an elf like this."

Essie gritted her teeth and somehow managed to keep her smile in place. She didn't know how to reply to that.

Mark shook his head. "Father. Please don't be rude. This is a celebration of our princess, regardless of the man she married."

"Hmph." Mr. Hadley snorted again.

As Essie made polite excuses and pulled Farrendel away again, she let out a breath. "That was close. I fear this is how the rest of the night is going to go."

Farrendel nodded and said in elvish, "My family rarely hosts the full elven court, but when they do, I fear our reception would be much like this. Worse, probably. I am liked by the elven court only marginally better than you would be."

He said it in a matter-of-fact tone. As if it was merely expected that a prince of the elves would find himself nearly a pariah in his own court. Never mind that he had been acknowledged and made an official part of the family.

It seemed that stuffy, judgmental courtiers weren't only to be found in human circles. For all the elves' claims to perfection, their imperfections of heart and soul were there as much as in any human. They just attempted to hide it better.

Essie directed Farrendel through the crowd, making sure they paused to chat with the key Parliamentary members and their wives. As expected, some did their best to pretend Farrendel wasn't standing right there. Some were genuinely trying to be nice, though their attempts failed when they either assumed Farrendel couldn't understand Escarlish or that he would speak a broken version of it and addressed him in baby talk or spoke extra slowly and loudly. Others simply avoided speaking to Essie and Farrendel altogether.

The best were the few who had estates in the north yet not right on the border. They had more knowledge of the elves but also hadn't suffered the privations and raids that the estates closest to the border had experienced.

As the time for dinner neared, Essie eased herself and Farrendel into a group of several Parliament members and their wives, including Lord Kranshaw and Lord Bletchly.

Lord Kranshaw turned away from Farrendel, his lip curling. But Lord Bletchly held out his hand. "It is a pleasure to meet you again, Prince Farrendel. I trust your stay in Escarland has been pleasant."

Farrendel's stiff shoulders were hardly noticeable beneath his tailcoat as he shook Lord Bletchly's hand. Farrendel must be getting used to all the handshaking. This time, he even managed a hint of a forced smile. "It has been."

"It must have been quite the shock, visiting our bustling, modern city after growing up in the barbaric wilds of Tarenhiel." Lady Kranshaw's smile was sickly sweet, like a poisonous flower whose lovely scent did nothing to disguise its deadliness.

Essie tightened her grip on Farrendel's arm, keeping her smile in place by force of habit. "It was a shock returning here after enjoying the elven sophistication in Estyra."

A tinkling bell rang, signaling the beginning of dinner. Essie swallowed back her sigh of relief. The past half hour of conversations had been one long, tortuous event. She wouldn't blame Farrendel if he made a run for it partway through the evening.

In the formal dining room, they located their seats. Thankfully, the seating was arranged by precedence, so while they had a few of the Parliamentary lords and ladies seated near them, her family and Jalissa were also sitting close enough to talk.

Their presence relaxed Farrendel's shoulders as well. He and Jalissa shared a look that seemed to commiserate over the agony of the evening so far.

Essie slipped into the seat to Farrendel's right, putting herself between him and Lord Fiskre. While Lord Fiskre was one of the nicer lords, a grandfatherly figure with white hair and smile wrinkles etched into his skin, Farrendel would probably appreciate sitting next to Edmund instead.

"Princess Elspeth, congratulations on your marriage." Lord Fiskre nodded to her as the salad course was placed in front of them by the serving staff. "It is nice to see elves and humans sitting at a table together once again. My grandfather used to tell stories about the time when he was a boy and elves and humans didn't have the animosity they have now."

"Thank you for your congratulations. Not everyone has been so supportive." Essie felt the first genuine smile since arriving at this ball.

"I, for one, find it refreshing." Lord Fiskre grinned. "Keeps both Escarland and Tarenhiel from getting too stuffy and stodgy, if you ask me."

Essie felt her own grin tug at her mouth. Lord Fiskre must have been a real adventurer in his day. His eyes still had that fire in them.

Next to him, Lady Fiskre patted his hand. "We wish you every happiness, princess."

Essie tapped Farrendel's arm. When he turned to her, she introduced him to Lord and Lady Fiskre. All four of them were soon chatting, drawing in Jalissa from across the table. The conversation remained interesting all through the soup and meat course.

As the serving staff placed the cheesecake desert in front of them, Averett stood and clinked his fork against his glass to gain everyone's attention. When the various conversations around the table fell silent, Averett faced Farrendel and Essie. "I would like to raise a toast to my sister Princess Elspeth and her husband Prince Farrendel. Yours was a marriage made to secure peace, but together you have built so much more. I am pleased to welcome you to the family, Prince Farrendel." Averett raised his glass. "To Prince Farrendel and Princess Elspeth and lasting peace between Escarland and Tarenhiel."

"Hear, hear!" Julien and Edmund raised their glasses.

Down the table, several of the Parliament members raised their glasses, joining in the cheer. Others raised their glasses, but less enthusiastically, as if they didn't want to let their king know they weren't happy about this. Still others crossed their arms, very purposefully boycotting their king's toast.

She hadn't expected everyone to be happy. At least a slim majority were cheering, if reluctantly.

The ringing ping of forks tapping glasses started in scattered places around the long tables. Beside her, Lord Fiskre picked up his fork and began tapping it against his glass.

As the noise swelled, Farrendel shifted, his shoulders tensing. Jalissa's gaze flicked back and forth, her fingers flexing on her fork as if she was debating the consequences of joining in when she didn't know what was happening.

Essie hadn't thought to prepare Farrendel for this. It hadn't occurred to her that this tradition would be put in place. This was something that happened when people were enthusiastic about a marriage.

"What is this?" Farrendel leaned close, whispering in elvish.

"A human marriage tradition." Essie also spoke in elvish, keeping her voice low. "When glasses are clinked like this, the newlyweds are expected to kiss."

Farrendel's eyes widened. "Right here? In front of everyone?"

"Yes, I'm afraid. That's how the tradition goes. Sorry, a quick little peck doesn't work. It needs to be a real kiss. Anything less will make everyone think you see me as just a duty." Essie slid her fingers through Farrendel's and stood.

Farrendel slowly glided to his feet as well, his shoulders tensed.

Essie rested a hand on his chest. "Smile. Try to look like you want to kiss me."

Farrendel cupped her cheek and eased closer. His kiss was gentle, light. Still toe curling, even in its sweetness.

When it had lingered just long enough, Essie pressed on Farrendel's chest. Just subtle enough that everyone watching wouldn't notice, but Farrendel would feel it.

He pulled back, but just far enough to press a kiss to her temple. "Did I do that right?" he murmured in elvish.

"Exactly right." Essie smiled up at him.

"I don't think anyone will doubt the two of you are disgustingly in love." Edmund managed to keep his gagging expression hidden behind his hand so that only Essie and Farrendel could see it.

Essie returned to her seat. "Admit it. You helped start the glass clinking."

Edmund smirked and polished off the last bite of his cheesecake.

The warmth filling her remained all through the rest of the desert and the official ceremony in the ballroom where Averett conferred titles onto both Farrendel and Essie. It was a ceremony that would have been done at the ball after the wedding, if they'd had a celebration ball then. Farrendel's title of prince was officially recognized. He was also made a Knight of the Royal Order of the Maple, a distinction all princes of Escarland had. Farrendel had been especially wary of the whole kneel and let Averett tap his shoulders with a sword thing, but he bore the ceremony without flinching when the time came.

Finally, both he and Essie got a whole list of titles from Duke and Duchess on down, complete with an estate along the northern border between Escarland and Tarenhiel. While the estate's main house was a crumbling, old stone castle, it had a smaller manor house constructed of wood that would be much more habitable for her and Farrendel, should they wish to stay there.

After all their worry, the ceremony concluded without any attempts by Mr. Charles Hadley or his cronies to hurt Farrendel or even protest his newly awarded titles. Perhaps he'd thought better of acting against a member of the royal family, even one by marriage, within Winstead Palace.

By the time the evening transitioned to dancing, Essie could tell Farrendel was just about done. Even her brothers' jokes weren't drawing much of a smile out of him, and he kept looking longingly toward the doors to the garden.

"You don't look that happy to be dancing with me." Essie leaned in close as Farrendel swept her through the simple steps of the first dance, a traditional Escarlish waltz. She had practiced the steps with him that morning, but he didn't seem to enjoy dancing, for all its emphasis on footwork and timing. It probably had something to do with feeling like he was on display and vulnerable. "Is it the dancing or the people?"

"Both." A hint of a smile tugged at his mouth, only to die a moment later.

"Let's finish this dance, then slip out of here and head back for the Cottage." This party might be for them, but they didn't have to linger. They were the newlyweds after all. Sneaking out of a ball early was somewhat expected.

Between the two of them, she and Farrendel eased their way through the crowd so that they were near the doors to the rest of the palace when the dance ended. Thankfully, Mother was holding court nearby. Essie caught her eye.

When Mother bowed out of her conversation and walked over, Essie gave her a short hug. "Farrendel and I are sneaking out early."

Mother glanced from her to Farrendel. "Will you have breakfast with the family before you leave for Tarenhiel?"

Farrendel nodded. "Yes."

It said a lot about the bond he'd built with her family that he agreed so readily. He probably would eat a first breakfast right away when he got up, then another one with the family later, but it was the thought that counted.

"We'll see both of you there." Mother stepped

forward, as if she wanted to give Farrendel a hug but couldn't with all the onlookers.

"Thank you." Essie smiled, took Farrendel's arm, and headed for the doors.

As soon as they stepped clear of the ballroom and turned the corner toward the family wing, she slid her fingers down Farrendel's arm until she held his hand as she'd longed to do all night. "Sorry this was such a long night."

"It was..." He trailed off, as if he couldn't figure out a nice way to say it.

"Excruciating?"

That brought a smile to his face. "Yes."

Essie leaned closer to him as they strolled across the green velvet rug covering this hallway. Various landscape paintings filled the walls. At this time of the night with the ball keeping everyone busy behind them, it was completely deserted, even of servants, leaving Essie free to relax and hold Farrendel's hand without worrying about anyone seeing.

This was their last night together before he left for war. A night to linger and savor their time together. Essie wasn't exactly sure how to go about telling Farrendel that she didn't want to have regrets tonight. That if, tonight, their kissing led to more...

"Princess Elspeth! Prince Farrendel!"

Essie halted and turned. Lord Bletchly was hurrying down the hallway toward them. "Yes, Lord Bletchly? Did you need something?"

"I saw you leaving and just wanted to give my congratulations once again on your marriage." Lord Bletchly turned to Farrendel and held out his hand. "It was a pleasure to meet you, Prince Farrendel. I look forward to the growing peace between our kingdoms."

Farrendel drew in a deep breath, probably bracing himself for yet one more handshake after he'd thought himself done with those for the evening. He gripped Lord Bletchly's hand, the tight sleeve of his tailcoat riding up his arm to expose his wrist.

Lord Bletchly swung his other hand up and clapped something around Farrendel's wrist. At the same moment, a door clicked open behind Essie, footsteps scuffing across stone.

Farrendel yanked his hand free, his other hand sparking with a weak blue fire.

"I wouldn't do that, if I were you." Lord Bletchly's genial tone turned hard, cold.

Something cold and round dug into the small of Essie's back. She opened her mouth to cry out, but a rag clapped over both her mouth and nose, smelling of something chemical and sickly sweet. She was yanked backwards, the back of her head pressing into a stranger's chest.

She scrambled, off balance, trying to get purchase for her feet so that she could stomp on her attacker's foot or kick him up higher. She couldn't reach her derringer, not without the men noticing.

Yet she needed to get free. To scream. To help Farrendel. To fight.

She couldn't seem to find her balance, and only her attacker pressing her head against his chest kept her from sliding to the floor. The sickly-sweet stench coated her tongue, filling her throat. She couldn't draw a decent breath past the press of his hand over her nose and mouth. Her muscles felt weak. Shaky. What was wrong with her?

Farrendel glanced from Essie and the person behind her to Lord Bletchly. His magic remained nothing but a faint swirl around his left hand.

"I was assured your power would be weak inside the stones of the castle, and that shackle should impede most of your magic. There's nothing you can do, not without risking her." Lord Bletchly stood all too sure of himself, as if he wasn't only feet from Farrendel's deadly, crackling magic.

Except that Farrendel's magic didn't hold the power it normally did. Lord Bletchly was right. There was a chance Essie was immune to Farrendel's magic. But that was a chance Farrendel wouldn't take. With the gunman standing directly behind her with a gun to her back, her body provided a shield.

Essie opened her mouth to scream. To tell him not to stand down. But all that filled her mouth, her lungs, was the chemical stench. A light-headed buzzing rang in her ears. She couldn't gather her feet beneath her. The hands she lifted, trying to claw the man holding her, scrabbled weakly at his shirt. She couldn't seem to raise her arms high enough.

Farrendel's shoulders slumped. His magic winked out.

No. Essie tried to scream into the man's hand. *No. Don't. Fight.*

Nothing but a whisper squeaked out.

Lord Bletchly forced Farrendel onto his knees, shackling Farrendel's hands behind his back. There was something about the shackles. They didn't glint like iron, and

247

when it clamped around his wrist, blood dripped, as if the shackle had sliced him.

Farrendel didn't resist as Lord Bletchly pressed a rag over his mouth and nose. He met and held Essie's gaze.

Essie blinked, trying to keep her eyes open. Heaviness filled her arms, her legs.

She was being dragged through a doorway. Lord Bletchly hauled Farrendel after her, keeping the rag over his face. The lord patted Farrendel down, removing knives from each of Farrendel's boots.

She was on the floor, blinking up at the man standing over her. Light brown hair, a slim face.

Mark Hadley. There was something significant about the fact that he was standing there. But she couldn't...quite...

Sleepy...dizzy...blackness...

TWENTY-TWO

H er head pounded. Essie groaned and tried to find a more comfortable position on her pillow.

Except that her head wasn't resting on her pillow. It was thunking against something hard in time with a clatter that almost sounded like...

Train wheels.

Essie blinked and pushed herself onto her elbows. Her head spun at the movement, her stomach lurching. She barely swallowed back the bile in time to keep from hurling the contents of her stomach onto the freight car's wooden floor. Still, the bile provided some relief in her far too dry mouth.

The train boxcar clattered again as its wheels rattled from one section of rail to the next, thumping her body up and down on the floor. Wind whistled through the cracks in the slatted wall, shivering against her skin.

She still wore her green silk dress, gloves up to her elbows, and dancing slippers on her feet. Patting her leg, she located the derringer still strapped to her calf. They must not have searched her thoroughly, not expecting a princess would be carrying a weapon.

Drawing in a deep breath to try to calm her nauseous stomach and hammering head, she pushed all the way to a sitting position and, slowly so as not to cause another wave of dizziness, studied her surroundings.

In front of her, the train car was dark and empty. Not even a pebble or a spare crate that could be turned into a weapon if her derringer's one shot wasn't enough. At least her hands were free. Maybe she could pry a loose board from the floor or the slats. Not that any piece of wood rotted enough to break off would be much use as a weapon, but it would be a distraction if thrown at someone's face.

A muffled groan came from behind her. She eased around as fast as she could in the shaking train with her head swirling and aching.

Farrendel lay curled on his side on the train floor, his back to her. Blood puddled on the wooden floor beneath his shackled wrists.

"Farrendel!" Essie crawled across the train car until she reached his side. She rested a hand on his shoulder. "Are you all right? Are you awake?"

He gave another small groan, curling and uncurling before he blinked up at her. "Help me up."

With his hands shackled behind his back, he couldn't push upright by himself. She heaved him upright and helped him shift back until he leaned against the wall of the train car.

She reached for his hands. "Let's see about those shackles."

"No, do not touch." Farrendel shifted to keep his

bound hands away from her. "These are not iron shackles. They are stone and ice, made by the trolls. I do not know what they might do to you."

Essie held up her hand. "I'm wearing gloves. And I'll be careful. Just let me see. You're bleeding."

He leaned forward, and she peered around his shoulder. The shackles clamped around his wrists, but the inside of each manacle was spiked, almost like the stone had claws digging into Farrendel's skin.

She couldn't get those shackles off. They were embedding themselves into his skin, just like he'd described the trolls doing to hold him captive fifteen years ago.

She sat back on her heels and tugged on Farrendel's neckcloth. "I can use this to try to stop the bleeding, at least. And free you from one constricting item, even if it isn't the shackles."

Tugging the neckcloth free, she tried to rip it. But fabric didn't simply tear when someone yanked hard enough.

"I still have a knife strapped to my back that they did not find." Farrendel leaned forward.

"Really? That will be helpful." Essie blinked at him a moment before realizing she would have to be the one to draw it. She blamed her still aching head. "Um, right."

Now to try not to make this more awkward than it already was. She wormed her hand beneath the collar of his tailcoat, then beneath his shirt. The tips of her fingers brushed the top of the knife, but she couldn't quite get her arm far enough down the back of his shirt with his tailcoat as tailored around his shoulders as it was.

He was doing a good job of hiding it, but his wince meant this was probably uncomfortable for him as well. His collar must be choking him.

"All right, new plan." Essie worked her hand free. "Let's get that tailcoat off. Actually, it will work even better than the neckcloth for stopping the bleeding since we can wad it up around the shackles."

"Do not worry about my wrists. The knife is most important." Farrendel flexed his shoulders, as if he could shrug the tailcoat free by himself.

It took her tugging and Farrendel wiggling to peel the tailcoat from his shoulders and down his arms. With her hands still gloved, Essie tucked the tailcoat around his wrists, wincing every time he flinched. She tried not to think about his blood soaking through her gloves to squish against her fingers. She refused to let panic lodge in her chest at the fact he was shackled with manacles laced with troll magic.

When she finished tucking the tailcoat into the manacles and around his wounds as much as possible, she peeled her gloves off her trembling fingers. She forced a smile to her face as she untied the ribbon binding his hair, then undid the first few buttons of his shirt. "Well, this night isn't as romantic as I thought it would be."

She'd hoped to earn at least a flicker of a smile from him. But all she got was his hard expression. His warrior focus.

This time when she wormed her hand underneath his shirt, she tried not to think too much about her now gloveless fingers brushing his warm skin. This wasn't the time for romantic thoughts. They were on a train captured by the Escarlish traitors. They needed his knife.

Her fingers located the knife's hilt, then followed it down to what felt like plaster bandages rather than a traditional sheath. No wonder the traitors hadn't found it. Farrendel had plastered it in place with bandages, making the knife lie flat beneath his fitted tailcoat rather than a sheath, leather straps, and buckles that would have caused telltale lumps beneath his clothes.

This was Farrendel's last ditch knife. It wouldn't have been easy for him to draw, even without his hands shackled behind his back. This was for when things went terribly wrong.

With a yank, Essie peeled the bandages and the knife from Farrendel's back, earning her a wince. At least it was some expression. His hard stillness settled like a weight in her stomach. He only became Laesornysh when things were dire.

Withdrawing her hand, she peeled the bandages from the knife. "I can use these bandages on your wrists, if the tailcoat isn't working as well as I hoped. Then we can use the knife to try to open the train car's door. It's probably a simple latch. We should be able to get it open. The train will have to stop sooner or later for coal and water, so we can jump out and make our escape then."

"Essie."

"I still have my gun, and you'll have the knife, though hopefully we shouldn't have to fight our way out if we're quick. And then we'll see if we can find a horse or a wagon or something. We're bound to be near a town."

"Essie."

"Unless Lord Bletchly had this train track specially built without putting it on the official maps of the train routes across the kingdom. Or maybe it was Mark Hadley. Do you think Mark is working with his father or is his father ignorant of what his son has been doing? I guess we'll have to find out after we escape. It shouldn't be that much longer until we stop. Trains—"

"Essie." Farrendel's voice rang harder, sharper than she'd ever heard him use with her.

She snapped her mouth shut. When she glanced down, she spotted her fingers, white knuckled and shaking, gripping the knife. Her breathing was coming far too fast, and the echoes from her voice was ringing too high-pitched.

Farrendel's face softened. "Essie, I need you to listen."

She drew in a ragged breath and sat facing Farrendel. "Sorry. All right, I'm listening."

"This train is not going to stop. Not until we reach the border." Farrendel leaned his head against the slatted wall. "It is powered by a magical device. I can feel it."

That meant they couldn't escape when the train stopped for coal and water. Essie had known the Hadley trains ran only on magical devices. Averett had mentioned it only the night before. "We can still pry the door open and jump—"

"Not at this speed. The fall would most likely kill us." His tone said it was something he'd already examined and ruled out as a possibility.

Essie let out another long, slow breath. He didn't need her to come up with ideas. He'd already sorted through all possible actions and settled on a plan. This was, after all, what he'd trained for as Laesornysh. Right now, all he needed from her was to listen. She crawled closer to him and rested her hand on his knee. "What's the plan?"

"They think these shackles will be enough to stop my magic. They were enough, fifteen years ago, and within the stones of Winstead Palace. But not now. When we stop, I will have enough magic to fight back."

"That's wonderful. Then we can—"

"Essie…" He dragged her name out. His expression

didn't look like this was a wonderful revelation. If anything, his tight mouth had turned grim.

"Right. Sorry. Listening." Essie squeezed her hands together.

"I will only have enough magic for one diversion. It will leave me weak." He drew in a deep breath, holding her gaze. "That is why, when I cause the diversion, you will escape."

"But you'll be coming too, right? We'll meet up later or...or..." She read the truth in his eyes, the taut line of his mouth. "I'm not leaving you behind."

"We know who the Escarlish traitors are. When this train stops at the border, we may find out whom the Tarenhieli traitor is. That information is vital to both of our kingdoms. You must escape, no matter what. You cannot risk being recaptured, not even on the chance to save me." Farrendel's gaze drilled into her. "Promise me you will escape. Our brothers need to be told, and you are the only one who can tell them."

She swallowed back her protest, forcing herself to think. He was not simply sending her away, like one of her brothers would have, because she was the helpless female who had to be protected.

His protectiveness played a role, but it wasn't only that. He was trusting her to be an important part of his plan. It made the most logical sense that he, with his magic, would be the diversion and hold off their attackers. Therefore, the duty to escape with the crucial information fell to her.

He was trusting her to be his fellow warrior in this. To do what needed to be done for the good of both their kingdoms. If she failed to escape, then his sacrifice would be meaningless.

His sacrifice...something inside Essie shook, but she forced it down. "I promise. I'll escape and give this information to our brothers."

They would have to act on this side of the border. If she escaped on the Tarenhieli side, the elven towns were much more scattered. She would have farther to go to fetch help, and the elves might not recognize her or help her right away.

At the Escarlish border, she wouldn't be far from an army outpost, even if it was only a watchtower with a few soldiers stationed there. It would still have a telegraph and fast horses to make sure those stationed there could give warning of an attack. They would recognize their princess and give aid without question.

"I'll come back for you. In may take a few hours, but I'll get help at the nearest outpost. I'll just need you to hang on until then." She let that thought send strength into her legs, her fingers. She wouldn't abandon Farrendel for long. Surely he would have enough magic to hold off Lord Bletchly, Mark Hadley, the elven traitor, and whomever else was waiting at the border.

"Essie." For the first time since they'd started this conversation, Farrendel's gaze dropped from hers to focus on the floor of the train car. "I do not intend to let them take me alive again."

For a moment, she could just blink at him. Surely, he didn't mean...he couldn't intend to...

But he still wasn't looking at her, his shoulders tense.

She gripped the front of his shirt, kneeling so close her knees pressed into his leg. "No, Farrendel. No. If you're captured, we'll rescue you. I'll rally both our brothers, and—"

"No." His gaze whipped up to hers so fast, she had to

catch her breath at the intensity. His silver-blue eyes glinted. "No. Do not let them try to rescue me. My father died last time. I could not live knowing my rescue cost your brothers or my brother their lives."

"But..."

"You said it was my father's choice last time. Please, Essie. This time, let the sacrifice be my choice. Please." His gaze fell to the train car's floor. "I cannot face that torture again, and I cannot let my brother die to rescue me."

Everything in her ached to argue. To beg him to surrender rather than fight to the death.

But could she ask him to surrender, knowing the agony he'd face? Could she ask him to face torture again for her? Who would demand such suffering from another person?

This was goodbye. Not just while he went off to war. But forever.

"Farrendel..." She tightened her grip on his shirt, then leaned forward and kissed him.

This kiss was tears and desperation. Her hands in his hair. The heat swirling between them. Kissing his mouth, cheek, neck, back to his mouth until she was breathless. From kissing or from swallowing back her sobs, she didn't know.

When she finally pulled back, it was only to see his eyes. "Please promise me this. That you'll try to live for me. If there's a chance you can escape after I'm long gone or you can hold out until I come back with reinforcements, then please try. And if they do capture you, then please survive. I will come for you."

"No, Essie..."

She cut him off with a quick kiss. "I know you want

to be the one to sacrifice this time. That it will kill you if me or my brothers or your brother died to save you. I get it. I'll do my best to make sure that doesn't happen. But I know my brothers. And I think I know yours. If you're captured, they won't rest until they rescue you, no matter what I say. So please promise me you'll fight with every breath in your body to get back to me."

As her hands were still in his hair, she felt more than saw his nod.

That took some of the frantic energy from her fingers. She rested her head against his shoulder, snuggling into him as best she could with his hands bound behind his back. "This won't be like last time, you know. The trolls will plan a trap knowing how your brother will try to rescue you. But they won't know how to anticipate my brothers. They are about to find out just how big a mistake they made in having us snatched from Winstead Palace's grounds." She curled one hand into his shirt while she reached behind him and clasped his cold fingers with the other. "I wonder why they did it. It is sure to bring Escarland into the war, and that can't be their plan."

"They want to incite a war between Tarenhiel and Escarland again." Farrendel rested his cheek against her hair. "My brother will be furious that I was captured while under your brother's protection. And if your body were to turn up abandoned in some ditch in Tarenhiel, your brother would blame mine."

Another reason Essie needed to escape. She wasn't about to let her corpse be used as a catalyst for a war. "We won't let that happen. If I can get proof that the trolls executed an operation like this on Escarlish soil, it will be an act of war. Parliament won't stand in Averett's way any longer."

"I do not know what we will find at the border, but I would surmise the trolls will have sent some of their soldiers. If they intend to take me alive back to Kostaria, they will need to provide the elven traitor with help to cross Tarenhiel." His voice vibrated in his chest beneath her ear. A strangely soothing sound, for all that they were talking about war and death and forever goodbyes.

"Then I will do my best to snatch something to act as proof, if I can do it without risking my life or my escape." Essie stifled a yawn. Her headache was going away, fading against the warmth of Farrendel's chest as the train continued to clatter rhythmically onward.

"You should rest. You will need to be alert when we arrive at the border."

"I don't want to sleep away our time together. Not if…" She couldn't finish. A tear coursed wet and scalding down her cheek and onto her chin. But she wasn't sure she could just sit here either, knowing each clack of the wheels took her closer to having Farrendel ripped from her. "I don't think I can do this. I don't want you to die."

The last word was a sob. She didn't want to be weak. She didn't want to fall apart into tears.

But she loved Farrendel and he was probably going to die and if that wasn't a good enough reason to take a few minutes to cry, then she didn't know what was.

He held still as she sobbed, his cheek against her hair, his fingers squeezing hers.

As she sniffled and hiccupped her way to silence, Farrendel pressed a kiss into her hair. "Please, no matter what happens, do not stop smiling. I could not bear it if you became broken. Not because of me."

Broken like he was. He didn't say it out loud, but that's what he meant.

Right now, she didn't know if she could promise that. She'd always thought she could smile through anything. That she didn't have to face life crying.

She couldn't smile about this. If he died, would she ever manage to smile again?

When she'd married him, she'd told herself her happiness didn't depend on him.

But it did. Oh, how it did. Love was painful like that.

She had to tell him something. "I'll try."

"I know." He kissed her hair again. "These past few months have been the best of my life."

It would've been sweet. Romantic. If he wasn't saying it because he thought he would die when this train got to where it was going.

Though, perhaps that made it all the sweeter.

"They were pretty amazing." Essie snuggled closer, tracing the end of a scar visible at the collar of Farrendel's shirt. "But far too short."

"If I had known, I would have skipped the months our brothers spent negotiating that meeting and offered to marry you right away."

That brought a smile. A small laugh, even. Not something she'd thought she'd manage right then. Making him laugh was her job. She hadn't expected he'd do it for her. Was it possible to love him more because of it?

She needed to follow his example. Did she want to spend her last moments with him crying? She could gift him this. Laughter. Smiles. Tears could come later.

She forced a lightness to her tone, a contrast to the weight in her chest. "It wouldn't have done you any good. I probably would have refused, suspicious why the youngest elf prince had suddenly decided he wanted to marry me. The whole arranged marriage thing only sounds like a good idea if it's my idea."

That earned her a rumbling, almost like a chuckle, inside his chest.

She curled tighter against him. In her flat dancing slippers, her toes were growing cold. Her fingers too. A silk dress would not have been her first choice of outfits to be kidnapped in.

"I would offer you my coat, but it is stuck." Farrendel rested his head on hers. "Is there a story of your childhood you have not told me yet?"

Essie had to think a few minutes before she thought of one.

They spent hours like that. Telling stories and chatting. Mostly about little things. Her favorite flower. His favorite spot in Estyra to watch the sunrise.

She must have dozed off at some point. She woke when the boxcar shuddered while the brakes squealed. She rubbed at her face and forced herself to sit up, away from Farrendel's warmth. "We're stopping."

"Yes." Farrendel's voice was steady. "We need to prepare."

Essie tucked the bandages around the shackles, both to continue to halt the bleeding and hide the bandages from sight. Once done, she handed Farrendel his knife, which he gripped in a fist beneath the tailcoat.

For her part, she tied back her hair using the ribbon that had been in Farrendel's hair since her hair had fallen from its pins.

Once her hair was out of her face, she pulled the train of her dress between her legs, then tied it around her waist, turning her dress into trousers. Very floppy trousers that bunched at her knees and exposed her ankles, but at this point, she didn't care. Hopefully Lord Bletchly and Mark Hadley would just assume she wanted to keep her long dress off the ground and not that she was preparing to escape.

Since having her dress hiked to her knees showed off her derringer strapped to her calf, she removed the holster and secured the derringer beneath where her dress was tied around her waist. It would be easier to draw from there anyway.

Beneath them, the boxcar shuddered again, this time accompanied by a louder squeal of brakes and the grind of metal on metal.

So little time.

Essie staggered back to Farrendel's side and curled against him, ignoring the cold of the wooden floor against her legs and the prickle of splinters against her knees. She rested her hands on his chest, but she didn't know what to say. She didn't want to say goodbye. That would be giving up hope too soon.

There was still a chance. A chance Farrendel could fight long enough for her to fetch help. A chance he'd be captured, and they could rescue him. A chance he could defeat all his enemies and escape.

All chances she clung to with every beat of her heart.

She gripped the front of his shirt. "I love you, Farrendel. Don't forget that."

"Essie, shynafir." Her elven title *fierce heart* turned into an endearment. Farrendel kissed her, long and slow, a lingering farewell. He moved his kiss from her mouth to her cheek, then whispered in her ear, "You, my love, are fierce enough to survive this."

She would've said something. Kissed him again. Burst into tears.

But with a squeak and the clatter of the rolling door, cool air blasted inside.

She spun to face the door but didn't release Farrendel's shirt. Couldn't force her fingers to let him go.

Lord Bletchly and Mark Hadley stood there with two men dressed in workers' garb, dull brown shirt and sturdy trousers.

Lord Bletchly's mouth curled. "I was feeling sorry I had to sacrifice you, princess. But it's clear you've actually fallen in love with the elf."

He spat out *elf* with the same venom someone might say *beast* or *monster*.

How had he managed to fool them so completely? He'd seemed supportive of the new treaty with the elves. He'd been pleasant to both her and Farrendel at Winstead Palace.

All just to get close enough to betray them.

Essie lifted her chin and stared right back. She wasn't going to dignify that comment with a response.

The two workers leveled muskets at Essie and Farrendel. Mark motioned. "Get down from there, unless you want us to drag you out."

There was no point to resisting. They needed to bide their time until the right moment, and Essie trusted Farrendel to judge when that moment would be.

She climbed to her feet and gripped Farrendel's elbow, steadying him as he staggered upright.

Was that stagger real or feigned? Even Essie wasn't entirely sure, and she knew how graceful Farrendel was normally. He could balance on a four-inch-wide branch without wobbling. Surely having his hands bound behind his back wouldn't affect him that much.

Except that the shackles contained troll magic.

At the door, she hopped out, falling to her knees as she landed. None of the men standing around her reached a hand to help.

Farrendel prepared to jump, but Mark grabbed his arm and yanked, sending Farrendel tumbling from the boxcar.

Farrendel landed on his shoulder, rolled, then lay on the ground as if stunned.

Essie scrambled to reach his side, but hands gripped her arms, holding her back. She wrenched, trying to break free, but they were too strong.

Farrendel's gaze met hers, and he tipped his head in a nod so slight no one would notice if they hadn't spent months living with the elves learning to look for such subtle expressions.

He was fine. Not as stunned and helpless as he appeared to be.

These men would expect her to be terrified. Hysterical. Helpless.

That's exactly what she would give them. Right up until the moment she drew her derringer.

"Unhand me." It didn't take too much effort to add a screeching sob to her voice. "I am your princess. My brother will hear about this."

"Oh, he will. When your murdered body is found across the border in Tarenhiel, the public outcry against the elves will be all he'll hear." Mark sent a sneer her way as he kicked Farrendel in the ribs before yanking him to his feet.

With one of the armed men leading the way, Mark and

the other workman shoved Farrendel in front of them. That left only Lord Bletchly guarding her. He gripped her arm, hard enough her muscles ground against her bones. "Come along, Your Highness."

Even though she was trying to appear helpless and weak, Essie swallowed back the gasp of pain. She didn't want Farrendel to feel like he had to act sooner than he should on her account.

Instead, as Lord Bletchly marched her past the engine house where the train was currently being turned around, she did what she did best.

Talk.

"Why are you doing this? What do you have to gain?" Essie tried to remember everything she knew about Lord Bletchly. "You had a son who died fighting the elves, didn't you? Please don't tell me you betrayed your country merely out of revenge."

Lord Bletchly snorted as they strode past a large, wooden warehouse. "Revenge is just the topping on the cake. You see, I have invested in many companies, especially weapons manufacturers. War is profitable. Even the threat of war is very profitable."

"But the new treaty with the elves would cut into their profits and thus your dividends." Essie nodded toward Mark ahead, using the motion to peer into a doorway to the warehouse as they passed. Boxes were stacked along the wall, marked with the army's symbol.

Weapons then. A warehouse filled with weapons all waiting to be shipped to the trolls.

Essie snapped her gaze away before Lord Bletchly would notice her looking. "I suppose that's why Mark is in on this. As the army's main supplier, his company has the most to lose. Is his father a part of this?"

Mark glanced over his shoulder, scowling. "My father is too patriotic for that. No, he intends to retire, taking all his money with him. Sure, he plans to leave me the company. But not a dime of all the money he's earned over the years. Says it's up to me to keep the business profitable and earn my own money. Well, that's exactly what I'm doing."

Money. Farrendel could end up dead just for money.

Lord Bletchly's grip on her arm squeezed tighter. "Selling to the trolls has helped boost the profit margins, but war will be astronomically more profitable if the company is selling weapons to both Escarland and Kostaria. If the elves that killed my son are wiped out in the process, so much the better."

Essie's stomach churned. Didn't he care about the lives that would be lost? The Escarlish soldiers who could go into a war started for money. The elven warriors fighting just to protect their homeland. "Don't you see how wrong this is? You've turned the army into your own personal money-making machine. It's not supposed to work like that. The army exists to protect the people, and their weapons are manufactured to give them that ability. It is a duty, a heavy burden. Not...not this."

"Are you truly so naïve, princess, that you think the world works like that? The world runs on money, nothing more. Ideals are just wishful thinking."

Maybe they were. But she refused to believe goodness didn't exist. That honor didn't exist. Maybe it wasn't in people's hearts. Maybe people were nothing but greed and evil.

But there was still family. Friendship. Love. They were real. They existed. And they were worth fighting for.

They cleared the end of the warehouse, finally

catching a glimpse of the Hydalla River ahead. A wharf extended into the river, a steamboat puffing smoke tied to it. Figures hauled crates up the gangplank, all but their forms obscured by the steamboat's smoke billowing between them and Essie.

Six figures strolled down the wharf toward Essie, Farrendel, and their captors while others still moved by the boat, loading crates. Four of the figures were trolls, with their white-blue skin and hair cropped short, revealing their slightly tapered ears.

But the two people behind them were willowy, with long hair flowing around their shoulders. Elves. One was a male elf with golden blond hair darker than Farrendel's that Essie vaguely recognized. Had she seen him around Estyra? Wandering the tree branches of Ellonahshinel?

It didn't matter. Not when her gaze snagged on the second elf, with her long black hair blowing in the breeze and her dark eyes focused on Farrendel.

Farrendel went stock still, causing Mark and the other man to crash into his back. His expression twisted, pained, as if he'd been stabbed. "Melantha?"

Farrendel's sister Melantha stared back at him, her mouth twisted in a sneer. Her gaze left Farrendel, as if dismissing him, as she turned to the troll next to her. "Here is Laesornysh, delivered as requested. I will provide you safe passage across Tarenhiel as long as you uphold your end of the bargain."

"Of course. We always honor our promises." The troll next to her dipped a small bow in her direction. He spoke with a thick dialect that shortened the vowels and came down harder on the consonants than the way the elves spoke.

"What bargain?" Essie succeeded in wrenching herself

free of Lord Bletchly's grip and reached Farrendel's side, resting a hand on his arm.

Farrendel was shaking. His gaze remained focused on Melantha. "You are my sister."

That snapped her flashing eyes back to him. "You are not my brother."

Essie felt Farrendel break piece by piece. She glared at Melantha. It would be so satisfying to march over there and yank Melantha's hair right from her scalp.

The four trolls were moving forward, probably to take custody of Farrendel. Or to pay Lord Bletchly and Mark Hadley for their weapons and betrayal. Two more of the trolls, who had been loading the steamboat, strode down the jetty. More reinforcements.

"Why?" Farrendel's voice was low, hoarse. "I have done everything I could to earn my place in the family. What did I do wrong?"

"Nothing," Essie whispered, tightening her grip on his arm. A family's love wasn't earned, and there was something so very wrong that Farrendel felt he'd had to earn his. How had Essie not seen it? She'd caught glimpses, but never put together how deep it ran.

"Father never should have brought you to Estyra. You ruined everything. You destroyed Father's reign and legacy. You soiled our family." Melantha's voice shook, her eyes glassy as if she were close to tears.

"I am sorry." Farrendel stated it quietly, as if he truly thought he was to blame.

"Farrendel couldn't help being born. None of the blame rests on him." Essie glared at the approaching trolls, the crowding Escarlish thugs. Couldn't they see this needed to be talked out?

"Just when I thought things were getting better, you

went and married a human. As if you needed to remind everyone just how flawed you are. Look at you. You even dress like one of them." Melantha's mouth curled. "If Jalissa and I are to have any chance of happiness, then I have to get rid of you."

Farrendel hunched, as if every word was a punch. Perhaps a physical beating would have hurt him less.

"By handing him over to the trolls? You know they are just going to overrun Tarenhiel once Farrendel is out of the way." Essie was shaking now too. But it wasn't pain or fear. She'd never felt heat quite this intense inside her chest before. Was this the anger people always implied she should have because of her red hair? Right now, she embraced it.

"All they want is Laesornysh to punish him for assassinating their late king. They have promised Tarenhiel will have peace if I turn him over to them. That is the bargain." Melantha waved from Farrendel to the trolls encircling them.

How gullible was Melantha? "And that ambush? I was there. They were trying to kill all of us."

"The only people they were under orders to kill were you and him." Melantha sniffed, not even looking at Farrendel. As if he was dog poop she couldn't wait to scrape off the bottom of her shoe.

Essie glanced at the trolls, catching the way they were looking at each other. The flick of their eyes, the smirks flashing, then gone.

There would be no peace for Tarenhiel. Melantha, the betrayer, was about to find herself betrayed.

Maybe later Essie would dredge up some sympathy. But she couldn't manage it right then, not with Farrendel's pain trembling through her touch on his arm.

"And the guns from Escarland? If their intentions were peaceful, why would they ask you to help transport guns for them?" Essie gestured at the crates stacked around them.

For the first time, Melantha shifted, as if uncomfortable having to face a truth she had been willingly ignoring. "They just needed the weapons to take out Laesornysh. Most of the crates have been food since they can grow so little in Kostaria."

The blond-haired elf behind her glanced toward the trolls. Something about his demeanor made Essie think that he knew more about the transport of the weapons than Melantha did. Was Melantha perhaps the traitor behind the information leaks about Farrendel, but this other elf the traitor behind moving the weapons and trolls across Tarenhiel?

Both Escarland and Tarenhiel had several traitors. It was an infestation.

Behind Melantha, Lord Bletchly and a troll who seemed to be the leader shook hands, exchanging a pouch that probably contained money. The troll turned and nodded.

The troll nearest Essie huffed. "Enough talk." He grabbed Essie, yanking her away from Farrendel.

Farrendel's head snapped up, his body going deadly still. His silver-blue eyes focused on the troll gripping Essie. Blue light flared at Farrendel's fingertips. "Let. Her. Go."

Bolts of power slithered up Farrendel's hands to his wrists. A crack split the air, pieces of shackle and black tailcoat peppering the ground around Farrendel. He dropped into a fighting stance, knife gripped in his hand.

Essie stomped down as hard as she could on the arch

of the troll's foot. His boot protected him, and her soft dancing slipper made it hard to get a good strike in. But it must have startled him enough. When his grip lessened, she wrenched free.

The troll scrambled for the knife strapped to his belt as he reached for Essie with his other hand. Just as he was drawing the knife, a bolt of Farrendel's magic blasted into him.

The knife landed at Essie's feet. She swiped it from the ground, then looked back.

Farrendel stood in the center of a circle of trolls, bolts of his magic crackling around him. He was panting, sweat beading on his forehead.

His gaze locked on hers. One last, silent farewell.

Then, she turned and ran.

CHAPTER
TWENTY-THREE

Farrendel's magic sizzled around him as he faced the oncoming trolls. His wrists burned with agony where his magic touched the troll magic lingering in his wounds. A few remnants of the stone remained buried underneath his skin, pulsing with pain even as he forced his magic free.

He needed to provide Essie time to escape. No matter how much it hurt, he must survive long enough to give her time.

Several of the trolls rushed him as the rest by the boat dropped what they were doing and raced down the wharf toward Farrendel. He counted ten trolls in total.

He flared his magic at them, making all but one stumble back. The remaining troll lunged, raising a sword made of stone flickering with magic. Farrendel blocked with a burst of magic, flinging the troll backwards. The troll landed hard and did not get up.

Farrendel grimaced at the numbness in his fingertips. If he remained cold and emotionless, he would not be strong enough to hold them off. He released the iron grip he held around his emotions, letting himself feel the pain of Melantha's betrayal. Her words sliced deep inside his chest. *You are not my brother.*

Not her brother. Not her family. Unwanted by those who should have loved him.

Did any of his family actually love him? Or did they all, deep down, feel like Melantha? Did they wish they could go back to a time when their family was whole and happy before he was born?

Unwanted. Not her brother. Unworthy.

Something in him shook, and he let it, unleashing the pain in a wave of magic. The trolls stumbled back, and one of them cried out.

A shield of troll magic burst around them. There were only eight trolls left, but one or more of them were powerful. With a power Farrendel had not felt since he faced the troll king in battle.

He should have expected the trolls would send a skilled warrior to capture him. Last time, they had thought sheer numbers and Escarlish weapons alone would work. And they might have, if not for Essie.

Essie. Essie loved him. He clung to that simple truth as if it was the only thing keeping his magic from consuming him. Even with all the magic crashing through him, he could still feel the bright connection of the heart bond warming deep in his chest. His entire family might secretly hate him, but he would not break because he could be certain Essie loved him.

He fought for her. To give her time to escape. To make sure her kingdom did not fall even if his did.

Magic burst from him, swirling higher, crackling with power. He cried out at the agony tearing through his wrists and arms, but he sank deeper into the magic. If it destroyed him, it would not matter as long as Essie survived.

The trolls crowded together. A wall of rock burst from the ground, rising higher.

Gripping his knife, Farrendel dashed toward the rock wall and leapt. He pushed off, the troll magic burning even through the leather of his boot. He shoved past the pain and flipped onto the top of the wall.

Troll magic burst upward, a hurried attempt at a shield. Farrendel wedged his magic into the gap before the shield grew large enough to shelter the trolls beneath. Flipping off the wall, Farrendel landed on the shoulders of one of the trolls.

The trolls were built more solidly than humans, and Farrendel's weight, even dropped from the air, only staggered him rather than knock him down.

Still, Farrendel drove his knife into the troll's chest, using the knife as a pivot to launch from the dying troll's shoulders to the ground. Farrendel kicked a troll's wrist on his way down, shoving aside a swinging sword aimed for his head.

A few feet away, one of the Escarlish traitors hunched behind a box, looking about ready to vomit. Farrendel did not see the other one. Had he chased after Essie?

Melantha huddled behind one of the wharf's pilings, as if she feared he would lash out at her next. But even if his heart ached, he was not about to turn his magic on Melantha. He still loved her as a sister, for all she hated him.

Thanfardil, the other Tarenhieli traitor, dashed to shelter behind a crate not far from the human traitor Lord Bletchly. Now there was an elf Farrendel would not hesitate to take down if necessary. He, more than Melantha, was responsible for Escarlish weapons in the hands of the trolls. Melantha only wanted Farrendel dead. Thanfardil betrayed his entire kingdom, knowing the death and destruction it would mean for his own people.

Farrendel sent a blast of magic in Thanfardil's direction. Thanfardil scurried deeper into the maze of crates with something like a shriek.

The air stirred behind Farrendel, and he whirled, ducking a swinging sword and plunging his knife into another troll's chest.

Troll magic flared to Farrendel's right. Farrendel raised a hand, meeting the flare with a blast of his own magic. The two magics met, exploded. Farrendel braced himself as the ground shook, and the air shattered.

When the debris settled, Farrendel found himself facing a tall troll wearing a thin, gold circlet. Something about his face was familiar, though younger and less lined than that of the troll king Farrendel had killed fifteen years ago.

The trolls had not just sent a strong warrior to retrieve Farrendel. They had sent their prince.

The troll prince gripped a sword in one hand, a dagger in the other. He stepped toward Farrendel, five more trolls at his back.

Farrendel could launch himself at them, even armed as he was with only a knife. But he needed to continue to draw them away from Essie. The farther he took this fight away from her, the better.

With a leap, he pushed up and over the rock wall again, dropped to the other side, and dashed several feet closer to the wharf and the steamboat.

Behind her piling, Melantha curled in a tighter ball, eyes wide.

Besides Melantha, there was no one here who should not die. Farrendel blasted his magic against the rock wall, leaning into it with all his strength. Cracks appeared in the rock even as troll magic scalded against Farrendel's. With a shout, he let his magic explode outward.

The top and sides of the wall shattered, sending debris hurtling into the trolls behind it. Two of the trolls went down, clutching sizzling wounds in arms and legs. Only the center of the wall held, the troll prince coating it with a layer of frosty magic, three trolls huddled behind him.

Farrendel braced himself and fell deeper into the crackling storm of his magic. It pulsed beneath his skin, burned behind his eyes, flickered to the ends of his hair even as it seared against the stone in his wrists.

With a twist of his hand, he sent a bolt into the box that Lord Bletchly sheltered behind. The box detonated with a roar of fire and smoke. Lord Bletchly went flying, blood coating his face and hands. Dead or badly wounded, Farrendel did not know.

Shards of wood and shrapnel from the weapons inside that box peppered the shield protecting Farrendel from being blown off his feet.

The weapons. He glanced toward the steamboat waiting at the dock. The trolls had been loading boxes onto the boat before they had arrived. More boxes stacked around them and on the wharf, waiting to be loaded.

He could not allow these weapons to reach the trolls. Even if he blew himself up in the process, the weapons had to be destroyed.

The trolls rushed him again, the troll prince leading the way. Farrendel poured a torrent of magic in his direction, forcing the troll prince to pour his magic into a shield.

With the troll prince occupied, Farrendel dashed toward the rest of the trolls, launched off one of the stacks of crates, and flipped over their heads. He shoved aside a sword aimed for his stomach and plunged his knife into the troll.

The troll prince shoved, and the magics exploded outward. Since he was in the air, Farrendel was blown backwards, landing heavily and rolling.

Leaving only a portion of his power directed at the trolls, Farrendel blasted the boxes stacked around them, forcing the troll prince to use his magic to protect himself and his remaining two trolls. The roar of explosions filled the air, ringing in Farrendel's ears, as shrapnel and splinters burst against his magical shield.

He staggered a few more steps toward the wharf. Had he bought enough time for Essie? He did not dare delay any longer to destroy the steamboat. Though as soon as he took his magic from the trolls, they would attack him. They would fill him full of stone and magic. Maybe they would kill him. Maybe capture him.

As long as not one more weapon reached Kostaria, it would not matter.

Hopefully Essie was far enough away. She would ensure that whatever sacrifice he made today would not be in vain.

He gathered his magic until everything inside him crackled. Then, with a deep breath, he drew the sizzling bolts of magic from the trolls and channeled everything he had toward the steamboat.

Blue lightning engulfed the boat, tearing at the boards,

seeking the volatile ammunition, even as footsteps crunched on the gravel behind him.

Troll magic dropped the temperature around him. The moment the trolls stabbed him, the power of his magic would be cut off.

Bolts of his magic burst through the steamboat, touched the crates stacked in the boat's hold. He sensed the ignition a second before the roar, the eruption of fire.

Farrendel reached for the last of his magic and shoved it into a shield around Melantha.

A shockwave picked him up and tossed him. He slammed to the ground, gravel tearing his hands, his cheek. His ears rang, the breath knocked from his lungs.

Shrapnel and burning splinters of wood rained around him. He managed a few, weak sizzles of magic to keep the worst of it from stabbing him. Gasping for breath, he craned his head, finding Melantha crouched in the protection of his magic.

All around was smoke and fire. He coughed, gathered his strength, and pushed to his hands and knees.

Essie must be well on her way out. Maybe he could escape, like she had asked him to.

He sensed a presence behind him. Reaching for his knife, he rolled and batted the troll prince's sword to the side.

The troll planted a boot on his chest, pinning him to the ground hard enough to knock the air from his lungs again. Magic iced the troll prince's sword a moment before he stabbed Farrendel through the shoulder.

Pain lanced to Farrendel's bones even as he lost feeling in his fingers. All the stones of the gravel beneath him stabbed into his back.

With a growl, Farrendel gripped the troll's ankle with his good hand and sent sparks shooting up the troll's leg.

The troll cried out and stumbled backwards, the leather of his boot smoking.

Farrendel rolled to his knees, dodging as one of the other trolls leapt for him. He needed to get to his feet. If he did not, he would have no hope of surviving.

The troll prince recovered. He and the other trolls rushed Farrendel.

Farrendel reached for his magic, but he could only get one of his hands to work. Blood slicked warm and wet down his back, pain lancing from the stones stabbed into his skin. He pushed onto one knee, lashing out with his magic at the two trolls behind their prince. The trolls were blasted from their feet, landing on the dirt.

The troll prince stepped forward, a knife of stone and ice growing in his hand.

As the troll prince stabbed down, Farrendel grabbed his wrist and used it to yank himself to his feet. He lunged at the troll and stabbed with all the force of his momentum.

The knife stopped an inch from the troll prince's shoulder, even as Farrendel halted the troll's knife with a crackling shield of his own.

They both shoved, magic crackling against magic, neither giving an inch. Sweat poured down Farrendel's back and under his hairline. Agony flared through his wrist as the stone there lengthened and burrowed deeper into his body. His hand on the knife shook while the bolts of his magic sputtered around his other hand.

Behind him, the other two trolls clambered to their feet, but Farrendel could not divert any of his magic or attention away from the troll prince.

The troll prince's snarl showed his teeth. "Murderer. No wonder your family turned on you."

It was a stab that shook Farrendel to his core. His magic faltered. It was only for a second. But it was enough.

The troll prince drove the stone knife into Farrendel's shoulder. Stone and troll magic grew down his arm from his shoulder, pinning that arm to his side. A wave of intense pain tore through him. The last bolts of his magic fizzled out. The knife dropped from his numb fingers.

One of the trolls behind him clapped a rag over Farrendel's nose and mouth.

That same, overly sweet stench choked Farrendel's nose and burned in his eyes. This was the might of the humans. They did not have the magical or physical strength of other races, but they had their inventions and their chemicals that even magic could not fight.

He could try to keep fighting. Maybe he could force the troll prince to kill him.

But, strangely, he no longer wanted to fight to the death. He wanted to survive, as Essie had begged. It was time to conserve his strength, bide his time, and put his trust in Essie.

As darkness closed in around him, he clung to the warmth of the heart bond. She was still alive, and she would come for him.

TWENTY-FOUR

Essie didn't look back. She raced the way they'd come, thankful her dancing shoes were flat, not the heeled shoes that were coming into style.

Footsteps pounded behind her. Too heavy to be Farrendel's.

She risked a glance over her shoulder. Mark Hadley sprinted after her, long legs eating the distance between them.

Essie dodged around crates and swerved around some of the smaller sheds in the dockside complex. The crackle of Farrendel's magic buzzed through the air. The ground trembled with the force of his magic unleashed.

Something exploded, shaking the ground and rattling the windowpanes in the abandoned guard shack as she raced past it.

As long as the explosions and fury of magic continued behind her, she'd know he was still alive.

"Princess Elspeth! Stop!" Mark Hadley shouted, only

a few yards behind her now. "There's no point in running."

Wasn't there? Lord Bletchly had flat out told her he planned to kill her. Why would Essie just give up to Mark Hadley knowing that?

"Stop!" His voice was even closer now. He would catch her in a few more seconds.

Fine. She'd stop. She was backed into a corner, and she'd come out shooting if Mark pushed her.

Spinning, she planted her feet, facing him. Running until the last second would only delay the inevitable. Better to face him now, while she had some distance. She stuffed the troll's knife into the knot of her dress at the small of her back and drew the derringer. When she pointed it at Mark, her hands were steady. "Don't come any closer. I will shoot you."

Mark slowed his pace, but he didn't stop. "Now, princess. You shouldn't play with weapons you can't handle."

As if he knew anything about her abilities. Her blood pounded in her ears, anger pulsing hot in her chest, but she shoved all of it away to keep her aim steady. "You just kidnapped me and my husband, threw us in a train without food or water or a water closet for an entire day, and then handed us over to his enemies to be killed. I dare you to take another step."

She'd have to wait for him to take a few more steps than that. Derringers didn't have a long range, and she needed accuracy.

He smirked and kept strolling forward.

A concussive boom tore the air. The force pounded Essie, the ground heaving beneath her feet.

She was on the ground, gasping for air, a ringing

filling her ears. Burning shards of wood and metal fell from the sky. A metal shard stabbed into the ground a few feet away.

Rolling, she located her derringer a few feet away and grabbed it. Only when she pushed to her feet did she feel the pounding at the back of her head and the pain flaring all along her back.

In the distance, a plume of smoke and fire rose into the sky. Was that the steamboat? The cargo of guns and ammunition waiting to be loaded?

Had Farrendel survived?

As much as she wanted to rush back and check, she'd promised Farrendel. Her sole mission right now was to get away safely with the identity of the traitors in both Escarland and Tarenhiel.

A few yards away, Mark Hadley lay face down on the ground, blood oozing around a foot-long shard of metal jutting from his back. If he wasn't already dead, he soon would be.

Some of the burning brands of wood had fallen onto the roof of the warehouse. If not put out, the whole warehouse would burn, exploding the ammunition stored inside.

She might as well help it along. She couldn't let those weapons fall into the hands of the trolls. Perhaps Escarland's army would get here in time and recover them, but she couldn't take the risk. Better to destroy them.

After gathering a few of the burning chunks of wood, she threw them into the warehouse's open door, watching as they landed on the stacks of crates.

When the fire ate through those crates and sparked the ammunition stored inside, this warehouse's explosion would make the previous one look small.

Hopefully Farrendel decided to escape by the river. If he was still here when this warehouse exploded, he most likely wouldn't survive.

She couldn't think about that. She needed to get herself out of there as quickly as possible.

As she rounded the end of the warehouse, she spotted the train, unhooked from the rest of the cars and now turned around to face back into Escarland. It even appeared to be shuddering with a slight vibration, as if powered up and waiting. Perhaps Lord Bletchly hadn't intended to stick around long. He would probably want to get back to Aldon as quickly as possible to allay any suspicion when Essie turned up missing, then dead.

As he was most likely dead, given he had probably been near that steamboat and Farrendel's magic, Essie was going to commandeer his train.

She dashed toward the train, then scrambled onto the engine's cab.

The engineer started, his eyes widening at her appearance. "Princess! What…"

She would've thought him an innocent who hadn't known his train had carried a kidnapped princess if he hadn't lunged at her.

She raised her derringer, halting him in his tracks. In her entire life, she'd never had such furious heat coursing through her veins. "Get this train moving. Now."

"If you shoot me, I won't be able to drive this train." The engineer eased closer, as if he still intended to jump her and wrest the gun from her fingers.

"I've toured enough trains and been given enough demonstrations, I'll figure it out." Essie kept the gun rock steady, pointed at his chest. The biggest target, as Julien had taught her. "Now that warehouse is on fire and could explode any minute. You can either die from a bullet or an explosion or you can get us out of here. Your choice."

His eyes widened yet again before he flicked a glance toward the warehouse. He sprang to the controls, yanking one lever back, then shoving another one forward as far as it would go.

A whining crackle filled the air, and the engine gave a shudder. Metal screeched against metal as the wheels struggled to turn against the iron rails. Slowly, inch by inch, the train crawled forward and gathered speed.

Essie didn't dare take her eyes off the engineer, not even to check on the burning warehouse. How long would it take for the ammunition in the crates to catch?

Agonizingly slowly, the engine gathered speed. Essie braced herself against the wall, counting each chug of the wheels, each beat of her heart.

The minutes ticked by. The train engine sped along the tracks now, the wind whipping past the open windows.

A roar sounded behind them. A gust of wind battered the sides of the engine house, blasting in through the windows. Moments later, the floor heaved beneath them, the car tilting.

Essie braced herself against the wall, a scream choking inside her throat. Were they going to derail? How badly would they be hurt if the engine went tumbling?

The wheels crashed back onto the tracks with a horrendous squeal. The whole train engine shuddered, then snapped into place, clacking forward smoothly once again.

After easing back on the lever Essie guessed controlled speed, the engineer turned to her. She expected him to say something. Perhaps ask a question.

But he grabbed an iron poker from its hook on the

wall, a leftover from when this train was steam-powered before its conversion to magical power. Lunging, he swung it at her.

She ducked and stumbled backwards, her back striking the wall of the engine house.

Nowhere left to run. They were going too fast for her to jump out, even if she wanted to hike on foot to the nearest town or outpost.

He rushed at her again, iron poker raised for a blow.

Essie braced herself and flexed her fingers on her derringer. He was bigger than her. Stronger. Even wounded, he could probably subdue her. She only had one shot. It had to count.

Raising her gun, she leveled it at his chest, held it steady, and pulled the trigger.

TWENTY-FIVE

Essie paced the quarters she'd been given in Fort Defense, the nearest military outpost to the destroyed warehouse. The commander said he sent soldiers, though he wouldn't let her go along. As if, after shooting the engineer and hiking her way here all by herself, she was a wilting flower who would faint at seeing the aftermath of a battle.

She'd seen one before, after all.

If Farrendel was there…if he was hurt…she could save him. She needed to be there, to grip his hand and use the force of their heart bond.

Rest, the commander had told her. *Rest*.

As if she could, knowing Farrendel was out there somewhere. Hurt. Captured. Dead.

It had been hours since she escaped. How long did it take the squad of soldiers to go to the exploded warehouse and back?

Boots sounded on the floor outside a moment before the door thunked with a knock. "Essie? You awake?"

Essie just about yanked the door off its hinges as she flung it open. "Avie." She threw herself forward and hugged him, burying her face against his shoulder as she used to do as a little girl. He was only seven years older than her, but since their father died, Averett had been her shoulder to cry on, her protector, her big brother. "I don't know where he is and he might be dead or the trolls might have captured him and they might be torturing him or he got blown up when I blew up that warehouse. What if I killed him?"

Her voice cracked on the last word.

Averett rubbed her back. "He's not dead. At least, they didn't find his body at the site. You didn't blow him up."

"Then they got him." Essie's voice fully broke this time. Farrendel's worst nightmare. Was he being tortured even now?

Averett hugged her tighter. "We'll get him back, Essie. We'll get him back."

Two more hands rested on her shoulders. Julien and Edmund, letting her know they were there for her.

Essie tried to choke back her sobs, muffling them against Averett's shirt. She shouldn't spend her time crying. Not when there was so much she should be doing instead.

Yet here she was crying anyway. Because her heart *hurt* in a way she'd never felt before. As if her ribs were about to cave into the emptiness in her chest. Logic didn't stop the tears. She couldn't simply will the ache away.

Finally, she managed to swallow back the lump in her throat, walling it inside her chest. It still hurt, as if her tears were pressing against her throat, eager to pour out again.

Essie swiped at her face, her skintight with all the dried tears. "Sorry."

"I've gotten used to it over the years." Averett handed her a handkerchief. His mouth had a ghost of a smile, even if his eyes were still shadowed. "At least you didn't wipe your nose on my shirt again."

"I haven't done that since I was six or seven." Essie took the handkerchief, wiped her eyes, and blew her nose.

Averett sighed and gestured to the couch. "Why don't we sit down?"

The report couldn't be good, not if it was a delivered-sitting-down kind of report.

Essie took a seat in the center of the couch, and Edmund and Julien dropped into the seats on either side of her.

Averett claimed the armchair, pulling it forward to better face the couch. "You don't have to do this."

Essie drew in a deep breath. Composure. She needed to be composed. Calm. Farrendel needed her to hold it together. "I need to know what they found there. Please. I need to know."

"Lots of bodies." Julien's voice rumbled to her right. "Farrendel put up quite the fight. I hear you didn't do half bad yourself."

It wasn't something to celebrate. She'd been desperate. Angry. Scared. "Who was killed?"

"Lord Bletchly, Mark Hadley, and two other Escarlish men. It looked like some of the trolls may have been killed, but they took those bodies with them." Averett rubbed his palm with his thumb. "We didn't find any elf bodies."

That meant both of the elven traitors had most likely survived. Essie clenched her fingers together. Would it have been better or worse if Melantha had been killed in the fighting? As bewildered as Farrendel had been, Essie was sure he wouldn't have killed her, but one of the trolls or the explosions might have.

"Based on your description, Jalissa thinks the second elf traitor is Thanfardil. He is apparently in charge of the train schedules in Tarenhiel." Edmund's gaze focused on the floor.

In all the pain of the past day, Essie had forgotten about Jalissa. Essie wasn't the only one suffering right now. Jalissa's brother was missing—probably captured—and her sister had been revealed as traitor to her kingdom.

"I thought he looked familiar. I must have seen him around the train station in Estyra." Not someone she had paid any attention to, but, apparently, that was what made him such a good traitor. He could schedule the trains to hide the fact that he was ferrying weapons to the trolls. "Was this news passed to King Weylind?"

"Yes, but we haven't heard an answer if he was able to stop the trolls from crossing Tarenhiel." Averett met her gaze. "All we know is he wants to meet on Linder Island tonight."

If King Weylind got the message, then there was hope. Maybe he had already rescued Farrendel.

Except that Melantha was working with the trolls. Even if this Thanfardil failed to secure safe passage across Tarenhiel, she probably still could.

Would she do it, after what she had witnessed? Would she realize in time that the trolls had no intention of peace now that they had Farrendel?

Even if she did, Thanfardil might have co-conspirators who would help him get Farrendel and his captors across Tarenhiel to Kostaria. Hopefully the elves would look into all of Thanfardil's contacts and underlings to see if any of the rest of them were also involved.

Seriously, a traitor infestation. Cockroaches would have been easier to eliminate.

"At least King Weylind knows who the traitors are. You succeeded in giving him that information." Next to her, Julien patted her shoulder, as if she was one of his soldiers who had done a good job. "When we conducted our raid, we discovered evidence that suggests Charles Hadley was unaware of his son's treachery. We found the doctored books in the son's office. We've already rounded up the other accomplices, both at the factory and in the army's receiving warehouse."

That was something, at least.

Yet, capturing the traitors didn't have the joy of victory she'd thought it would. Maybe because the price had been so high.

"Is Jalissa here?" Essie's voice came out flat, ringing hollow inside her chest. She couldn't feel. Couldn't think. Just exist. Breathe in. Breathe out. One moment at a time.

"Yes. She's waiting on the train." Averett gestured toward the door. "We need to board the train now to make it to the meeting with King Weylind on Linder Island this evening."

A part of her just wanted to keep sitting there. Moving, even to stand, was too much effort.

But she couldn't stay here. She was still a princess, and she still had a duty. King Weylind would be furious, and Farrendel would want Essie to do her best to talk him down.

With a deep breath and the last shreds of her strength, Essie pushed to her feet. "Let's go."

Her brothers clustered around her as she strode down the stairs and out the door of the commander's quarters. Gathering her composure, she managed to put on a princess smile and thank the commander of the outpost for his hospitality, as if she wasn't shattered and hollow inside.

Essie kept the brittle smile on her face all the way until she climbed the stairs into the privacy of the royal train waiting on the outpost's siding.

Yet she couldn't break, even here. All three of her brothers were there and watching. Down the hallway, Jalissa sat in the parlor of the royal car. And, down the train tracks at Linder Island, Essie would have to face King Weylind and try to stop him from starting a war with her brother over losing his brother.

It was so tempting to turn into one of the compartments and hide away. What she wanted to do was curl on a bunk and sob. Preferably while clutching a piece of clothing belonging to Farrendel. That would be the tragic, romantic thing to do, right?

Past the compartments, Jalissa perched on the padded bench seat, perfectly still, staring at the dark green carpet on the floor as if it held the answers to all of life's problems.

Essie couldn't just hide and ignore Jalissa's grief. Jalissa was stuck in a kingdom not her own, surrounded by a family that wasn't hers while she dealt with her sister's betrayal and her brother's capture. Essie was the closest thing to family Jalissa had right then.

Since marrying Farrendel, Essie had focused on how

Melantha and Jalissa kept her at a distance. How they didn't embrace her as their sister.

Yet, how often had she thought of them as her sisters-in-law? She'd always thought of them as Farrendel's sisters, not hers.

It had been different with Paige. Since Paige was already Essie's best friend, that friendship had only deepened with sisterhood. It hadn't taken an effort to build that relationship.

Essie hadn't put in the effort for Melantha and Jalissa. Perhaps she could be excused since it had been necessary to focus on building her relationship with Farrendel first.

But it was time Essie stepped up and was the sister Jalissa needed.

Essie eased onto the seat next to Jalissa. She didn't speak. Even she couldn't find the words for this moment.

Perhaps, silence was best right now. An understanding silence of just being there, ready to listen if Jalissa needed to talk.

Jalissa clenched and unclenched her fingers into her skirt. The layers of wrinkles already there spoke to how long she'd been sitting there doing that, over and over again. "I cannot believe Melantha would do this to us. Why would she betray her own family and kingdom?"

"She thought she was doing it for the good of Tarenhiel. I think she believed—or wanted to believe—the trolls when they said all they wanted was Farrendel." Essie's words rang hollow as the train shuddered into motion, sending vibrations through her feet and the couch she sat on.

She wasn't defending Melantha or making excuses for her. No, this was for Jalissa to try to help her come to grips with a sister's utter betrayal.

"Even so, how could she do this to Farrendel?" Jalissa's fingers squeezed her burgundy skirt into a ball, and this time, she didn't unclench her fists. "He is our brother."

"She said she doesn't see him that way." Essie had never felt particularly close to Melantha, so the betrayal didn't hurt her the way it did Farrendel and Jalissa. But she'd tried to imagine Averett, Julien, or Edmund doing something like this.

She honestly couldn't. It was too unthinkable.

Not simply because they were her brothers, but because her whole family's culture wouldn't allow for something like this. The tragedy of losing their father had knit them closer together, far closer than most royal families.

Perhaps it was because she was an outsider, but Essie had been able to see how Farrendel's family had been shattered at its core. King Weylind had done his best to pick up the pieces. Jalissa looked out for Farrendel, and Melantha had pretended to care.

But due in part to the large age gaps between the siblings and the elven culture that so disdained Farrendel for simply being born, it had been a difficult, nearly impossible task.

Jalissa turned shattered, dark brown eyes to Essie. "Does she not remember the little one we helped raise? How we fell in love the first time we held him as a tiny infant?"

"I bet Farrendel was an adorable child." Essie clasped her hands to stop herself from reaching for Jalissa. Her elf sister-in-law wouldn't appreciate the contact the way Paige would have.

"He was." Jalissa's voice grew rough and scratchy.

"He was not always like he is now. He was always quiet, but he would smile and laugh and sometimes even chatter with us. When he would look up at me with those blue eyes of his, it was nearly impossible to tell him no."

"I can imagine." He hadn't lost that kicked puppy dog look as an adult. Though, it was hard to think about Farrendel laughing and doing enough talking to count as chattering. "It's amazing he didn't end up spoiled rotten."

Jalissa's brow wrinkled for a moment, then smoothed. "Life would not let him. That scar on his face?" She touched her own cheek. "He did not receive it from the trolls. That happened in Estyra when he was fifteen. That was when he stopped smiling and laughing and talking."

Fifteen. It would have been young for a human to experience something traumatic enough to leave a scar. But for an elf, that was the equivalent of seven or eight years old.

It must have been traumatic for him. Bad enough that he had yet to tell Essie about it, even though they'd talked about his torture at the hands of the trolls. But an injury done at the hands of his own people?

No wonder he felt he had to earn love. Honestly, it was amazing he'd ever become Laesornysh, willing to lay his life on the line for his people, rather than become a traitor himself.

"How could Melantha have forgotten that day?" Jalissa twisted her skirt as if trying to strangle it. "How could she remember the blood dripping from his face and the tears he was trying so hard not to cry and still do this to him?"

Essie swallowed back the lump in her throat, heart aching inside her.

"Father packed up and moved to Lethorel with

Farrendel that same day. He spent most of the next few decades ruling from there with Weylind taking over most of the day-to-day responsibilities in Estyra." Jalissa swiped at her face, dashing away the single tear that had trickled down her face. "I spent most of my time in Lethorel while Melantha stayed in Estyra. I did not think anything of that until now."

Essie rubbed her fingers against her dirty dress, sneaking a glance at Jalissa. "Weylind loves Farrendel, and he spent just as much time away from him while Farrendel was growing up as Melantha did. It cannot be only that."

"No, I suppose not. But Melantha had been free to visit in a way he was not. She could have chosen to spend more time in Lethorel if she had wished. Weylind was already married at the time, but she was...well, had been..."

"Had been what?" Essie remembered Melantha had said something about how her and Jalissa would never be happy as long as Farrendel was alive. Was this what she was talking about?

Jalissa drew in a shaky breath. "She was betrothed. He nearly broke it off once Farrendel's birth was revealed, and she managed to convince him not to take such a drastic measure. But when it became clear after that attack that Father was not going to banish Farrendel and our family would forever be labeled as tainted because of it, Melantha's betrothed broke it off and married someone else less than a year later, a scandalously quick wedding for elven standards."

"That would be scandalous even by human standards." Essie couldn't help the wry grimace. If less than a year was scandalous, her and Farrendel's marriage was horribly gossip-worthy.

"Neither Melantha nor I have ever gotten another offer. None of the respectable elven families would wish to marry into ours, for all we are royalty. I did not realize Melantha blamed Farrendel for that. I certainly do not." Jalissa finally unclenched her fingers and smoothed the front of her dress. "I was only a hundred and two when Farrendel was born. I had not yet established my own life like Weylind and Melantha."

"I know you and Farrendel are close." It made sense, since they were the closest in age. For Jalissa, the age gap between her and Farrendel was the same as it was to her and Melantha. Not so for Melantha or Weylind.

At a hundred and two when he'd been born, Jalissa had been roughly the same age Farrendel was now. An adult, yes, but for an elf, barely an adult. She'd been like an eighteen-year-old human. An adult on paper, but still living much like a child under the parents' authority. It had been easier for her to be a true sibling to Farrendel in a way it was harder for Weylind and Melantha.

Jalissa turned, facing Essie. "I am sorry for the times I have been harsh to you. I was not as welcoming as I should have been when you married Farrendel."

Essie pushed away the echoes of Jalissa's words from back then. "You love your brother and were worried for him. I know I'd be worried if one of my brothers married a girl he'd never even talked to."

"I still should have trusted that my brother knew what he was doing. He must have seen something in you that first day to make him so certain."

"He told me it was my smile." A ghost of that smile

flickered on her face before dying. How could she smile when Farrendel was out there somewhere? Hurt. Captured. Maybe undergoing torture.

Jalissa nodded, as if Farrendel being attracted to Essie's smile made perfect sense. "You have been good for him. I have not seen him happy and smiling like this in decades. Not since..." Jalissa's voice faded as her eyes shimmered. She looked away as a tear escaped to meander down her cheek onto her chin.

This time, Essie couldn't help herself. She wrapped an arm around Jalissa, giving her a side hug.

"He was so broken last time." More tears slid down Jalissa's face. She gripped Essie's hand painfully tight, her tear-filled gaze swinging up to stab into Essie. "He is still alive, is he not?"

"I don't know." Essie rubbed at her upper chest, as if she could relieve the ache there. How she wished she knew if Farrendel was alive or dead. This place stuck between hope and fear tore her apart.

Jalissa's brow wrinkled. "You should be able to tell. But perhaps the elishina does not work that way with humans."

The heart bond. It hadn't occurred to Essie to use it to find out if Farrendel was alive or dead. She assumed she could only feel it when they were physically touching. How much was there to this heart bond that she still didn't understand?

Essie drew in a deep breath, trying to calm the churn in her stomach and ache in her chest long enough to feel the heart bond. She'd only felt it when touching Farrendel. Because she was human, did that mean she wouldn't be able to access the magical connection without him there?

"I don't know." It was such a horrible answer to have to give. For herself and for Jalissa. "I think I may need some time and quiet. I've never tried something like this before. But, I think...I think he must be alive. Surely I would have felt it if he died."

Or was his death that aching hole she felt even now in her chest?

"You would have. I have heard the feeling of an elishina breaking is unmistakable." Jalissa swiped at her face again, even though the tears continued to drip down her face. They were the silent tears of someone trying to hold back the depth of their emotion and succeeding for everything but those telltale tears. "My parents had an elishina. Did Farrendel ever tell you that?"

"No, he didn't." Why wouldn't he have told her? Perhaps because the elf queen hadn't been his mother. Perhaps he felt guilty, somehow, for the breaking of that heart bond even if he'd had nothing to do with it. The elf queen had already been dead for several years by the time Farrendel was born.

Except that Essie saw this for what it was. Evidence that Farrendel was his father's son. He loved like his father. Completely. Whole-heartedly.

Jalissa gave both of Essie's hands a squeeze. "In these past months, I have become thankful you are what Farrendel needed. Now, it seems you are also the sister I needed, *iscienata*."

Little sister. For the elves, saying brother or sister was an endearment used among family members. But the added *little* wasn't a denigration but signified even more affection than if Jalissa had simply called her *sister*.

There was only one response Essie could give to

Jalissa. She pulled her hands free and hugged Jalissa as she would a sister.

And, surprisingly, Jalissa didn't pull away. Her return hug was tentative, light. But she didn't let go as both of them cried onto each other's shoulders.

CHAPTER
TWENTY-SIX

By the time Essie stepped from the train at the military outpost across the river from Linder Island, her face had been washed of tears, her eyes less puffy and red after multiple rounds of cool cloths pressed to them. Her emotions remained buried deep. This was not a time for tears but action.

She still wore the same dark green dress she'd been kidnapped in, complete with torn hems and singe marks. Let King Weylind and the other elves judge her less-than-perfect appearance if they wished. She didn't care.

At least they would see what she'd been through. She hadn't been a helpless, crying maiden while Farrendel took all the danger. She had fought for her escape even as Farrendel had. She'd only left him behind because the information she knew was too vital to risk.

To complete the ensemble, she strapped her rifle across her back. It didn't exactly go with the dress, and King Weylind might be offended that she brought a weapon to this meeting.

But since Averett didn't dare bring a weapon, she would. She would show the elves that Escarland was ready for war. Not against the elves but alongside them.

Jalissa joined her, tall and beautiful, her face smooth and composed.

Averett led the way from the train to the jetty where the steamboat waited, smoke already puffing from the smokestacks. Across the river, the elven boat also waited, gangplank lowered, as figures glided on board.

This was all so much like that meeting several months ago, yet Farrendel wouldn't be there to greet them on Linder Island.

Essie raised her chin, clenching her jaw to stop her chin from trembling.

Averett, Julien, Edmund, Jalissa, her guard, and Essie boarded the steamboat. Essie leaned against the rail, needing the cooling, late summer air to wash over her as the steamboat pulled out into the river.

She squeezed her eyes shut, digging deep inside her chest. Farrendel. Concentrate on Farrendel. Remember that zing of magic she'd felt at that wedding and try to find it somewhere in her chest.

Something shifted. It was brief. A whisper, nothing more.

But she felt *him*. Like she had when she'd gripped his hand and willed him not to die.

Hold on, Farrendel. We're coming for you.

She didn't know if he would feel that she'd reached for the connection. But she would will as much encouragement and strength his way as she could. Even if she didn't know where he was or what he was going through.

He was alive. That was the main thing she'd needed to know.

She whirled from the railing, casting about until she spotted Jalissa at the railing closer to the bow of the steamboat. Essie dashed to her and barely restrained herself from grabbing Jalissa in another hug. Instead, she gripped Jalissa's shoulders in the elven hug. "Farrendel's alive. I managed to feel the heart bond. It was brief, but there. He's alive."

Beneath Essie's grip, Jalissa's shoulders sank, muscles relaxing. Jalissa gripped Essie's shoulders and squeezed, her mouth working like she wanted to say something but couldn't find the words or force them past a lump in her throat.

After a moment, Jalissa released Essie and turned away, back to the railing in the direction of Linder Island and, beyond it, the forested shore of Tarenhiel. "Good. Knowing he is alive may be the only thing that will calm Weylind at this meeting."

Elves might appear calm and serene, but when they got angry, it was fierce and simmering. And, for an elf, Weylind had a temper. Perhaps he should've been the one stuck with the flaming red hair. He fit the stereotype better than she did most of the time.

The steamboat chugged alongside the wharf now built on Linder Island, its wheels frothing as the captain threw it into reverse to slow, then stop their momentum. Deckhands tossed lines around pilings, tying the boat in place, before lowering the gangplank.

Essie's stomach knotted even more than it had that day over three months ago. This time, she couldn't dredge up a smile. Perhaps she had been innocent and naïve back then. She'd blithely told herself she wouldn't let herself end up heartbroken because of her arranged marriage.

Yet, here she was, hollow and aching. Not for the lack of love, as she had feared, but because of an abundance of it.

She followed Averett and Julien down the gangplank with Edmund and Jalissa and several guards falling in behind them. They strode past the stone blockhouse by the wharf that provided shelter for the telegraph operator and dock workers stationed here to pass along messages and shipments of goods across the island to the elves stationed only a few yards away on the other side of the island.

As Averett approached the center of the island, King Weylind stalked around the small wooden building the elves had built. His black hair flowed down his back, parting around the hilt of the sword over one shoulder, a quiver of arrows over the other. The buckles on his leather armor glinted as he prowled closer. The two elves marching in his wake also wore armor and weapons, their faces hard as the rock of Linder Island beneath their feet.

Behind Essie, hammers on muskets clicked into place. Boots scuffed as soldiers elbowed past her to hurry to Averett's side.

"Stand down." Averett gestured to the soldiers, holding out his arms as if planning to physically hold them back.

"Your Majesty. You need to be protected." The lieutenant in charge shifted his feet, as if torn between stepping in front of his king to protect him and obeying his king's order to stand down.

"Stand down. The elven king will not attack. Not yet." Averett stood tall, his crown glinting in the late afternoon sunlight. Gone was whatever uncertainty he'd shown in his last meeting with King Weylind. Perhaps the better understanding of the elves Essie and Farrendel had provided was giving him confidence. Or maybe he was filled with the same raw-edged, borderline reckless determination that was filling Essie.

"Jalissa, isciena." King Weylind raised his voice, speaking in elvish. "Step away from them."

The churn in Essie's stomach knotted tighter. How angry was King Weylind if he wanted Jalissa out of the way? What was he planning to do?

She'd known he'd be angry, but it had never occurred to her that he would actually attack Averett right here. Surely he wasn't planning to assassinate Escarland's king right here and now.

And, he'd only asked Jalissa to step away. Not Essie. Whatever progress she'd made toward him thinking of her as his sister-in-law had apparently vanished in his anger.

Averett glanced over his shoulder. "Translation?"

Jalissa held her head high. "He wishes for me to join him on that side of the island."

"I see." The lines around Averett's mouth deepened. "I will not stop you if you wish to join your brother. I want peace between our peoples. My brothers and I are not armed. Only Essie carries a weapon, and she belongs to both my people and yours. More, I intend to join this war on your brother's side, if he will hear me out."

Jalissa held Averett's gaze for a moment, perhaps searching for the truth in his words. Finally, she gave a clipped nod and faced forward. "Weylind Daresheni, I stand with them. They wish for peace, and I ask you to hear what they have come to say. It is what Farrendel wanted."

King Weylind didn't relax. If anything, his posture

and expression turned harder, colder. As if just the mention of Farrendel's name sent his big brother protective instincts into a fury.

"I am going to walk to the center of the island with just my sister. She is armed, but I am not." Averett stared at King Weylind across the short expanse of the island's rocky surface separating them.

"Your Majesty..." The lieutenant almost sounded like he was in pain as he dragged out Averett's title.

"The elven king will not attack while his sister is with us." Averett didn't glance away from King Weylind, though he waved a staying hand as some of the guards swung their guns toward Jalissa. "No, she's not our hostage. Lower your weapons. Be prepared in case the elven king attacks, but I don't believe he will."

The lieutenant's face pinched, like he was trying really hard not to roll his eyes at his king's naïve approach to politics. But he lowered his musket and took a step back.

"Essie." Averett motioned her forward, but he didn't hold out his arm. She wouldn't have taken it if he had. Perhaps he realized that now wasn't the time to treat her as a princess that needed an escort but as one who had fought and survived.

She was, after all, the only witness to Melantha's betrayal. King Weylind had every reason to want to disbelieve Essie's report, even if the physical evidence of Farrendel's disappearance, the troll knife Essie had taken, and the types of information that had been leaking to the trolls all corroborated Essie's story.

Together, Essie and Averett marched toward the center of the island. Across from them, King Weylind stalked forward. Even though he remained well-armed, he came alone, the two elf bodyguards remaining on the far side.

This time, when Averett and King Weylind halted in the center of the island facing each other, there was no fancy meeting tent set up. No chairs and tables and diplomats. And no Farrendel standing cold and deadly at King Weylind's back.

King Weylind halted only a foot from Averett, looming over him with every inch of his slim, angry elf height. If he had been human, he probably would have jabbed Averett in the chest with his finger. As it was, he leaned close, as if to intimidate with his breath and piercing eyes. "I trusted you to keep my brother safe. Instead, you let him get snatched right from your own palace."

"My own sister was taken as well." Averett crossed his arms. "Believe me, I am not happy with what happened either."

Essie gripped the leather strap holding her gun across her back and tried not to shift.

"Yet here your sister stands while my brother is still captured." King Weylind glared.

Averett glared right back. "Because of your brother's courageous sacrifice."

"You do not know what they have already done to him." King Weylind's mouth twisted, his eyes pained, even as he reached into his tunic and yanked out a package of folded canvas. "The trolls left this at the northern border."

Essie's stomach churned. The canvas wasn't stained red, so hopefully King Weylind wasn't about to reveal Farrendel's severed finger.

King Weylind flipped open the canvas, revealing a cascade of something glinting and silver-blond.

Farrendel's hair.

Essie's breath caught. The trolls had chopped off his

hair. She reached out and tentatively stroked a strand of it as it lay across King Weylind's palms. "Farrendel depends on his hair when he fights. This will be like robbing him of one of his senses."

"An elf warrior's hair symbolizes his honor. It is considered a dishonor to have one's hair shorn. It is a shame done to traitors and cowards." King Weylind cradled Farrendel's hair across his palms. "Farrendel is not the one who should have suffered this."

No. Melantha was the traitor. She was the one who should have been subjected to that humiliation.

Instead it had been Farrendel shoved onto his knees, a troll grasping his hair, slicing through it with a knife.

King Weylind's gaze was pained. "Last time, they did not cut his hair. He was tortured as part of his capture, but back then, the trolls had been focused on using him as a trap for our father. This time..." King Weylind held up Farrendel's hair. "They have many reasons to wish revenge on Farrendel. They will torture him for the sake of causing him pain. This will be worse than before."

The torture had already begun. Essie hugged her arms over her stomach. Farrendel's worst fear had come true. He had been captured by the trolls.

Survive. It was the one thing she'd asked him to do. Just survive.

How long would it take to rescue him? Could he survive the days—weeks—of torture? How much of her Farrendel would be left when they rescued him?

"This"— King Weylind jabbed Farrendel's hair forward, stopping only an inch shy of Averett's chest— "is what your failure to protect him has cost. I trusted you, and you failed to protect my brother."

Averett faced King Weylind without flinching and shouted right back. "He's our brother too."

King Weylind blinked. He straightened. Blinked again.

"He's our brother too," Averett repeated at a lower volume and waved to Julien and Edmund standing behind him with arms crossed. "And we intend to get him back. You can either help us or you can get out of our way."

King Weylind's gaze searched Averett's face before he turned to Essie and spoke in elvish. "Does he speak the truth?"

Would King Weylind believe her if she said yes?

Yet, he had asked. King Weylind wouldn't have bothered to ask if he didn't believe she'd tell the truth. "Yes. Farrendel is a part of my family, and my brothers take care of their own."

King Weylind's expression softened a fraction. "What exactly do you intend?"

"Operating on Escarland's soil, as the trolls did, is an act of war. As soon as I return to Aldon, I will be declaring war on Kostaria, and Parliament will vote to approve. After one of their own proved to be a traitor and with all the evidence we have of the trolls meddling in Escarlish politics, the vote will be close to unanimous." Averett stuck out his hand. "I would like to expand our treaty and fight alongside you to defeat the trolls together."

King Weylind stared at Averett's hand before he tipped a slight bow and touched his hand to his forehead, mouth, then chest. "Very well. We elves will accept your aid."

Typical elves. Even now, King Weylind managed to sound condescending toward humans.

Yet, Essie now recognized the significance of the forehead, mouth, chest gesture. It meant something along the lines of good thoughts to each other, kind words to each other, and loyalty to each other, and meant more than the coldly formal mouth to forehead motion.

King Weylind folded the canvas back over the remnants of Farrendel's hair and turned to Essie. "Is he still alive?"

"Yes." As of a few minutes ago, at least. "I know that much."

Essie gripped the strap of her gun, heat building inside her chest. The trolls had turned Melantha against her own brother. They'd organized several traitors inside Escarland and Tarenhiel. And now, they had Farrendel and would torture him.

She reached deep inside herself until she could grasp the connection she had with Farrendel. For a flicker of a moment, the connection snapped into place, real and alive and thrumming with a sense of Farrendel's heart beating in time with hers.

But this time, she also caught a sense of blinding pain shivering beneath her skin.

No, not her pain. His.

Survive, Farrendel. Just survive.

The trolls had taken her elf, and she was going to get him back no matter who stood in her way.

Don't Miss the Next Adventure

DEATH WIND

Essie should be planning her happily ever after, not planning a war.

Although they once were enemies, the humans of Escarland and the elves of Tarenhiel have allied to fight the trolls from the far north. But alliances are tricky things even in the best of times, and with Farrendel, the elves' foremost warrior and Essie's husband, captured by the trolls, the circumstances appear dire indeed.

But Essie won't give up, and she will make her two peoples work together to fight this war if it's the last thing she does. One way or another, she will get Farrendel back, no matter what it takes.

Buy Now

FREE BOOK!

Thanks so much for reading *War Bound*! I hope Essie's and Farrendel's story touched your heart and brought a smile. If you loved the book, please consider leaving a review on Amazon or Goodreads. Reviews help your fellow readers find books that they will love.

If you want to learn about all my upcoming releases, get great book recommendations, and see a behind-the-scenes glimpse into the writing process, follow my blog at www.taragrayce.com.

 If you sign up for my newsletter, you'll receive a free novella, *Elf Prince* (*Elven Alliance* Book 1.5). This novella shows the beginning of *Fierce Heart* from Farrendel's point of view.

Farrendel Laesornysh, prince of the elves, never expected he would marry, much less that he would marry a human princess.

When a marriage alliance is the appeasement the humans of Escarland demand, this marriage is a price Farrendel is willing to pay, even if it is probably a trick by the humans for some devious purpose. It is either marriage or war, and Farrendel has already killed enough for a lifetime.

The human princess is probably a spy. Or an assassin sent to kill him on his wedding night. Yet if he can make this marriage work, as his grandmother seems to think, it might be the first breath of hope Farrendel has had in over a decade.

Sign up for my newsletter now

You will also receive the free novella *Steal a Swordmaiden's Heart*, which is set in the same world as *Stolen Midsummer Bride* and *Bluebeard and the Outlaw*!

ALSO BY TARA GRAYCE

ELVEN ALLIANCE SERIES

Fierce Heart

War Bound

Death Wind

Troll Queen

Pretense

STOLEN BRIDES OF THE FAE

Stolen Midsummer Bride

A VILLAIN'S EVER AFTER

Bluebeard and the Outlaw

PRINCESS BY NIGHT

Lost in Averell

ACKNOWLEDGMENTS

Thank you to everyone who made this release possible! To my writer friends, especially Molly, Morgan, Sarah, Savannah, Sierra, and the entire Spinster Aunt gang for being so encouraging and helpful. To my dad for making sure Farrendel's fight scenes are climatic instead of blah. To my mom for encouraging my creative side. To my sisters-in-law Alyssa and Abby for adoring Essie and Farrendel. To my brothers for reading these books even if they have a bit more romance than action. To my friends Bri, Paula, and Jill for always being excited about my books no matter what I write. To my proofreaders Tom, Mindy, and Deborah, thanks so much for helping to eradicate the typos as much as humanly possible. And, most of all, thanks to my God for giving me so many blessings.

CPSIA information can be obtained
at www.ICGtesting.com
Printed in the USA
LVHW092019200222
711571LV00010B/136/J